Invisible Insurrection of

Invisible Insurrection of a Million Minds

A Trocchi Reader

Edited by Andrew Murray Scott

© Introduction Andrew Murray Scott 1991
© All other material The Alexander Trocchi Estate
First published by Polygon
22 George Square, Edinburgh

Set in Lasercomp Sabon by Alden Press, Northampton
Printed and Bound in Great Britain by Redwood Press Ltd, Melksham

British Cataloguing In Publication Data
Trocchi, Alexander 1925–1984
Invisible insurrection of a million minds: a Trocchi reader.
I. Title II. Murray Scott, Andrew
828.91409

ISBN 0 7486 6108 5

The Publisher acknowledges subsidy from the Scottish Arts Council towards the publication of this volume.

Contents

Introduction	vii

Part One

Pages of an Autobiography	3
The Earthbound	36
Fragments from a Diary of a Man Found Gassed in a Glasgow Slum	43
Tapeworm	46
Peter Pierce	55

Part Two

Letter to Jack	71
A Meeting	74
The Rum and the Pelican	87
Eileen Lanelly	97
The Holy Man	104
Foreword to Vol. 5 of Frank Harris' *Memoirs*	113
Letter to Samuel Beckett	115
Extract from *Young Adam*	117

Part Three

A Being of Distances	125
Wolfie	137
Letter to Terry Southern	141
Extract from *Cain's Book*: 'Jody'	148
A Note on George Orwell	168

Part Four

The Invisible Insurrection of a Million Minds	177
Sigma: A Tactical Blueprint	192
Letters to Hugh MacDiarmid	204
Letter to William S. Burroughs	207

The Junkie: Menace or Scapegoat?	210
Notes from a Diary of a Cure, 1965	216
How I Came to Want to Get Off	218
Uncle Hamlet, Quite Gone into Middle Age . . .	220
Acknowledgements and Sources	222
A Trocchi Bibliography	224

Introduction

Even after his death in 1984, Alexander Trocchi, the author of *Cain's Book* was not allowed to rest in peace – his ashes mysteriously disappeared – and later, many of his papers were burned in a fire for which no cause was ever found, just as *Cain's Book* itself had been burned in 1963 by order of the courts. So Trocchi's remains are nowhere or everywhere. It is strangely appropriate as an end point. Or a beginning . . .

For many years Trocchi had been ostracised by the literary establishment. He was regarded as dangerous, an anarchist, one who might suddenly begin to inject himself with heroin in public, or make love to someone's wife on the sofa. Or begin a revolution. Or something equally unexpected and embarrassing. Then, too, he was ignored by some Scots because of the heat of his headline-making exchanges with Hugh MacDiarmid at the Edinburgh Festival in 1962. MacDiarmid, hardly an establishment figure himself, had not read a word of Trocchi's work, but had dismissed him (and William Burroughs) in a drunken aside as 'cosmopolitan scum'.

When Trocchi received a Writer's Grant of £500 from the Arts Council in 1970, which rescued him from considerable debt, the tabloid newspapers decried this on their front pages as 'Money for Junkies' and 'Cash for Drug Fiends'. But Trocchi's notoriety as a heroin addict with a twenty-five year addiction should not be allowed to obscure the versatility and quality of his literary talent. As editor of *Merlin*, the influential Paris quarterly magazine (1952–55), his friends included Henry Miller, Samuel Beckett, Robert Creeley, Eugene Ionesco, and Pablo Neruda.

Trocchi was the foremost British writer of the Beat era, the first 'prophet of permissiveness', leader of the British cultural underground and a prime mover of many of the cultural events which characterised the 1960s and 70s, including the sigma project and the London anti-university movement. He sacrificed his own literary output between 1963 and 1977 to sigma – an iconoclastic and diffuse 'movement', even by the standards of the sixties. In the fifties he had been a prominent figure in the expatriate literary circles of Paris – the only British member of the Situationist International, and one of the founders of the Beat community in Venice West in California.

First and foremost however, he was a brilliant novelist, whose novels explored and ultimately rejected the basic rules of novel-writing, and the conventions associated with producing literary 'product'. From his earliest days at Glasgow University, where he had been described as 'a student manifestly of genius', he was at all times an innovator, outrageous, larger-than-life.

This collection of his writing includes some published essays and short stories, and previously unpublished fiction. Trocchi has left behind work of quality. The Reader has been compiled in tandem with my full-length biography (*Alexander Trocchi: The Making of the Monster*, Polygon, 1991) to make better-known the work of one of Scotland's most deserving talents. While his novel, *Cain's Book* – described by Edwin Morgan and others as one of the twenty greatest modern Scottish novels – is still in print as are *Young Adam* and *Sappho of Lesbos*, most of the material in this collection will be new even to those already aware of the dozen or so books Trocchi published in his lifetime.

Beckett was perhaps the biggest single influence on his writing, although, while Beckett moved inwards, almost beyond the scope of language, Trocchi took Beckett's original 'outsider' or existentialist stance and moved outwards until his canvas encompassed the entire political situation of the Western World. His commitment to social change concentrated on undermining fixed patterns of thought and response, which, he believed, were restricted by the terms of expression of their own consciousness. All of Trocchi's work contains elements of rejection of the status quo; the political and moral establishments; what Trocchi called the 'Auntie (or Grannie) Grundys' or the 'bow-leggeds of Grundy'. This is accomplished subtly, from within, by concealing it in narrative guise or in the plot, where the expected regular certainties are overwhelmed by elements of nihilism. He referred to himself in his notes as 'a polluter of the wells', and a cultural subversive, whose aim was the undermining of all fixed assumptions, accepted forms, traditions, stereotypes, but R.D. Laing was not alone in regarding him as 'an ultra-conservative counter-revolutionary', and 'a romantic utopian'.

The first section of the Reader opens with episodes set in Glasgow from an unpublished autobiographical novel which describes his childhood and early romances, and in which his own persona is named 'Nicolas'. His older brother Jack and his cousin Victor both feature under their real names. The eldest of the three brothers, Alfred, died in the Isle of Man in 1971. Jo Christie, his best friend from school days at Hillhead High School (and Cally House, Gatehouse of Fleet whence they were evacuated during the early days of the war), was in real life Cecil Strachan, and while the real-life counterparts of Mollie, Isobel and Sylvia are unknown, his first wife Betty or Elizabeth is often given her real name, although she also appears as 'Judith'. In the two short stories and prose piece which follow, 'Nicolas' is living variously in a cottage at Garronhead near Balfron in the Campsie Fells and in a flat in Glasgow with Betty. Thus far, we have a reasonably accurate record of Trocchi's early life and first marriage. The short story 'Peter Pierce', written at a later date in Paris, is also set in a Scottish milieu and has been described as his best short story. It prefigures the mood of *Young Adam*, the novel which he began at Garronhead in 1948 and which saw critics compare him to Camus and Chekhov.

The second section introduces a new persona, James Fidler, a rather repressed and unglamorous clerical assistant of early middle age, through which Trocchi could speak and address issues less directly related to his own life. Of about six unpublished novels, this is perhaps the most conventional in stylistic terms and betrays the influence of James Joyce and George Orwell. The short stories, 'The Meeting', 'The Rum and the Pelican' and 'Eileen Lanelly' were originally sections of the novel. The story, 'The Holy Man' shows the influence Beckett had upon him in Paris where he lived from 1950 to 1955. He was regarded by Beckett as a young protégé and they were on friendly terms. The story has a similar structure to *Waiting For Godot* and the 'holy man' like Godot does not appear. The 'Foreword to Vol. 5 of Frank Harris *Memoirs*' reveals the success of his satirical rewriting – a 'labour of hate' as he later described it – a hoax upon a writer 'whose literary style or lack of it' he deplored. The letter to Beckett relates to a slight cooling of their friendship following Beckett's complaints over a text which appeared in *Merlin*. The extract which follows, the very first pages of the novel *Young Adam* sets the scene of the novel and shows the deft way in which Trocchi handled naturalistic description within an existentialist narrative. The action is precise, detailed, yet is reported by an observer, almost a voyeur, who is detached, remote though never dispassionate. Many reviewers described the novel as the most accessible of Trocchi's work and it is both a murder thriller, an attack on the British system of justice and capital punishment as much as a portrayal of loneliness and isolation and the central 'hipster' character/narrator.

The third section commences with 'A Being of Distances', a short story in which 'Christopher', another of the author's alter egos, measures the distances, both geographical and emotional, between himself and his father. Parts of the story recur in *Cain's Book*, the 'novel' or manifesto cum autobiography, which took him six years to write and which absorbed much of his earlier output of short fiction. 'Wolfie', a wonderfully descriptive piece of writing sees Trocchi, the Greenwich Village junkie, taking a long subway ride to the Bronx in search of heroin. It was a trip which was to end in arrest and his imprisonment, yet again, in 'the tombs' – the cells of the New York Police Department. 'Jody' is an extract from *Cain's Book* which describes the Greenwich Village drug scene in which Trocchi participated. His insights into the motives and behaviour of drug-addicts make this one of the best pieces of writing to deal with that milieu. His essay on George Orwell, first published in the *Evergreen Review* became highly regarded by Eng. Lit. students in America for its succinctness and originality. His correspondence with Terry Southern, a 'hipster' friend from Paris days, is outrageous and amusing. Southern is a successful novelist and movie scriptwriter and while both were, in the mid-fifties, willing to churn out formula soft-porn novels for the Olympia Press, they shared a conspiracy to revolutionise the literary novel and were comrades-in-arms against the establishment, during the writing of *Cain's Book*.

Part Four of the Reader sees Trocchi settled in London, having narrowly escaped from the FBI and a mandatory death sentence. He is married to Lyn, his second wife, and has two sons, Nicolas and Marcus. The two essays, 'Invisible Insurrection' and 'Sigma: A Tactical Blueprint' are possibly his best-known and most reprinted non-fiction works. Their visionary quality and the extravagance of their literary style, which coalesces the tone of decadent writers such as De Quincey and Coleridge with the most modern of the 'post-beat' avant-garde, meant that they were much imitated and extremely influential. 'The Junkie: Menace or Scapegoat?', first published in *Ink* magazine in 1970 sets out with clarity his views on the drugs issue. But there was a price to pay for having been so long at the cutting edge of cultural revolution, for having had to live it all on a daily basis; the 'Notes from a Diary of a Cure, 1965' and 'How I Came to Want to Get Off' and 'Uncle Hamlet, Quite Gone into Middle Age . . .' reveal the depth of his exhaustion. He had literally 'committed a kind of spiritual hari-kari' and felt that he had nothing more to say. The last piece, written as a Christmas Eve note to Sally Child, is wistful, almost as if aware, even in 1978 – more than five years before his death – that he will never complete *The Long Book*. From then on, he was searching for a 'plausible end'. I hope that this collection will encourage readers to seek out more of Trocchi's work and that public interest will result in the reprinting of his novels. His writing, like his extraordinary life, is always exciting and worthwhile.

Andrew Murray Scott
January 1991

Annie and Alfredo Trocchi with Alex aged three
on Sauchiehall Street, Glasgow, c.1928
(Courtesy: Jack Robertson)

Part One

Alexander Trocchi was born in Glasgow on 30 July 1925. The family had relatives who were important in the Vatican but Alfredo, their father, who had been a concert pianist and bandleader, became unemployable due to arthritis. Life soon became a struggle to keep up the appearance of respectability . . .

Pages of an Autobiography

Faded now. The lost gentility of another century. A street of old houses, respectable in its location towards the west of the city. A street of bank-clerks, insurance agents, shopkeepers. The women of the street, tired, genteel, dignified, poor. Husbands, for one reason or another, not quite unsatisfactory. Their sins abroad in conversation. An affair of rumour and unfinished sentence, because outside their respective houses they were neat men, dandy men, polite in conversation. And no man collarless. As the years turned the faces of the younger women became more hollow, tongues sharper, lips less red and soft. The ruin of women's faces in a street of surprised, indignant men. To a stranger the street must have given the impression of peace. Underneath passed a procession of sad days, plagued by the curse of respectability on a small income . . .

The houses were built of grey stone.

Ours was a main door house. Enter through our own garden – a small plot of wiry grass that was never green, hedged in by a sparse privet hedge – or by the back entrance in the close. My father was very proud. As compared with his brother's flat! Only a hole in the wall. There was a backgreen also which we shared with the people above. The grass didn't grow there at all. It was reduced to a patch of scabrous black earth by the feet of children. It was one of my mother's ambitions to sow seed there. Each winter she would talk of planting it and warn us that when she did we should not be allowed to devil it with our feet. For some reason or other she never got round to it. She contented herself with planting nasturtiums in the front garden. They flowered untidily for a few weeks each summer. And she looked forward to those weeks and to the appearance of lily of the valley which grew at the front steps beside an old seashell.

On my father's instructions only the adults of the house were allowed to use the front entrance. The children, even those of the 'paying guests', and tradesmen were required to enter by the close. When my eldest brother left school and went into an office he insisted that it was one of his rights as a wage-earner to enter and have his friends call for him at the front door. He was allowed to do so. As we grew up and my father's dominion became less secure this caste-system of privilege was one of the first things to disappear.

We came to this street during my first year at school. My cousin, Victor, led me round all the lanes and dunnies, and it was he who first took me below the Caledonian Mansions down to the banks of the Kelvin. His first love was the daughter of the stationmaster at Kelvinbridge Station. A slim little girl with hair like a bluebell. He pointed her out to me one summer afternoon as she stood in the doorway of the station with her legs crossed and her hands clasped behind her back against the wall. She stood all alone there in a short print dress –
*Vielleicht sind
deine Fransen glücklich fur dich –,
oder über den jungen
prallen Brüsten die grüne metallene Seide
fuhlt sich unendlich verwohnt und entbehrt nichts.*
And then she began to bounce a ball against the brick wall of the station. We watched her round the edge of the building, and when I pretended I was going to shout to her he blushed and pulled me out of sight. One day, he said, he was going to speak to her. He never did.

The year was 1931.

We gathered fragments of gaily coloured china. Beads and artificial jewellery which we would separate according each a distinct value. We collected glass marbles. Red with delicate sinews of purple and white. All in a glass ball. We saved foreign stamps. But it was the colours, the stranger, more vivid patterns that excited us. The stamps of Egypt, Persia, Zanzibar.

Winter came. And with it the brittle music of the weather. The creeping fingers of frost and fog. The houses were blacker. The ribbon of sky grew more narrow, yellower. It hovered over the ice-struck street like the ominous shadow of a bat. We were allowed out for only an hour after tea.

In the mornings the sun seemed to have lost all its power. As insignificant as a glass lens. And the fog stuck in our noses and made it difficult to breathe. We did not run so much then. Our throats became dry more quickly and there was no clean air to slake them with. Even the stones seemed harder. The wind cut at our clothes like a scythe. It was not until the snow came in January that the death was lifted from amongst us and the air and the leafless branches of the trees seemed to stir again with life. And then the snowdrops and the first crocus. A slender jewel-spear. Delicate as a woman's eyelid. Still packed round with snow. The green of its leaves like swordblades cloven into existence. The sun growing in splendour. A huge amber ball of life and power and joy. Mummie! Mummie! I saw a crocus today . . . purple and yellow and I wanted to bring it home to you Mummie but I didn't want to take it because it wouldn't like it in the kitchen would it Mummie? The snow began to melt and a new land was disclosed. A land which radiated plumes of sound and colour, involved in a mystery of growth and breathing. The colour of the buildings had changed from black to grey again, and the air was alive with the laughter of girls in new frocks and leather sandals.

There was a goddess in our street.

Can't remember her name. But it should have been Jasmine or Isis or Miraldoqc. At first she was a girl. Always surrounded by the older boys of the neighbourhood. She didn't play like the rest of the girls. She came out each evening and stood watching from the mouth of a close. Soon all the older boys – she must have been about ten years older than I – had left off their playing and had gathered round about her. The rest of the girls hated her. A priestess with a train of inferior priests in her wake. One day she left school and went to work. We didn't see her for a week. And then one evening when she came out the transformation had taken place. She wore high-heeled shoes, very sheer silk stockings and her body with its sudden contours was mature like a red rose.

She had always been disdainful. Now she was the unapproachable goddess from a strange planet, the mistress of the moon. Her cold beauty struck the street like a javelin. A sudden presence of witchcraft. Hectic. Risen from the stones.

A silence had fallen on us. We stared. Slowly, embarrassed, we returned to our play. No boy dared to go over to her.

Instead she came herself. She chose a victim and engaged him in conversation. Soon the game had stopped and she was surrounded. Following her, we went through a close and into a dunnie. She lighted a cigarette and leaning against the wall she spoke softly to the older boys who surrounded her. I wriggled my way through the crowd until I was very close to her, until I was involved in the strange exciting smell of her make-up and her clothes. Then I heard her say: Get these kids out of here! The first time I felt like a pariah dog.

About a week later a sports car began to call at her house. Each evening we had a glimpse of her shapely legs as she stepped inside. As the car moved off she didn't glance to either side. We followed it with our eyes until it was out of sight . . .

October came. And Hallowe'en – when we dressed up as pirates and carried daggers and cutlasses and turnip lanterns like grinning skulls. Went from door to door begging for ha'pennies. Subjected to the agony of singing in well-lighted rooms in front of girls of our own age. Blushing beneath our greasepaint. Sometimes, forgetting the reward for our efforts, trying to escape humiliation. A laughing father barring our way. Subjecting us again to the cruel joy of his tittering daughters. Extracting the last shameful drop of blood from us. Sometimes apples, nuts, a few coppers, sixpence if the degradation had been profound enough. From the hands of a pretty girl of our own age. Perhaps her father thought we'd be back in twenty years time. That his daughter needed practice in playing Lady Bountiful. Who knows? Perhaps we will too . . .

November, November, remember, remember the fifth of November! Gunpowder, treason and plot! Burned Guy Fawkes on a piece of wasteground, whooping round the effigy like red Indians, hurling firecrackers, demons and rockets into the flames. Afterwards, when the fire was dead and the embers were slowly blackening, we eluded the cheeky zigzag of the last squib.

Christmas Eve. The smell of mincemeat and pastry. The kitchen all littered with sugar and spices and nuts. The smell of the ham boiling, of the plucked white flourdusted flesh of the turkey on the dresser. Of the kitchen grate stoked busily to redness. When will you make the sweets Mummie? In a wee while Nicolas, after the baking's done. Don't be impatient dear. He twisted on his heel away from her, his nose in line with the dresser. Looking at the big bird. He poked his finger at the rubbery flesh. With his nail he scraped at one of the little pimples of the skin. Don't do that Nicolas. You'll break the skin. Why don't you run along to Christie with your soldiers and when you come back you can help me with the sweets. He frowned. I wanted to take some sweets for him. You can go along with them tomorrow dear. You can take them in the morning some time. He lingered and said: How long'll you be? Come back about half-past eight, she said. You must be in bed by half-past nine. You'll be up late tomorrow night.

When he was in bed he fell asleep listening to the Salvation Army. Outside in the street they were playing 'Holy the Night' – he wanted to get to sleep quickly . . .

Again the movement of the year into birth, into a red and white fantasia of fear and shame and joy. The pink coil of worms. Green flower-fuses. The anonymous face of a beggar. Smeared with a blue growth and the pain of the eyes, hollow and slanting like poles of shadow in the empty sockets of a skull. Creeping round corners. Hesitating at the edge of sex and its pale fleshly perfection. Leda. The swan twisted into the chattering blue-grey mass of a pneumatic drill chipping the surface of stones. Frantic. Demented. With dust and noise for feathers. The black hardness of the street for a lover. The lust of metals. The carping bentness of a nail. – Between the fissure of the old brocade curtains he allowed the night to enter with its silk green breasts. Asked her when she would take him away. When she would allow him to put the honey to his lips and feel the soft fragrance of her pollen. She entered between a wedge of fabric and drew away from him in a mist of floating objects and sounds. Coiling together like a nest of multi-coloured snakes. And then shutting off like the sleek descent of a guillotine. He was alone and the night was black and nothing more. Not even a pinhead of light to break its weight. He turned to sleep when he heard the footsteps of his mother in the corridor.

In the morning and every morning he was demoralised by the unfriendliness of things. The starfish and the little crescent-shaped units of sensation were gone. Nothing but the day and the hours of school and the morning sharp as a tack. To school with his leather satchel and his diminutive resentment. The canker of himself. He hated the smell of classrooms.

It was the hesitation in himself that frightened him. The broken gesticulations. The gawky half-movements. The desire for symmetry. For the symmetry of certitude like the music of Wagner. Like the sky-fixed crouch of the hawk. Like the dart of fishes. To get beyond the first step. Or the beginning of a smile. The immense frozen hesitation like the rising of water in a cistern. Ominously green. Growing internally. The sudden fracture of one's continuity – the freak spasm to the unfinal twist. Have you looked at the eye of a bird? Like the ball of a bead. The vision broken in fear. Elegant. Tremulous. Like the pistil of a lily. With a wetness about it. A soft warm sylph-sap – you know it's alive . . .

He didn't know what he meant, but that he meant something, something like leaves and colours and glittering slivers of glass, like the tropical sun and the moon like a ripe yellow cheese – a spectral knowledge. The noise of the bees told him that. All day long round the flower garden a drone of certainty. But that was when he was alone, with a primitive pineal loneliness in the north . . .

It was the violence of the colours mainly. The small nests of corruption. The flower blades which fought for existence at the base of the buildings in a husk of dry earth, as black as soot, as sour as the stench of metal foundries. Speckles of surprise in the eyeless dead hulk of the street. Colours more than voices or smells. Ivory, alabaster, rose, ultramarine, turquoise, violet, gold, topaz, emerald, cyanic. The dramatic irisation of things. The red red electrifaction in the midst of chimneys, iron railings, vendors, automobiles, gutters, stanks. A garden of incest in the House of God.

Felt different even then. Couldn't imagine myself growing up and surrendering myself to this business of life in which all the members of my family were respectable failures. All, that is, except Uncle Anthony who was a cross between Prince Charming and auld Nick, a spiritual overlord who refused to consider life as any sort of business at all. For him life was love and danger. For him was 'no life save when the swords clash' or when he saw the silver movement of a thigh in the darkness. By God, Papiols, then the wine tastes good! But all this invention. I never saw Uncle Anthony. Perhaps never existed at all except in my imagination. But it doesn't make any difference. The air was alive with him. He grew like a tumour in the stones. His poison was flowers and sunlight and joy.

Sometimes I used to sit alone in the cellar at the end of the backgreen wondering what I would do when I left school. I would light a candle and watch the twin points of yellow flame as it swayed like a snake's tongue. Making the wall alive. Irrupted with change. The cellar was overgrown with silence, a sacrificial silence such as I could not experience elsewhere, born of decaying brick, a silence which lived in darkness, in the fabulous orange texture of the walls. To my horror I discovered that I was not interested in doing anything. Didn't want to be a farmer or an engineer or a lawyer or a doctor. Sometimes I pretended. But even then I had no ambition unless it was to be Prime Minister or God Almighty or something of that nature. And this because I knew that anything short of this would describe merely the limits of my servitude. Later, when I came to understand what it would mean to be Prime Minister, I decided that that career was probably less suited to my nature than any other. Always impatient with idiot-opinion of lowest common denominators represented by unions, parliaments and suchlike institutions. Only the autocracy of God remained undefiled by the limiting contagion of the mass. Unfortunately, this ambition did not provide me with an answer to the kindly enquiries of my relatives. To the question: What do you want to be when you grow up, I could hardly have replied, Oh, I'm going to be God – they wouldn't have understood . . .

In the cellar he had returned again to the primitive beginnings of life, to the primeval spring wherein his ego was rooted. The flame of the candle pulsing in the centre of the old table was itself a centre from whose magnet locus radiated green tentacles of light. The arteries of the cosmos. The flame was as strange, as uncanny as a salamander. It fascinated him. It possessed the strange obliquity of an eye, not a human eye – the eye of a Javanese idol. A cruel despotic goddess whose flesh was fish-scaled in gold and silver, whose limbs moved with the subtlety of a python. It was a pale flame. Phosphorescent like the ghost of a rose. Prophetic as the lip of Tiresius. Often he watched it burn itself out to a heap of viscous wax, blue for an instant before it sizzled out. And then he would light another candle or unlock the cellar door and let in a wall of light. In summer he could watch the sun set from where he was sitting. As though the air which during the day had been composed of one element – a fresh radiant blue air – were beginning to decompose like curdled milk. Its flesh was lighter, less blue. Containing long strands like tapering islands of red. The blood run out into estuaries. Later, when the sun had disappeared, all that remained of this mysterious chemical change in the atmosphere was two shades of grey – a fire extinguished – the grey of its flesh and the darker grey of the scars where the blood had run out. When he thought of the sky, of course, he was thinking of that fragment of it that was visible between the blocks of tenements. The space was not as restricted as it might have been because between the block in which they lived and the next block there were two sets of backyards and a lane which ran between. Along this lane came the dust-cart each morning to collect the refuse from the two blocks of tenements. Sometimes he would sit alone in the cellar with the door opened or closed depending on his mood. During winter he would close the door and lock himself in. Only in winter when it was dark outside in the evenings so that no light filtered through the cracks in the old walls was it dark enough inside for the candle flame to dominate the interior completely. In summer the spokes of green light which it generated were interrupted and disintegrated by white dust-laden poles of sunlight entering through cracks. Thus he could never during the summer believe in the absolute power of the flame. Couldn't absorb the unadulterated mystery of its green strands. The flame itself was a dull eye. Almost insignificant. And although he was alone, he was not alone in the world, because during the summer the world extended along the poles of sunlight beyond the walls of the cellar . . .

Not alone in the world. Nicolas looked up at the crucifix. The brass Christ was dull, turning green at the corners. Thinking of Judith. Can't imagine her face somehow. I say to myself – she had grey eyes. She was very beautiful. But these are abstractions. Nothing to do with the existing woman to whom I was married. This woman is not even a memory. I can almost see the suspension bridge. I can remember it. With Judith it's different. I have a set of words which perhaps I applied to her in the past when she was there at the other side of the room or sleeping beside me with the flesh of her neck exposed. I repeat these words now. But they are meaningless. Empty generalisations. Signs signifying nothing. Could apply them to this woman or that or to the picture of an actress in the newspaper. If I say – the sea is green, that is equally meaningless. I can never bring the black shock of the existing sea into myself. I remain all the time in a sort of adjectival delirium . . .

Uncle Anthony became for me the symbol of adventure. Compared with him my other uncles were no more than the respectable suits they walked in. Prosaic buggers with one dull memory. Remember them coming to our house and sitting in an armchair with their legs crossed and socks with clocks on them. Yes, they would take another cup of tea. Half a cup because time flies and I must be getting – did you hear about Mrs Derwentwater. Nasal catarrh you know. What's that? What did you say? Something wrong with her ugh navel? Ah, nasal! Less compromising. Yes, I will have another spoonful. They're going to operate. Remove her nose. Cut it off. Far more sanitary. Is it really as late as that. Well I must be getting, must be getting, must be getting along . . .

Years passed with a falling of leaves and rain. And something else was falling away. More significant. Protective scales of myself. An involuntary discarding of my layers of certainty and laughter. I felt myself becoming gradually more naked. Even in the cellar. Exposed. The rain raced in the gutters of my mind with a flotsam of dead symbols . . .

. . . perhaps when you are my age, the priest was saying, you will realise that only God can be in you. Men can be with but never in you. And women too. To men and women you are always another. That is why you can be most lonely with the person you love most. A frantic desire to be absorbed. Impossible. That is the root of heresy.

Nicolas turned to look at him. The grey hair in small tight curls at the temples. He was looking at the crucifix.

La Belle Dame Sans Merci, Nicolas said. But there it is. The separateness is there. And so is the desire to end it. You won't eradicate it by calling it heresy. You merely transfer the desire to a God you have invented. You can elide with Him, perhaps get the illusion of not being alone, because He doesn't exist. He is in you already, created by you. So the elision is not difficult. But. It's got nothing to do with existence. I don't know your God. And I'm not interested in creating one for myself. If I can't elide with a woman with a belly and eyes and blood, one that laughs and smells like a woman, with feet and hands and hair like a woman, then I'll derive no comfort from an imaginative fusion with a symbol. I'd rather be free and alone and conscious of my isolation.

It's not that you haven't understood, Father Doherty said. You have chosen evil. Like Tristan you have chosen to destroy yourself.

Nicolas walked over to the window and looked out at the rain. At least I have chosen, he said . . .

I shall write about the steel in the flute.

I shall write a symphony in blood.

I shall write about Uncle Anthony!

Stood watching the crowds getting on to the tramcars. Home for the evening meal. The city gradually emptying itself. An illusion of purpose about all the people. And a lonely feeling at the base of my stomach. A faceless alien here. Like my friend Kapinski was. His shoulders wet and a strange prayer on his lips. Only a bloody foreigner after all – I am here and I am standing and there is nothing but the sound of water in my boots. Doing nothing because you see I haven't a penny – alone with his Slavonic suffering – and I am thinking that I will perhaps be in France again, but there is something in me you know that I cannot leave. No more than a shadow on a wall. One of the faceless. Leaving the city it is as though you have never been there at all. No severing of ties. No ties to sever. Faceless because unrecognised. Unremembered. No exit from oneself.

Started to walk. Perhaps the first time I felt I had to walk. A temporary relief. You have the feeling you are doing something. There is no question of indifference. Not in the beginning at least. You must move. You must act. And therefore you walk . . .

Found myself walking in the direction of the same café where Cathro and I used to sit for an hour each evening. Found myself opening the door and going in. As good a place as any. Sat at a table near the door. Somehow it seemed safer that way. Although of what memory or apparition he was afraid he had no notion. Something in the atmosphere. A familiarity that through time had become unfamiliar. Returned unrecognised to the place that shared your defeat. The faded clowns on the walls stare back at you. Subrisio saltat.

The coffee cold and tasteless. The cup cracked, leaking on a yellow saucer. Almost he thought time stopped altogether. The rain at the doorway blew in with the man framed there in hesitation. Tall. The blue suit wet and baggy at the knees. A white face pitted like the rind of a lemon. Hastily he closed the door. Paused, sat down immediately opposite me. Smiled as if to excuse himself and then he drifted back to his own thoughts.

I watched him raise a newspaper between us with the finality of a camera shutter.

Four fingers on each side of the newspaper on the back page of which black letters followed out a rigid procession of days and voices in anger. Frightstruck to the trapeze in the Arlington[1] I swung high over backgreens where my brother Alfie with blood streaming from his nose fended off four ragged urchins with curses and blows – I'll beat the daylight out of you! he screamed, swinging a big boot to the bottom of one. Alfie! Alfie! my mother cried from the kitchen window. Leave him alone you young hooligans! Later at the table he sat with defiant red hair swearing eternal enmity against all trespassers. My brother Jake placed a large dux medal with a blue ribbon on it on his side plate and stuffed a cream cookie into his mouth. A few moments later a glowering dog entered and sat in my father's place where, with the silver fork of my father it wolfed three chops by means of a clicking dental plate and with a black look all round went out again to get drunk.[2] When the shadow had passed the silence was broken by Jake's strong munch and by the tinkle of his medal against his cup. He sat there with a leer twenty years too old for him, his little finger hooked through the blue ribbon of the medal which he swung backwards and forwards against the cup. I'd like to see him break his teeth, he said gently, cocking his ear to hear the front door slam.

At that moment the man opposite moved the paper and he returned again to the café where the clowns were still derisive. He looked at the man. Didn't know who he was, or why he was

1. Trocchi was a regular attender at the Arlington Street Baths.
2. This is not a factually correct description of his father, who drank alcohol only in moderation.

there. But the newspaper that he raised between them was the prohibiting vacuum between two planets, a shadowy no-man's land inhabited only by the voice of a dying civilisation, the broken hulk of a vessel sinking on a yellow sea.

At sixteen I knew my enemy. Sat there at the café table and wondered what it all meant. I hated the man – oh, not that man particularly, I could see alright that he was merely one of the hoard of red-eyed rats that slunk on to the quay when the ship made its last voyage, something at the edge of the tragedy, strictly irrelevant, like the charwoman who must have mopped up the floors at Elsinore after Shagspur got bloody at the end of the play. Perhaps he didn't even come into the café. Perhaps I'm telling lies. I'm good at that too. That's not the point. I was on the verge of a great discovery, only it was just a bit beyond me. Not until I read that story by Lawrence, The Woman Who Rode Away, about a year later that I began to get the hang of it. And not all at once either. It's a slow process, this business of becoming alive. I began to see that the modern world is two worlds. Two layers of history. Interpenetrating. Distinct. The one inhabited by professors, doctors, politicians, trade unionists, bank clerks, butchers, fishmongers, journalists. The other by people like the woman who rode away. The sun-addicts. The moon-men. The helmeted men. The Vikings. The lovers. Of the dead and of the living . . .

Father Doherty had risen. He was standing now, his back to the fire, with his hands clasped behind his back. Do you think, Mr Kradnor, that you are alone in being able to choose? Nicolas at the window was hardly listening. Shaking his head vaguely – Not alone. Others too perhaps. And granting that you are exceptional in having the power consciously to choose, the priest said, are you not committed to choose what is right? Nicolas turned to face him. I would have to have known already what was right, he said. And that's impossible. Even if right and wrong did exist, it would be impossible to know what they were. I can't live historically existing as I do into a future that'll certainly be absurd. Will it rain tomorrow? And the day after that? And if you say that right is something that each man knows for himself, then I deny it. The word 'right' is not in my vocabulary. I feel nothing. Perhaps I'm pathological. But I do feel committed. I do feel guilty. No matter what I had chosen I should feel guilty. Just because I exist, because I am separate and because some day I shall tread on a cat because I wasn't looking where I was going when I crossed the street to give sixpence to a pavement artist. Do you understand Father – I stand before the future like a child who is mortally afraid of being again projected into a room where everything is fragile. But surely, Father Doherty said, there are some things for which we are not responsible. Nicolas said, one has usually acted before one has time to make any metaphysical calculations. Otherwise one would never act at all. The diagnosis comes afterwards.

Nicolas turned away again towards the window. Back towards himself and the years that sloped away from him into the streets . . .

Over the old beat. Almost a routine job now. Walking and wondering. Drinking and fornicating between times. And still unable to get what's to be said said and time gurgling down the stank like gripegreen sewage. Stick your nose in it you bastard as it drops there to the belly of the cosmos! It is an extremely long streak of yesterday's spaghetti. A spiritual menstruation. Exclusively of your own manufacture, you bum! An affair of brief encounters, tortuous liaisons in back rooms of the city, of reading and eating and drinking and writing and sanitary towels. The steel on the anvil. Sand propelled along the crust of a naked track. An affair of colours and voices, of half-remembered melodies – when will the city's snarl make my throat utter?

Rain crawls on tenement roofs. A slow bleeding on café windows, down walls over dark pavements to the gutter. I am sitting in Renucci's making a coffee last against time. It is milk-muddily English. But it is coffee. I am feeling pretty low. There is really nothing to feel high about. The rain in the evening, the empty pockets, the slow tumour of loneliness festering somehow all around me. Renucci placed his large hand across his eyes. He said nothing. Whether or not he understood me I couldn't say. Perhaps he did. Renucci was nobody's fool.

In the evening my mother prepared for church. Behind her along hushed Sabbath streets. At six-thirty p.m. the bells will ring out again all over the city. Monotone. And black-coated, white-collared men, women with pot-shaped hats with black macaroni or crowfeathers on them, umbrellas ebonyhandled, silver-banded as a sign of respectability, will trickle along the streets beside pointed leather shoes. Outside the church Mr Oglevy will ponderously unpocket his solid-gold chain watch from about his thick midriff, and he will say politely to Mrs Oglevy, to the Misses Oglevy, to Master Oglevy, to young Mr Smith and to Edith Gowdie (spinster) that it is time to enter. Introierimus ad altare dei.

At the other side of the city men in smooth-checked caps, white-scarved and sleekly barbered will smoke into the slow-moving night. Sandy Forbes will break away from his group – introierit ad altare Phyllis. A big red-headed tart. Grey-white marble skin. The others will watch after him. Men without God.

Minuit sonne. Mon père prend le couteau et coupe le pain.

At midnight a city stirs in its sleep. Husks fallen. Eyes see. Limbs loosen. The rebirth. The city has thrown off the damping yellow sickness of yesterday. The streetlamps are brighter. Less chaste. They hiss in derision. At the Central Station the newsboys are untying bundles of fresh-printed crisp white newspapers. The homeless, the restless, the sleepless drink coffee at the wagon-stalls in St Vincent Street. And read tomorrows news. Old care-worn women falter in and out of the shadows. The taxis wait. The morning light breaks along the street, darkly, incognito. The homeless, the restless, the sleepless prepare for another day . . .

And how should I begin?

I could start with the dog-eared man. The one with shiny pants who tried to sell insurance. Nothing like being safely insured, he used to say. If a man can't have a decent burial . . .

Nothing like the thought of a decent burial to buck a man up when his belly's empty. Or when his eyeballs bulge. Like old Mrs Croat there at number 24. Got everything arranged she has, right down to the flowers. Lilies and violets. Just waiting for her pain to burst. And she's even left instructions about who's to be pall-bearers and who hasn't. Not taking any chances.

I tell you Mr Nicolas, the dog-eared man said, it must be a great comfort to have things all tied up neatly like that. It must indeed. And he is already fingering his briefcase with a hopeless look in his eyes. The kind of look a guy must have when he sees the judge put on his black cap. It's his bread and beans after all. And although I show signs of wear and tear after all these years I don't suppose it looks as though I'll curl up and croak just after he's gone. This one, I can see him thinking, is good for ten years at least. And maybe he's right. Unless I get bit by a mad dog or something.

And it'll only cost you sixpence a week, he says. Prolonging the agony. He knows. I know. He knows I know. We are just making polite conversation on a fine spring morning. He is being led along to the hangman now. But he keeps right on talking because you never know. Why, I might look up brightly and say: Certainly Mr Dogear. You are the very man I have been looking for. I have set my heart on a really swell funeral. And you are just the man to look after it for me. And if God was really good I might pay him a month in advance. I might, I say. If I had a private income of sixpence a week. But there, I haven't. And he knows I haven't. So he keeps right on looking hopeless but talking all the same. And to be sure he's got to talk. He talks nine hours a day six days a week. And on Sunday mornings for good measure. Yes, I said, very reasonable, very reasonable indeed. But . . .

Sharp as a weasel he has intercepted me. I see you are an intelligent man, Mr Nicolas. Why, he says, at our price every person can be assured of a decent funeral. And no burden to the dear ones you leave behind. He looks at me fit to make your heart bleed. Sure, sure, I say. Die happy. Nothing on your conscience. With no bag of bones around to cause a smell. And all for sixpence a week. It's a wonder your company makes any profit at all. That's a fact, Mr Nicolas, he says looking at me suspicious like from behind the drop on the end of his nose. In fact, I go on raising my eyes slightly in reverence, I am overjoyed to hear that a big corporation like yours takes so much thought for the dear ones we leave behind. It is certainly very generous of them. Is this not evidence that the death of our Saviour was not in vain? Nosedrip has begun to smell a rat. From the corner of his eyes he contemplates my vest pocket. The one with the soup stain on it. Slowly the eye comes up, a hairless eyelid like the rind of a melon and a small round bloodshot eye. A question mark. Of course, he says, it's a business proposition. A fair deal for both sides. The dog-eared man is uncomfortable. But what a risk, I say to him. Have you thought of the risk? He nods his dome wisely. Why, I say, what if all your clients died tomorrow? Say a bubonic plague. Have you thought of the sorrow and suffering it would cause the shareholders? And all because they set out to relieve the sorrows of others. You must be very happy to work for such generous men! The dog-eared one looks as though he has his own opinion of the shareholders. But he doesn't say so. He thinks I'm crazy. But he doesn't say that either. He says instead rather slyly: Would you be interested, Mr Nicolas? Oh no, not for myself. I couldn't allow complete strangers to take such a risk on my account. I'm suffering from cancer. And anyway, a good oak coffin with a brass plate on it would be wasted on me. Too grand. Make me feel very small. He is about to say something very rude but he perks up a bit when I say to him: But why not come and have a drink with me Mr Dogear? I'm sure you could do with one as much as I. Well, Mr Nicolas, he says, that is a very kind thought indeed. I shall be glad to come with you. And so you shall, Mr Dogear . . . that is, if you will be good enough to return my kindness and lend me five shillings until the end of the week. I expect my cheque will come tomorrow. Delayed in the post, you know.

I must have said something to shock his sensibilities. He is looking at me very indignantly. I sympathise with him. It is surely a bad thing that a bum like myself should exist in the same world as those generous shareholders. Nothing but an ungrateful heel. Anti-social. A pimp, a parasite, a crawling thing. In a thin voice he says that he has just remembered an important engagement and he falls out of the door like a spilled skittle. Mr Dogear was a bit of a moralist in his own way. And besides, his mother told him never to lend money . . .

I could start with the dog-eared one, or with my father's false teeth for that matter. I've got all the time in the world, and a set of false teeth clacking somewhere about Capricorn might come in very handy during a dull moment. Comic relief, the critics call it, and they're all agreed that Shakespeare was the very one. You know: 'To my wife, my second best bed . . .' as Anthony said when he moved in with Cleopatra.

But it's a question of key. And volume too. I don't want to start piddling away with the flutes when I should open like Wagner with a crash of trumpets. But that's dangerous too. Because in a work of this length I'm liable to develop waiter's feet before I've worn the pile off the carpet. So keep it gradual, bum. Show a few scabs first. And then, when they're just beginning to show interest, shoot the works and send for the ambulance! This advice to myself who won't profit by it because I never take advice anyway . . .

The sky is yellow with swine fever. The sun paler than a disc of glass. A young man whose name is Nicolas and who reads too much looks at his shoes. Down under Central Station Bridge where lilies don't grow any more and the flowers have pear-shaped bare legs and wear lipstick.

In a glass of dull beer he has a vision of a table and a typewriter unused for a long time. Brewer's alchemy. The future like an unwanted tail is exposed when you take off your underpants.

Spoils the fun of it. Later, when he has extricated himself, the light still limpid on quietly cold streets, he begins to think of his mother who died of dysentry out of a tin of pilchards . . .[3]

Once a year perhaps, a small nipped woman on a Clyde paddle-steamer telling us not to lean over the rail too far . . .

In the eye of the morning there is an elision of dead consonants. Mist huddles on a yellow river. River of many dredgers. Exits and entrances. Bluebottle tugs on yellow oilwater. It is six o'clock in the morning trala trala trala . . .

Cold in the North with a coldness fit to cause lockjaw. The philosopher Keyserling who is rather an expert on the life-cycles of transplanted races could doubtless recommend a sort of spiritual 'Sloan's Linament' – as used by my father on his inevitable flesh – to keep the cold out. Extremely trying for an Italianate Scotchman like myself. The toxic frigidity filters through blood and soul contracting the latter to the hard black bead of Calvinism. Ice. Solid. Freezing tooth and gut. A hardening of the arteries in the lines of a face that was always forbidding. String for lips. The granite of Albion. Don't let them persuade you otherwise. The barking of my father provides a useful percussion effect in the bleak symphony of the North . . .

Six o'clock. Few places open for breakfast at that hour. Workingmen's places. Sad, grimy-capped workmen. Sallow porous faces. Men with no wives. Or whose wives don't make breakfast. Sinews permanently overstretched. Hook-fingered. Eat porridge and sausages. Drink tea. Brown like bootpolish. Cold th'smorning. Same as yesterday. Her eyes hopeless. With no expression in them. She scooped the coppers into a large red hand. First customer. Atmosphere reminding me of the time I worked in Oban. On my uppers. A job in a hotel . . .

3. Annie Trocchi, the writer's mother, died on 4 January 1942 of acute bacillary dysentry and the source of infection was discovered after a post-mortem to have been a tin of pilchards.

He left the ship at four o'clock in the afternoon. Into the slake yellow mists of the East Coast. Along a bald concrete strip of frost and black telegraph-poles. Pole-tops caged, sunk in the frozen yellow mass of the day. Christmas Day. On shore-leave.

The others had gone off earlier. To their pints and their women. He, in a sentimental mood, with a wistfulness behind his eyes, remained on board. He stayed behind, thinking to explore Christmas with a noggin of rum and a book of poetry. But the words were dead and flat. Lightless like spent bulbs. The words were as uninfectious as the broad yellow tongues of fog which moved a graveyard in the superstructure of the ship.

After the Christmas meal those on duty slung their hammocks in the messdeck. He sat alone at the table close to the bulkhead. With a noggin of rum and a book of poetry in front of him.

A yellow Christmas. A very yellow Merry Christmas!

About two o'clock he went on deck. He leant on the rail. Saw the land stretched out into the fog like an uneven pancake. And the sea whitely breaking against the shore-wall in the distance. The sound that clung around the ship even at anchor – even when the deck was deserted – the dynamo, the heart of a body asleep. The sound of electric lymph in the metal of the ship. An occasional gull. Sometimes two or three. A congerie of toothless hags cackling at an anecdote which, always meaningless, had long since ceased to amuse. Somewhere behind the rim of land a town of fishermen. Half-industrialised, growing inland over flat country. Christmas in the flat country. Behind blinded windows, with only the thin fragmentation of light and sound striking the isolation of the street. He had never felt lonelier. He couldn't remember ever having felt lonelier . . .

There was nothing he could do until four o'clock until the next tender came alongside. And then he would go ashore and try to lose himself in the town. How he hated the ship! The constrictions, the metal everywhere, the paint, the hawsers, the chains, the studded plates of the deck, the nightmare of iron and steel which ran his mind to limits all about him. And the cold air which lay along the ship forcing the mind to an intense consciousness of its isolation. He would go ashore at four o'clock. Until then, two hours, two heavy Christmas hours, five hundred yards even from the tail-end of voices that pass you on the street. With a book of poetry, instinct with one's own extended pain. Christ! to get away from those false shambling shadows and into the sun! to get away from words that followed him like footsteps down his own mind! to get away and into the laughter of the open street! To escape from thought and ideals and words. He dropped the book into the water. He watched the pages slacken and bend wetly downwards, half-sunk, where the hammocks of the sleeping men . . . – Christ, he said, it's fucking hot in here. He looked at Nicolas. – Not getting your head down?

Nicolas shook his head.

– Me either, the other said. Going ashore are you later?

– Yes. Four o'clock. Wish it was four now.

– Going to make some char, the cook said, going out again. Come to the galley in a while if you want some. He went out.

Last Christmas I was at Portsmouth. Four of us walked along to Southend. A canteen there. And a dance. Office girls mostly and a few Service women. The ping-pong tables drawn back. The last dance came quickly. We took our girls home. Kissed them goodnight. Couldn't blame them. There was nowhere we could have taken them. And it was a cold December night. We talked for a long time before we went to sleep. Mostly about women. Because we didn't have any . . .

It was cold on the tender. It moved slowly away from the side of the ship through the flat water. He leant on the guardrail and buttoned his overcoat up to his neck.

He got into the town about quarter to five. He looked around for an hotel and in the lounge he sat sipping whiskey and soda. He had a small round table to himself. The only person sitting alone. Who else would be alone at Christmas? The rest of the people in the room were grouped in little parties. All jolly and laughing and friendly amongst themselves. A girl at one of the tables caught his eye momentarily, smiled . . . he smiled back, half-blushing to be alone . . . and then she turned back to the conversation at her table. Another five minutes and he went out. Afraid she would look at him again. He didn't want to be pitied.

He found a canteen. Inside it was all decorated with streamers and tinsel string. There was holly and mistletoe, and the long refectory tables were spread with cakes and Christmas buns. Some of the older ladies of the town were officiating, smiling at everyone, pouring tea from huge brown teapots, all very busy and happy to be doing something for the boys and girls who were on leave. Some were dancing in a small cleared space to a gramophone. He sat down to watch. One of the girls reminded him of a girl at school, a girl older than himself. Margaret Meade. She had danced with him often. His head only at the height of her breasts. He remembered how the lower part of her body moved heavily against him coaxing his steps. He remembered being fascinated by her slow silent mature resilience and he wondered at the power in her limbs. Athletic limbs of a girl four years older than himself. He was learning to dance then. He turned his attention away from the dancers and looked at the rest of the people in the room. Mostly couples. Too many men.

The whole school watched her as she ran there with swift clean movements, a small black dog at her heels. I watched her all the time. From the moment she set foot on the lawn until she disappeared behind the trees. And even after that. After she had gone. Because I could still see her. I could see her in the gladness of the lawn which came alive in her presence and remained alive like grass after a summer shower for the rest of the day. Like myself, the lawn lived for her as it lived for none of the other girls from that day to this. It was her creature as surely as I have always been.

When he thought about it afterwards he wondered whether he had got things upside down. – Do you know what I mean? he wrote in his diary: She radiates life. It emanates from her pores . . . a scintillation of sound, animal, vegetable, mineral. She has violins in her flesh. Perhaps she is an instrument. The lovely instrument of the earth. The symbol of the earth's fertility . . .

He turned away from the lawn when his imagination could sustain the atmosphere no longer, when the bankruptcy of the grass and the trees and the distances apart from the life of her body forced itself upon his mind. He turned away from it because he couldn't bear things out of relation to her. Green and gold, the graceful rhythm of her. Or else some fool interrupted him. Following his eyes to the empty lawn, seeing nothing, suggesting a game of table-tennis. And he couldn't explain it to anyone. Couldn't explain, that is, without being presented with a lot of abortive parallels which didn't seem to him to be parallels at all but merely inferior. Infinitely so. Not even a difference of degree at all. You can't love in a bowler hat. He became a poet.

And then five years during which he avoided her. It was easy to avoid her because she was not looking for him. And, anyway, he returned to the city only during his leaves from the navy. But even in the navy he wrote long letters to her which he never posted. Instead he showed them to Ginger Bacon, because Ginger, in spite of his squat dwarfish exterior, had a soul. A big soul. As big as a sunflower. And he played billiards and he drank beer and he could look after himself. He was a person. And what was perhaps more important, Ginger gave him hope. – If I were a girl, Ginger said, I couldn't resist that letter. If she has any imagination, she'll answer. If she hasn't, then it's high time you found out. Believe me, Nick, if she's anything like you say she is, she'll answer. He grinned. She'll kiss your feet! Nicolas smiled. He shook his head. – Not yet, he said. I'll not post it yet. It's no good trying to rush things. I missed the first time. I want to be very sure before I try again. I won't try before I am sure. – And what if she gets married meantime? Ginger said. You don't want to be a bloody Hamlet all your life. – I don't give a damn if she gets married! She's mine! I don't give a damn if she gets married and has four children. I'll take her away from him. We'll run away to the moon together. As sure as I shall write a great poem some day, I'll have her. I'll dedicate my life to it, every minute of it. Have you read Stendhal? I'll scheme like Julien. Only I'll do it to make her love me. Do you understand, Ginger? I haven't got anything else to live for. Nothing else matters to me. Ginger laughed. – You'll do it, Nick. I know you will. You don't want to try to convince me. I was convinced before you said a word.

He had gone to the old galleries to see an exhibition with two friends. Epstein, Rodin, Daumier, Matisse, Picasso, Cezanne, Degas, Manet, Gauguin, Velasquez, Rembrandt, Seurat, Italian Primitives, vases of Sung and Han, old English silver and Dresden china. The gift of some patron or other to his native city. They had finally got round to the tearoom. There had been fifteen originals of Degas. They were elated. He was just crushing his cigarette in the saucer to rise and join his friends who had already risen when he saw her sitting alone at another table.

She had seen him first. She was smiling at him. He hesitated. She was alone. She was smiling at him. Perhaps she was waiting for someone. She was still smiling. He was going over to her. She had spoken to him. He heard her voice say 'hello', soft, surprised, delighted.

– Hello, Betty, he said.

They were looking at one another. Someone spoke at the next table. His friends were waiting for him. Hesitating at the entrance. They moved outside into the galleries. Lingering. Someone pushed past him carrying tea. She was still the same. More lovely than ever. And smiling still . . .

And then suddenly they were both laughing. It was he who spoke first.

– I haven't seen you for a long time, he said.

– Five years. Her eyes wide, grey, friendly.

– Are you alone?

– Excuse me, a voice said to him, but do you mind sitting down. You're upsetting our table. The man at the next table was fat, bald and red.

– Sorry, he said absently.

– Sit down and have some tea, Betty said.

– Just a minute, he said. I've got two friends. I'll go and tell them.

He came back alone.

In the past two years he had thought less about her (he had a passing infatuation for another girl . . . Mollie in a teashop in Canterbury, in the evening when she combed her wet hair in front of a flickering fire). Somehow, she had passed out of reality into myth, her image was confused with a shapeless, persistent undercurrent of certainty, fertility, joy within himself, with the animal certitude that nothing was beyond him. Her image was sunk in the depth of him, like the vague and ubiquitous images of spring, of harvest, of fulfilment. Like the vague magnificence of the lemongrove:

> Fifty men own the lemongrove
> And no man is a slave.

He would find fulfilment in action, and when he was ready to approach her, to win her for himself, he would take her and wear her like a red rose on the crest of his armour. Old gods spoke to him. Quetzalcoatl, Saturn, Poseidon. Beneath the tired, faithless nihilism of his civilised self he felt the bubbles of a darker power . . . the power of the concerned animal as it turns ferociously on its persecutor. Somehow he associated her with this power; she was at once the power itself and its predestined victim.

But now, sitting beside her, close, talking of Scarlatti and Bach and harpsichord music, the myth was exploded, and he felt the animal magnetism of her presence steal over him again like a sickness. Only this time the sickness was not painful. He was no longer hopeless as he had been at school. He had changed. His words were unembarrassed. The views he expressed were tinged with a faintly amused dogmatism bred of the certainty of his intellectual superiority. His voice was soft and controlled like the flight of an artist on the trapeze.

She sensed the change. She felt that he was her equal, that he was no longer the boy whom she had pitied for his devotion. Although she felt that he still loved her she sensed that he would never admit it. She knew that. Not, at least, until she had capitulated herself. He was impregnable. Like a bright young god who is sure of his omnipotence because he is omnipotent. He would never relinquish control of himself, never compromise himself, and he would leave her with the same calm certainty with the same faintly amused curl of his lips unless she surrendered first. She knew this and she became uncertain of herself. She knew that. She knew that he was attracted. But then most men were. And he was the only man she had met whom she knew would leave her without being committed. With the same softly persuasive certainty as he was speaking now. If she wished him to confess then she would have to confess first . . . she wondered whether she had already decided to do so . . . tacitly, but beyond doubt. For between man and woman there cannot be two deities. Someone must submit. To other men she had always been a goddess. This young man was calmly proclaiming his superiority, inviting her to worship. She who was Diana. Who moved with the grace of a planet through the stratosphere of men's souls. For the present, anyway, he would accept her only as a woman. If she liked she could sacrifice herself to him. If she didn't, he would pretend to be interested in the moth on the window or in the saucer where his cigarette ash accumulated. He would defend his isolation. Plunge only when he was sure of striking. And yet she knew from the tone of his voice that he loved her. She could feel the immense gravitational wanting beneath the formal meaning of his words. When he said – I prefer Mozart to Beethoven, he was saying also: You must come into relation with me of your own accord. When he said – Have you seen *Roses* by Juan Gris? . . . when he described their colour and texture so that she knew that Gris must be a great artist, he was saying more urgently: We can come to live only if you accept. And the softness in his voice suggested colour, sound, light, love and a hundred other filaments of being, a vast, unexplored boundlessness towards which she was drawn inexorably like the silk of a dandelion into wind.

He looked at her, Eyes, hands, hair, lips . . . talking at the same time of poetry, painting, music, ballet, anarchism, aristocracy. He realised that no names of mutual acquaintances were mentioned as usually happens when two people meet after a long interval as though trying to establish a reason for speaking to each other. On the contrary, Betty talked only of him and of herself as though everything else were irrelevant. And everything else was irrelevant. Art in any form was irrelevant except in so far as it provided a useful and effective medium for the secret transmission of more personal meanings. Like a secret personal language. He knew what he was doing, what they were both doing. The ambiguity of the conversation enabled them to establish an almost physical contact without overtly venturing from their isolation. It enabled him to consecrate himself, to confess his love for her, lifting the weight of it from himself without actually doing so at all, so that what she might suspect, know even, with part of her, she would doubt, wonder, perhaps fear, with another part.

There had been a girl at school. A girl called Sylvia. At night, immediately after the master had made his rounds to see that the lights were out, he fixed his mind on her. In the safety of his bed. Where no one could see his thoughts. Sometimes he stripped her. Sometimes she came to him naked. But the cinematograph broke down with loud laughter from the other side of the dormitory. And during the day, hating her for being the nightly assassin of the values which daylight and popular romances inspired in him, he hardly looked at her, and then, in the sight of all, demonstrated how little she meant to him. During the day his thoughts, although hopeless, were for Elizabeth. All in white and orange blossom. But it was never Elizabeth whom he held in his arms in the secrecy of his bed.

Outwardly it was the same during the year after he left school. Although he knew that it existed, he refused to recognise that part of him which longed to be the slave of a mistress – the triumphant slave to be sure – the jealous hating slave of a woman who only interested him carnally. During the day he repressed the dark impulsive force which strove to expel all irrelevance, which sought to persuade him towards the pure mystery of sex. Outwardly he recanted. He forced himself to look at faces. And when he looked at the face of Sylvia he saw only the stubborn obscenity of her desire.

He arranged to meet her after dark one evening so as not to be seen in the town with her. She had already acquired a reputation. In a mirror in the service room in which he and his father lived together he admired a mask of sophisticated cynicism. He dwelt with satisfaction on his daring, on the cut of his clothes. He did not see the contempt which lingered in the mirror after he had gone out.

His mask was waiting for her at the corner. She had expected it but said nothing.

— Where shall we go?

She shrugged her shoulders. Watching the chemical activity of his face.

— Let's go for a drink, then, he said. He waited for her answer.

— I don't feel like drinking tonight, she said casually. She witnessed the momentary decomposition of the mask.

He lost direction. Checkmate. He fled from the voice which came over to him — Recreate the past. Prostrate yourself at her feet.

She sensed his conflict. She sensed that his will was set against her. His being with her was a compromise, a guilty concession to the outlaw in him. And she despised him for it. She felt like slapping his face.

— What'll we do then? he said to her.

— We could go to a dance, she said. Her voice was deliberate. A public place. She wanted to humiliate him.

— If you like, he said. There was no way out of it.

They danced well together. In his dancing there was none of the self-conscious restraint which existed beneath the surface of his conversation. No conflict was reflected in his movements. He danced with a primitive grace. And Sylvia was still the best of dancers, lithe, slow, unconscious. They danced nearly every dance.

During the interval they sat drinking coffee. They were closer than they had been at the beginning. They talked of the past as though it contained no skeleton. He found his own voice. And when he paid her a compliment with it she recognised it as his own and softened towards him.

It was when he looked at his watch and found how late it was that he remembered his mask. He remembered why he had asked her to meet him. Again she saw a subtle catalysis in his face.

She allowed him to lead her into the park, but his advances were hasty and clumsy. She held his wrist firmly. He walked home with her dejectedly. He was amazed that he had not been able to seduce her. When he kissed her before she entered the house she said that he kissed perfectly. She did not add 'like a passionate rodent'. And he was unaware of the irony in her voice.

It was only afterwards that he understood everything.

He received his calling up papers with mixed feelings. He had no illusions about the kind of life that was in store for him. He resented interference. But at the same time he was glad to get away from the city of past failure. He left Christie behind. Christie didn't pass his medical. They saw each other occasionally, whenever Nicolas was on leave. And when he was demobilised it was to Christie that he returned . . .

Nicolas led her into the tunnel by the most obvious species of rationalisation. He took her hand and led her away from the dance-floor where the rest of the holidaymakers were dancing in sports jackets and tennis frocks. He put his arm round her. They walked beyond the road over a few fields that were green and singing. He was very conscious of his mask. Conscious of the deliberateness of his words. Meanwhile, Isobel, slim, with young animal flanks and her hot-house beauty, made the decision. She felt very superior to him, a determined, anxious youth who made bold with words that were not his. She took pleasure in her knowledge of what was about to pass. His words, each of which concealed a question, the either-or, skirted his purpose with monotonous insistency. He wished to appear very reasonable, to suggest irrationality with a calm, logical precision. He spoke of repression and sublimation because he feared his desire to touch her breasts. She, on the other hand, had already decided. She knew intuitively how she would react, how she would give herself, how she would take him. But she let him continue, wondering whether he would suggest the tunnel or the old mill, watching with a cruel part of her mind how he led himself into arguments which he managed very clumsily. She didn't say – Shut up, Nicolas! Here I am. If you want me, take me. She said instead – But what proof Nicolas is there that there's an unconscious mind? She might have added that she wasn't interested anyway, that she wanted to get to wherever he was circumspectly leading her as quickly as possible, that she wanted to lie down and open her legs wide to him. SHE KNEW. She knew intuitively. The barbaric heat of her body demanded him. She wasn't interested in his embarrassed circumlocutions. She might have said – These cumbersome scientific terms are irrelevant. It's a question of blood. In fact it isn't a question at all. It just is. A terrible cosmic propulsion. Only she would have expressed it by sounds and not words. But she remained remote and she said – frankly, Nicolas, I don't believe it. And she laughed in his face. He became angry. He said – It's not a question of belief, I'm talking facts.

– Your facts, she answered still laughing at him. They seem very silly to me!

– I can't help that, he said. You're a woman, and you haven't read about these things.

She agreed. She didn't read much at all she said. It bored her. She wondered when he would forget his pride, when he would stop talking like a schoolboy and come to meet her. She had been watching him while they walked, watching the studied seriousness of his face, the cynical Don Juan expression which came over it as he talked easily about repressed women, and she saw in him a civilised wasp afraid of its own sting. She had watched him triumphantly weaving the net in which he would entangle himself, not her. She had the delicious feeling of his involving himself in her woman power, of his compromising himself, laying himself, abject, at her mercy.

– Look, Isobel, he said suddenly, don't let's argue any more. Come and sit down and smoke a cigarette. He led her towards the tunnel.

So it was to be the tunnel after all. He was afraid of the sun. She allowed herself to be drawn towards the entrance. And when they were out of sight she slipped off her tennis skirt and drew his head down to her.

For years afterwards Nicolas wondered about her. It was the only one of his affairs that he never boasted about. Even at the time he was unsure whether he was the victim or the seducer.

And really the doubt hardly existed. He had been raped. Not rudely by an Amazon, but cunningly, lured into depersonalisation, through extinction. For a period of time . . . five, ten minutes perhaps, he had lived only by her, through her, for her, as surely as if he had been the foetus of her womb, he had existed merely as a chrysalis in the warm air of her being.

And she had laughed at him. Before and after she had laughed at him. Not, he realised now, with the voice of a silly girl who can't be serious. She had been serious. Deadly serious. Her laughter had been contemptuous. She despised him for his beastly little intellect. She despised its circuitous attempts at justification. And she revenged herself on it by enticing it to justify itself out of existence. She spat on his obvious cleverness. She drew forth its denial out of him and destroyed him. And her laughter proceeded from the animal dogmatism of her nature.

Now, years afterwards, he had learnt humility and he was eternally grateful to her. A girl, only eighteen, who had just left school, a girl two years younger than himself, whose inferiority he had taken for granted. But she was old in the instinctive wisdom of her sex. Under her power he underwent an unconscious and degrading depolarization. But she had taught him the meaning of life. And now, three years afterwards, he wished he could meet her again, slim and proud in her white tennis skirt. But he knew only that her name was Isobel and that she was the daughter of a schoolmaster who lived somewhere in Cardiff.

Faces out of the past like the masks on the walls of a theatrical shop. The odour of grease-paint, coconut-butter and a floating of false gesticulations. The mask of Isobel. Remote and pure in her desire. The mask of Anthony. Fearing the passing of time and the iron bars which divided him from it. The mask of my father. Fallen now with age and dried-up gums. A thousand masks. A thousand microcosms, each with a distinct centrifugal force, distinct perceptions, helplessly sandwiched between the layers of Saracen, forming colours on a grey crust.

When he left school in 1942 he took his own mask with him, an ill-fitting mask with the cracks of the years daubed with inferior putty. He walked unsteadily between two worlds with a volume of Bradlaugh in his pocket and later defended Aldous

Huxley against Christie who didn't like that author for the wrong reasons. He was a pacifist but joined the Fleet Air Arm because he remembered a conversation. Chowdrie and the rest at the hall fireplace at school and Elizabeth saying she would marry a pilot. He walked in glory which he didn't particularly want down the Wilhelmstrasse of his imagination.

The year passed quickly. A kind of marking time, a constant frustration. At the edge of things at the University. Unwilling to go in. Cursing his isolation. He seldom went out with girls because he couldn't break down the original barriers. He moved towards women with the guilty secret of his sex hidden in the back compartment of his wallet. It made him feel grown up. But it was his scab too, a terrible birthmark which made him hypersensitive to denial, a stigmata, self chosen, worn voluntarily behind the fear in his eyes.

A hungry sun. The angry yellow tiger spurting dust on city pavements. Hating his prey. Burning. Unconsuming. In hard bent shoes I walk the gutter-graven road. Along an edge of stone. The air contracts. Glare, gold, glint, glass, gash, score, in tired brick where black bones walk. The ulcer of the undamp air.

No light on the land now. No spark of friendly frost to raze its crust. Dead eyes to see the light. Dull skin to feel its breath. Its voice bursts brasking from a throat of clay. Its shoots are scaffoldings gaunt against the year's dead bulk! For I have known the dull-green baize, the smoke-sick air of billiard salons, I have known the suffocating tedium of tortuous days when my medium of expression was the potting of a ball. The lights that splay their cones in oblong rooms dissect the hours. The pack is cut. Eyes of men whose lives consist in parlour trades, Phoenicians of an evening in a room, reflect, dilate, rescind, in horror load the last and watch it sinking . . .

In the early season the seeds were big. In retrospect cabbage-seed and food for farm-beasts. A hacked crop and gladly locusted. That was a long time ago. I have been walking since in foreign lands. Along avenues of kings. I have small mind to return. And wish to be gone where the orchid is proudly impure. A decision revised and over-revised, I am yet undecided. Unbrave battler of the streets. Too hard to bear. Meanwhile unretracting along the edge of stone I over again decide I know my enemy! Through long territory of the past he has driven me, through goals of sunlight with harsh geometric precision. In the darkness I eluded him. Only there. Merely elusive. When the winds struck and I saw the grey prison-house he had made for me I became decided. Now it is only a question of time . . . The stale smell of the River Kelvin, twisting tortuous, through a time-blackened city. On the grey banks of Kelvin I first knew myself . . .

The Earthbound

'The thing's stuck!' Nicolas moved his foot unfixing four papery slates of a dirty colour sluttering suddenly downwards. 'God!' he said, and smiled.

'Heaven roo . . . ining from heaven . . .' Christie grinned the grin of smokesoaked teeth, precisely picking fragments from the rusted rone. Wide-jowled, he stood with buttocks jutting rudder-rubberoid on a soapbox. His left arm supported him. 'Manna,' he said gravely, retreating to ground level. 'Unleaven bread.' He fingered it to flakes and spread it lightly on the lean grey-green grass. 'Hey, wumman!' He thrust his big round head in at a small window. 'Ah'm feedin yur burds!' Unapplauded, he extricated himself and walked the length of the cottage with his head bent and his long white hands at prayer. 'Mocho lo agradezco, Padre,' he intoned through his fine nose and looked up at the roof where Nicolas, inattentive, was half-encased in chimney.

He turned to Judith as she emerged with a bucket of loamy soot. His dark metallic eyes engaged her definitively through his niggerbrown-rimmed spectacles.

'Your late husband,' he said, 'is being sucked into the black belly of original night.' He indicated the trunk and straddled legs which bent forth from the broken chimney.

Judith, from where she stood behind him, glanced up at the lengthy lower half of her lover. Fixed as a bent nail. Body taut.

'Nicolas!'

She stood there violet-eyed in paint-splattered dungarees.

'Come out of there at once! That's your last clean shirt!'

'The wages of sin,' Christie said, shaking his head. He seated himself on the soapbox to watch the proceedings.

'And you get up from there,' Judith said. 'There's a spade in the woodshed and we need a pit to put the rubbish in.'

'Pshaw!'

Christie placed one hand at his belly and the other at the small of his back and lifted himself, an unclean thing, from his seat.

'Radix malorum est femina!'

He let his pink tongue dangle from his lower lip and slunk off spluttering, leperlike, to his task.

'And mind you don't tread on the crow!' she called after him. She lifted her pail. As he entered the shed a vague half-articulated sound of 'kill' came back to her.

'Nicolas!'

Cooper opened out of the chimney like a pocket knife. In a proud masculine voice he shouted, 'Got it Jo! It's unstuck now!' He commenced to pull up on a dirty piece of rope and produced a frayed tatter of red cloth and an hairless brush from the vortex. 'Bugger it!' He sat abjectly down with one leg on either side of the gable. A pair of compasses.

'Your bloody-well-chosen stone's got stuck, Jo! I've lost it.' He held up the sad fragment of cloth which had been a bag as evidence.

His wife laughed at him.

Sootsmeared, gollywogic, he peered down at the source of derision.

'Where's Jo?' he demanded.

'Round the back digging a hole for the rubbish.'

'Good,' he said. He lit a cigarette in his strong broad hands and looked over across the moor where the heather sprouted in purple tufts. Treeless and almost fenceless, it stretched away in a gradual scabrous dome. Over there worldwise villagers with cracked winter faces had gone at night, secretly, to the whisky still. Not quite sixty years. From where he sat he could see Jo Christie's slow figure bent hard to cut the spade into the tough turf. He dug steadily, the hermit, hurling Provençal curses at the earth.

'Come down now, Nicolas. Breakfast's nearly ready.' Brushing her hair back, she shielded her eyes from the crisp white glare of the morning.

'What about the stone? It's probably stuck in the middle.'

'It wasn't big enough,' Judith said. 'It'll be in the fireplace.'

He was doubtful.

'Come down anyway.' She blew him a kiss and went into the house.

In the low brown-beamed kitchen she stirred a pot of thick mealy porridge. Sabbatical, it bubbled and spluttered against the sides of the pot. She spread some newspaper on the dung-coloured table and set it with oddments of crockery and cutlery. With all my worldly goods I thee endow. An iron double bedstead with creaking rustcrusted springs. The engines of love. The table with knobbly matchstick legs and a gallon of superior creamgloss paint. Two falling chairs and four alabastery tallow-candles. Let there be light. Myself too, he said afterwards. And the crow of course. The young crow which couldn't fly. All beak and gullet. She looked at the old Paris-plaster patched walls, damp-eclipsed, drawing together all layers of history in a peeling splotch of colour. Ochre, canary, heavygrey, webbed by cloudy veins of the original brick-red keel, varicose, at the surface. The kettle for tea.

'Porridge ready?' Nicolas appeared at the doorway.

'In a minute,' she said. 'Wash your hands at least.'

'I'll go and get Christie.' He went out.

Christie was still digging when he arrived. Kneedeep in an oblong grave.

'Alas, poor Yorick,' Christie said as he approached.

'Found anything?'

'My limitations,' Christie said. 'I have lost all my original brightness.' He twisted his face in a sudden quick leer. Rising, he threw his spade on top of the rootwoven turf and climbed out. He was a big-boned ball-jointed man with long feet. 'Tomorrow morning,' he said, 'I shall sleep till midday.'

'I have never been able to understand,' Christie said at the breakfast table, 'why people talk of the sanctity of work. No one ever talks of the sanctity of lust. And yet neither appeared until *after* the Fall.' He smiled with lingering insinuation at the man and the woman who were his hosts.

They talked about that during breakfast. Nicolas suggested that Christie should write an essay about it.

'I will. I will,' Christie said. 'I shall call it "Her Twin Delights".' He appraised Judith with the eye of a satyr and was pleased at the slow flowerlike blush it brought to her cheeks. 'I shall subtitle it "The Breasts of Tiresias" or "How Gertie Gorman Got Her Breasts Felt". Which do you prefer, Nicolas? Which has the more metaphysical ring to it?' Through the thick lenses of his spectacles he thrust a jesuitical stare at his friend.

Judith didn't like Jo Christie. She saw the heavy sexual scar of the celibate. The young female in her distrusted him.

Jo Christie didn't like women. The sullen secrecy of their sex was repulsive to him, and he was afraid of it. His tone was sarcastic and hysterical at the same time.

Nicolas, chewing toast, was aware of the opposing forces. Obliquely, within the fine white sprinkle of sunlight which pricked out dust-motes in the atmosphere, Judith and Jo were at war. The disputed territory was himself. Jo, his childhood friend, resenting the intrusion of the girl. And Judith, the girl, the slim sensual girl with the strange eyes, feeling outrage at her belly and her flanks. Ever since he had arrived, two days before, she had hated him. She hated his long yellow hands, his ridiculously big head, his heavy literary humour, and she hated his continual probing over sex as though it were a particularly obscene beetle whose ludicrous movements under the probe were to be enjoyed from a distance, intellectually, in laughter.

Nicolas didn't answer because Christie didn't expect an answer. But he smiled because he was amused. Jo Christie always amused him.

Judith poured a long spout of pale brown tea into each cup. She was angry. She was angry that Nicolas didn't see through Jo Christie. *She* saw through him. Oh, how easy it was for a woman to see through him! She would have liked to shock him. She wanted to shock the obscene little over-civilized male in him who was afraid of women!

Longly on his chair, Christie tilted, his myopic glance coming to rest on the girl.

'You don't approve Judith?'

Nicolas was looking, trying to read her face.

'I don't think it's funny, if that's what you mean,' the girl said. She was conscious of blushing again. But she couldn't explain. If Nicolas had said it she would have thought it was funny.

'She doesn't think it's funny,' Christie said, but he didn't go on because Nicolas was frowning.

After breakfast Nicolas and Judith went down to the farm where they kept the car and drove into the village for supplies. Judith, sitting beside him as he drove, looked straight ahead at the ribbon of road.

He didn't look at her but he said 'Why don't you like Jo, Judith?'

'I just don't like him, that's all,' she said.

'But there must be a reason surely?'

'Why must there be a reason?'

'You can't dislike a person for nothing at all.'

'I don't know. He laughs at *us*. I can feel him laughing all the time. He doesn't laugh at you but he laughs at *us*.'

'Oh, you take him too seriously, darling,' Nicolas said.

'He *is* serious,' Judith said. 'He doesn't like me so why should I like him? You don't see it but I do, he is laughing at us all the time.'

'Do you want him to go?'

'How can you make him go? You can't ask him to go, he's your friend.'

'I don't want you to be unhappy,' Nicolas said.

He said in a street, in the mouth of a close, in a cafe, long before she met Christie, that he didn't want her to be unhappy. And she hadn't been. They were poor but she didn't regret anything.

The little box-like Austin chugged on towards the village.

When they got back it wasn't necessary to say anything to him. He met them at the door and they knew from his face that something had happened. He handed a telegram to Nicolas.

'My father died early this morning,' he said.

Nicolas drove him to the station. For a while they didn't speak and then Christie, removing the cigarette from between his thick protruding lips, said that he supposed they would be glad to get rid of him.

Nicolas flushed.

'Don't think that, Jo,' he said.

The thick glasses stared straight ahead.

'What's the use, Nicolas? You know it's true as well as I do. I wouldn't be going now just for my father. My father meant nothing to me.'

'Don't talk rubbish, Jo. You've got to go for your father. He's dead. You've got to go for him.' He kept his eyes on the road. There were cows in front. He slowed down.

Christie was laughing softly, mirthlessly, his arms folded across his chest and his head tilted back.

Nicolas put the car out of gear and waited. A girl with big breasts in a print frock was coaxing the cows through the gate with a stick. She had bare legs and they were muddy. Steel's daughter.

'How virginal!' Christie said. 'How earthbound women are! Imagine that one white and smelly with her brood round about her!' He looked quickly at Nicolas, sideways. 'I don't *have* to do anything. My father never did anything for me. Why should I follow his coffin?'

Nicolas didn't answer. He thought the big-breasted girl quite attractive. Vaguely, he desired her.

'No, Nicolas,' Jo was saying in his hard hysterical voice, 'I'm not going because of my father. Let those who loved him bury him. Anyway, I hate funerals.'

The car moved forward again. Nicolas didn't know what to say. They followed the road over the hill past the small derelict church and on towards the station. Neither of them spoke.

On the platform they shook hands.

'See you some time,' Jo said. 'I'm going to Spain after the funeral.'

'You're going then?'

'Where?'

'To the funeral.'

'Oh that? I suppose so. I've got nothing better to do anyway.'

'Write me from Spain,' Nicolas said.

'My dear man,' Christie said, 'I never write letters. When I leave a place I do so purposively. Afterwards, I'm not masochistic enough to indulge in regret.' He stepped primly into the carriage and leaned out of the window. He smiled down at Nicolas.

'Good luck then,' Nicolas said.

As the metal of the train creaked forward Christie remained in the window, smiling.

Nicolas waved his hand. The last carriage turned out of sight behind the signal box.

He bought some stamps in the village. He had a manuscript to get off and he thought perhaps he would write a letter to Christie. He could say he was sorry anyway.

He drove slowly on the way back with both windows down, allowing the wind from the trees and the fields to enter the car. As he passed the farm where the cows had halted him he caught sight of the pink movement of the big-breasted girl as she disappeared into a barn. He thought of Judith, and at that moment, listening to the distant insectal sputter of a tractor at work, he was glad, he was suddenly very glad that women were earthbound . . .

Fragments from a Diary of a Man Found Gassed in a Glasgow Slum

Raining outside. Grey buildings all splotched and running. A coalman leading an old steaming horse. Another man on the cart. Sitting on top of the coalsacks with a coalsack over his head against the rain. The grey Capuchin.
    For a week now my mind has refused to hold onto things. Time and again I've sat down to work at the book or to make notes for something or other and got nothing done. Time moves. I am growing older. A coil of half-turns and shadowed exits. A moving that is nothing. A stasis that is merely a vague sense of unrest at the season's passing. Allowed events to catch me up again. To go on without me. Can't see the past for the present. The present for the future. Listening to a foreign language of which I understand only an occasional word. And those words meaningless because they're lost in a shifting stream. Vaguely I make an effort to intercept a meaning somewhere and to follow it through its development – why take for granted a development? – I miss. And time runs out of reach.
    A soiled raincoat, a dirty saucer, papers, books, empty bottles. A brush on the floor – like an inventory clerk I take stock. But nothing of all this signifies anything. There is no point at which I can enter into the series of perceptions. It is not I who impose upon fleeting impressions the series of labels – raincoat, saucer, books. An automatic recitation. Unlike an inventory clerk I have no immediate interest. No suggestion of possible value to be attached. No column of neatly written figures to be added up. No result to arrive at. Papers merely. Books merely. Bottles merely. And soon even the names cease to suggest themselves to my mouth. I am lost in anonymity. I am merely the unpleasant feeling of the presentness of it all. Something

going on. I am its consciousness. And yet to one side. Slightly apart. Yes. Distinctly apart. With a faint feeling of nausea that is all that is left of me.

And this woman. I shall go to the cinema with her this afternoon. Don't really know why. Except that in some obscure way I am involved. Involved in her desires. In her consciousness of me. We shall talk across continents. Of nothing. For nothing. I can give no meaning to this relation. It is there. Like the red leap of sun on the sea at night. The big strength of her. Of her purpose. Part of my personal inventory. One alarmclock, two cases, one typewriter, Mrs Reid – just like that – without a fragment of a reason. And I am already committed.

Later I shall come back again. No comment, no change – reasonless as a weather report. Absurdly I have come to exist in her mind. Just by existing. And I myself will be moved, persuaded, judged in the person that exists only for her . . .

Still raining. Whirlpools and rivers on the street. The rain whips flatly against the window.

I am alone. But my other faces are abroad, spoken in the lips of others. A thought. A faulty recognition. Death shall have no dominion.

At my mother's death. The last vital link with existence cut. Lowered into a grave that was my extinction. Men and women in black. Brothers. Aunts. Uncles. Lingered on the green slope like quavers on a musical score. Sixteen at the time. And my father said to me: You will never see your mother again. Like a drain running out. But she continued to exist. Her death was my direction.

Time begins to exist with me. All it contains or has contained exists in my existence. In the slow passing of the hours, between nightfall and nightfall, there is no existence other than my own. Love is a bad joke, Christie once said to me . . .

You destroy another existence by creating it. You create her whom you love, destroying her own existence. Two poles of experience. And ours so truly parallel – there is no elision between their separatenesses – a conjunction of the stars! Love is the desire to elide like sounds in language. But the desire is conscious and it is consciousness that has created the vacuum.

The curse of otherness, someone called it. The stigmata that each existing self bears unto itself even beyond death. Affecting – like the deathmask of my mother – I exist after death. Erased from the consciousness of the world only when history ceases to be meaningful, gradually, as the past in its detail loses its presentness and comes to be as a closely printed page, vague and illegible from a distance. Whatever I do I become involved. Whatever I choose, whatever slant I give to the future, an impersonal mechanism is set in motion – perhaps because I walked down a street or plucked a flower or lit a cigarette. Events outrun me. Guilty in every decision. Not to decide – even that is a decision. I am again involved. My existence spreads beyond itself. Affected. Affecting. Absurdly born. My slightest movement provokes a chaos of reactions. Like a stone dropped into water I am dropped into existence. I watch the ripples move away from me. Unable to recall them I watch them break against the shore. I didn't ask to be born. But I was born in my mother's agony. Not ask for life. But sucked at it like a leach. I am a scorpion with a sting in my tail . . .

Tapeworm

Desire for opium, alcohol – any narcotic or woman or power or the cigarette you finished two hours ago and the empty packet in front of you. The past is dead and useless. There is a tapeworm in your bloodstream. The crocus has faded. Doesn't matter what anyone else says. And this coldblooded bastard inside saying write write write, all over and over again when you'd much rather get hold of the bottle and sink into the state when all you want is some shapey piece of the other sex to play the flute with. But then you haven't got the money for that all the time. In fact you've got about two quid and then you're flat and all the while this lump of psychological cancer, this impersonal hook of worm has got you dangling like a piece of dead beef at the end of a butcher's chain. And it is not going to let off the pressure – not a dog's chance – until you sit down and write two thousand words that you can read over again without belching. So you don't write? Alright. You go to the pictures. It is a picture for adult audiences or at least that is what the censor calls them and you see some bugger who doesn't get seen getting into bed with some other bugger's wife but who is found out afterwards by circumstantial evidence and then the fireworks begin and the drama leaks oozily on via two violent deaths (crime does not pay) to a final stasis where the wronged bugger gets himself tied up again to another piece of skirt whom we are led to believe is some sort of suburban Desdemona who has no interest in these things and whose papa is going to get the wronged bugger a job in a bank where he can earn enough money to support his wife and breed children. She is the type of bitch who is going to keep one large burst eyeball on him and who is going to ditch him for some good clean bloke if he gets his shirt dirty. But of course that doesn't happen in the picture and the lights go on and you are left sitting in the one and ninepennies with nowhere to go and a sick feeling in the pit of your stomach.

And now you go outside and the night is cold and the rain is coming down like a box of blue rivets. You think of Bach and the second movement of the concerto for two violins and how many children he had and you wonder how that guy ever did it. You move into a doorway for shelter and you find that it sells fish and chips. You go to the counter and you are served by one of the sweetest little curls you have ever seen. Oliveskinned from Napoli. She is about seventeen and she has dark crinkly hair like most Italian girls. Her eyes are black diamonds with a touch of the snake about them and she has lips like those things you see advertising various beauty products. Only hers are real. They move softly like a slow-bleeding wound. But you don't get any ideas because her old man is standing there at the chiprange and he has a neck like a gnarled oak and a forearm like a ten pound cod. And anyway you have only two quid in the whole world and your tapeworm has got St Vitus dance. You go out and your feet are walking to wherever you left your typewriter. You are crucified and you have got to make the best of it. You know that what you write is going to be no good and that if it is good it won't be published because it is immoral. And you begin to wish you'd bought that bottle after all. And then you get to thinking you've had a bum deal and this merely puts you more clearly on the romantic side of the fence – you've got to believe a helluva lot to be a classicist, that is to say if there are such people. Which is hard to believe. And you begin to think that Rimbaud was dead right when he migrated. That man was dead right in a lot of things. But then you've got no guns – you swapped the Luger you brought back for Mario Praz's *Romantic Agony* so now you can't even blow your brains out – and you wouldn't know where to get any. And anyway the niggers are a lot smarter now and can probably get guns easily enough without making you rich by playing the intermediary. So it seems this tapeworm's got you nailed alright. It seems you've just got to fiddle away and snatch something to drink, eat or sleep with between meals – the tapeworm's meals, I mean, the hungry bastard!

You are walking slowly because you are a man as well as a bloody poet. You get to thinking that this whole set-up does not delight your nostrils. At the same time you do not want to change anything except perhaps the colour of your shoes. You walk too much. Your shoes get dusty and you could do with another half-inch of sole on them. But you do not want to build bridges or societies for the pacification of the nations. Let them bleed themselves white. The process of disintegration will at least provide some punk of a historian with a job and furnish at least four philosophers with a brand new philosophy of history. Incidentally it will provide men like yourself with some very interesting and variegated pigments for a mural or something. Viz. Guernica. Very interesting. It is very interesting indeed how superbly coloured are some of the most hideous diseases under a microscope. The orchid is fatal. You think to yourself that there is positively no use being indignant about it. You decided long ago to accept everything. Even the tapeworm. To do him justice – though God knows if a tapeworm deserves justice – he is very good when he is satisfied with his fodder. He sleeps then. And you are compensated by a sharp tingle of pleasure somewhere between your navel and your throat and by a supercharged desire for Betty your wife. It is then that you derive an intensified electric pleasure from her moist body. She is magnificent. You accept then. Past, present and future. They are all part of the present after all – what you wrote yesterday is as good as it is today – and the present is you. The future is as much part of you as your own daughter. You are the future. All of it that concerns you anyway. It does not appear suddenly in company like an unpleasant diarrhoea. It is here, now, at this instant. It exists in embryo as the product of your own perverted copulation, and if it turns out to be a bastard, well, you know who to blame! You should look after your wife better.

You get to thinking a lot when you are being probed on the backside by the tapeworm. Perhaps it's a sort of defence mechanism. Something glandular. You begin to think in circles. You think for example that the whole set-up stinks of stale meringue, musty taffeta and faded rosewater. A distinct odour of decay. The aforesaid items having originally been introduced to tone down the smell. You needn't have worried! The original stink disappeared long ago when its source solidified, that is to say when the apple disappeared down old Adam's gullet. By the time that pimp had reached the stage where he swallowed more than an apple, well, that was that as some folks say who want to be conclusive. By that time he was as dead as the bird who fell on his head on a concrete surface. After that he was worrying only about the next world and the price of a ticket on the bus. And incidentally he was the first silly bugger to clamour for the right to hard labour. Dead from the brainpan downwards. No. You needn't have worried about the smell. The hard, the dead, the negative exhales no odour. But then you get to thinking that perhaps this cadaverous hulk is made more interesting by the sham scent treatment. And this is the way you've got to argue if you're going to accept. You can have no truck with those coons who talk big about accepting one minute and produce a fistful of blueprints the next. And you have a sly thought to yourself that there is a lot of these bastards. So long as you're not a member of the official school of British Watercolourists you can accept the hypocrisy of a cheap blonde's mascara, and what's more, love it! You remember reading somewhere about the scarlet women of Ancient Egypt and what these janes didn't know about magnetizing the female torso you could put in your tooth. After touching it up with gold, green, grey and blue paints and draping a smoky-coloured something about as dense as a spider's web from hiplevel the guaranteed magnetic locus was upwards of four hundred yards. And if some modern skirts object in principle to these artifices, then it probably wouldn't be very practical for them anyway.

You are now reaching the hovel where you have temporarily installed your typewriter and your wife. You hesitate darkly at the bottom of the gaslit stair waiting for the woman whom Eliot said was also hesitating somewhere about the streetlamp. But of course she doesn't show up. And she is probably very mercenary anyway. So you light a cigarette and give the rudder to the tapeworm who is by this time about as sleepless as a lion rampant. You enter and Betty greets you with a big smile and a cup of coffee, and looking at her standing there like one of those enchantresses out of a fairy book you decide that if Caesar Borgia had wanted that little Italian curl at the chip shop then he would have been welcome to her as far as you are concerned. You decide that your wife has got all that it takes. After a while when she has shown a bit of leg and generally indicated that she desires your conjunction in the dance of the seven veils she begins to realise that this is one of those nights when the tapeworm has got you nailed. She is a good kid. Quietly she goes off to bed by herself and leaves you about as happy as a gooroo on a desert island.

You are sitting there in front of the typewriter. Like all other machines this wonderful invention needs an operator. You stare at the keyboard and it stares back at you as though it was disgusted. You big helpless bastard, it says, why don't you die? Sometimes you are sorry you have not pawned this contraption. It is one of those eternal manifestations of the cosmic pressure. But somehow it was always the last thing you had to pawn and you never needed to pawn it. At last you have a brainwave. You will play a game of solo. The more you think about it the more you like the idea. You have been alone a long time. Always as far as you can remember. Except perhaps sometimes when you are making love to Betty. You are alone now. And you begin to think that that is OK by you – at least you should know how to play solo . . .

My deal. Up through the hollow shadow-ribbed vault as far as the darkness. The bent ones. The feared ones. The edge of the rain metallic, final, a drawn dagger. And cold wet bodies under sodden smelling undergarments sticking to the expectant skin of soft-bellied harlots. I make a cut. I win. The cataracts are loosened as far as the flesh of my brain. I listen blackly to the drip drip drip of oil of cloves in the cavity of an old tooth. The pain sinks. I swell into being. I am the chancre of the cosmos. They hate me. But I have all the aces. I am an old hand at this game. With my terrible lever I shall prise their balance into Limbo. Not that I give a sweet damn really. Just that they get in the way – these moral philosophers, university professors and youth leaders, all the carbolic-soaped legion.

Men call me mad. It is true that I love bad smells and all sinful unclean things generally. I love bandits and poets and raped women, chinks and lascars and diseased negresses. Everything in fact from the navel downwards. Above the navel I am not such an expert. But then who really wants to be except moral philosophers, university professors and youth leaders? And you know what you can do with them. I can argue on their ground too – these buggers who worship the big brain and hide their penis in the urinal at the end – but who wants to argue with them anyway? Not me, by the good St Michael, not me! But perhaps I am mad too. If upside down means mad. I hang by my tail from the high wire. I put five fingers to my nose. Don't worry. I won't fall. You see, I've got the aces. I like a full fleshy thigh better than algebra. Laugh that one off you knackerless punks! I like sexy jube-jubey women better than pencils or metaphysics and what's more, I think deontology stinks! Put that in your pipes you noumenal jackanapes! Further, as logicians say, I like to trace with my tongue the soft line of down hair faintly over flesh from navel to cunt – I like to do that better than all your psychological bellyache with space-time and ultimate essences. I prick a balloon. I turn over my wilkies. I buy myself a packet of fags and a good stiff drink and I say to hell with thinlip, scragneck, knock-kneed virgins of thirty-five and their masculine paraphenalia. Agreed. May they inherit big brains and walk on tubular crutches till the cows come home. Then Charon ad holocaust. Pull the plug on them. They HAD their chance. Let them wallow in their own spume. Me? Give me a bed and a woman who knows when to take her scanties off – I'll be alright! My trick, gentlemen, I t'ink!

The man with the blue chin leads his queen. He is very, very efficient. He has studied economics at one of our liberal universities. They say he has fixed an automatic tabulator inside the lobe of his left ear. I hear it ticking now. He calculates he can trip me. The poor misguided bastard hasn't seen my fist! But this much I give him. He's thorough. He plays according to the rules. If I'm long-suited in Clubs he's caught me with my pants down. But as it happens I've got four aces and a string of trumps as long as a chorus-girl's leg. I grin. I take the first space-ship as far as Jupiter and I talk Rimbaud to the Caliph's daughter whose hips look like something out of Matisse. She is a very interesting conversationalist. But she is more interested in the practical than the theoretical. Which is as it should be. I don't disappoint her. As I have remarked before I am not interested in the pure in mind, flesh or spirit. May they inherit nothing. I am not interested in the white radiance of eternity. Later I decide it's about time to take a sock at this blue-chin with the university education. I flick an ace. I bend down and grab hold of his right shoe and twist it upwards towards the roof. He is hanging like a stuck pig from the chandelier reciting Karl Marx and Harold Laski. I tell him what he can do with these birds below plain level. I tell him what he can do with the London School of Economics and with this slow fungus he calls the proletariat. I draw my tomahawk and I remove his scalp. It is a very bloody business. Somehow the operation is not a surgical success. The top of his skull is hanging open like the lid of a box and I am surprised to see what this lug uses for a brain. It consists of two rotating wheels not unlike typewriter spools and a ribbon perforated like one of those pianola things winds from one to the other. By the length of it I guess this bastard must have taken an honours degree. I close the lid and stick a label on it – returned empty.

A smiling fat priest with face-flaps like a bulldog has just revoked. I can see that by the glassiness of his cheap-bead eyes. I decide to watch this bird very carefully. I consider him a lot more dangerous than the blue-chin I have just scalped. He is one of those chameleons who changes the colour of his coat to suit the company. He has read St Paul and likes being a Roman very well. But if this cheapskate thinks I am not going to notice he has revoked then he had better offer me a percentage. Otherwise I'm going to blow him. And on due consideration I decide I'm going to blow him anyway. I don't like his crap line about the negative value of this world. I think this world is a very nice place indeed. I have no desire to change it. I leave that to the moral philosophers, the university professors and the youth leaders and I hope that the imposition breaks their bloody backs or something equally unpleasant. A Christian is a bastard who refuses to accept the present in and for itself, that is to say, to accept life in all its aspects. In the conflict between sex and death he swings a club on the side of the latter – as if the said latter needed any boob to swing a club for it! This sack-faced bird in the white collar is extremely eloquent in his demands for (a) mutilation – a detruncated man, and (b) a general diminution of intensity in living, catabasis; life minus its mysterious pointed flame. And I have no use for this philosophy which is anti-orgasm. The orgasm is the fire in the black vault, it is the dark deed in the hotel bedroom. I look up a dictionary. Orgasm: n. immoderate excitement or action (Gr. orgasmos, orgao: I swell). And now we know. Orgasm defines the vibrant, the vivid, the volcanic, the living, the Antichrist. Dilation, expansion, pregnancy, brutalization, nakedization – Orgasmos the Galegod! I look this guy right in the eye and I say to him that he is all washed up. I tell him I am going to blow him which I proceed to do in the name of the good god Orgasmos with a stick of dynamite which I always carry round for that purpose. When the air clears I think to myself that some day I shall write a history of religion. But then I got to thinking that I could do that in three or four lines and I decide to do it pronto. So here goes. Some bastards begin to find life tough. The cosmic pressure is too tough for them and as they are weak-livered skunks they don't see that they can do very much about it. So they begin to deny that it is one hundred per cent authentic. It is to be considered as a sort of insurance premium, something for your own good like a bad bottle of tonic. You can cash in on it later. There is no more efficacious method of getting rid of a bastard than by denying his reality. But it is difficult to see what you can do with an impersonal bugger like death. So a good God is invented and He will see you alright. Then these guys got to thinking that there are some bright moments too in this world, e.g. sex. But as they had already written off this world lock, stock, and barrel as a 'mere transient thing' they had to levy a tax on this world's pleasures. And that is where the sin of the flesh comes in. But as these birds have only had experience of transient pleasure and as that is all bound up with sex they find it very difficult indeed to say just what this supersubstantial pleasure in the next world will be like. And so they say it is playing harps. And they call that symbolic. A history of heresy is far more interesting. It is the long struggle of sex and life against the death-instinct implicit in Christianity. I dedicate this history of religion to the schools and the colleges and suggest that they remove all the rest from their libraries. Don't those buggers know there is a paper shortage?

I am now leading out my string of trumps. I am pulling teeth like a dentist with thirty years' experience. This young man with the thick-lensed spectacles is looking decidedly uncomfortable. He is a poet and for this reason I spare him. But at the same time he is one of those coons who accept one minute and who talk of the utter dearth of all moral values in the modern world just a moment later. So he has got it coming to him. I can't allow him to pervert the minds of the young. So I compromise. Without saying anything I prod him a quick left to the solar plexus and send him home to his mama. I have now thirteen tricks in front of me and I decide that solo is a very interesting game!

You sit back and you are very happy to realise that the tapeworm is having a drop of shuteye. You smoke a cigarette. You go to the bedroom and you find that Betty is still awake. She gives you a long look and in a few moments you decide that the world is a very rosy place indeed.

Peter Pierce

My only contact with the outside world during my period of 'retirement' was through the ragman. He lived in a room above mine at the back of the house. He was called Peter Pierce.

He was a small man with an obvious limp. His brown-bristled chin was as sharp as a knife and it was always tilted to enable him to see better with his one eye. His other eye had been removed by a surgeon, skilfully, in an operating theatre which he described to me. The blind side of his face had a vacant, stricken look, almost supplicating, like the profile of a saint in an early Renaissance painting. Where the eye should have been was a concave tube of flesh, an empty socket, shiny and violet-pink, which looked as though it had been made by somebody pressing his thumb downward and inward from the bridge of the nose where the skin had a hurt, stretched appearance. He was really very ugly.

I told him I had to stay out of the way for a while because some men were looking for me. I had put something over on them and I had to lie low for a while. I told him I would pay him something if he would buy my food for me each day. He said there was no need for that. He would do it anyway out of friendship. But as he always insisted that I eat the evening meal with him, I said I would pay for it for the two of us, and he agreed to that. We ate upstairs in his room and sometimes he brought a bottle of beer.

His room was crammed with an assortment of junk. A bundle of assorted rags, old newspapers tied neatly into bales, pots, vases, busts, broken clocks, and stacks of books. I was glad of the books. I borrowed a few each day to read while he was out on his rounds.

He told me that he liked reading himself but that he couldn't read much because with only one eye he found it a bit of a strain. He was sorry about this because one of the busts he had was a bust of Carlyle, and he had noticed that there were some of his books in the pile. He asked me if I didn't think that having a life-size bust in front of you of the man whose books you were reading wouldn't give you a clearer impression of what the man was like who wrote the books. I said I had never thought about it but that I supposed there was something in what he said, for the books a man writes are part of his behaviour. He nodded his head eagerly. He said he wouldn't mind, sometime, if it wouldn't bore me, hearing what Carlyle had written, because ever since he had had the bust he had wondered. If I would read to him he would be very grateful.

But we agreed to leave it off for a while, for at least a week, because that week his round was on the other side of the town and by the time he got back and cooked supper for us there was only enough time left to check up on what he'd collected and sort the rags and papers into bundles. I suggested that I could do the baling during the day while he was out collecting. He was delighted about this.

That night, before I went downstairs to my own room, he had cooked some kippers for us, and afterward, while we sat back and drank the beer which he'd bought, he suggested that he would be willing to have me as a partner in the business. I could do the sorting and baling like I said, and he would do the collecting and the selling. The proper disposal of the goods was important, he said, but for the moment at least he himself would attend to that. I wouldn't need to go out of the house at all.

There was only one thing. He could use a bit more capital because sometimes he couldn't afford to buy what he was offered.

I said it seemed only fair to me that I should put some capital into the business because, after all, he was doing the hard work and there was already a lot of stock in the room.

In the future we can use your room too, he said.

That had not occurred to me but I agreed because, although some of the stuff that he brought in smelled rather strongly, I didn't see how I could reasonably object to the arrangement.

I asked him then how much he thought would be fair for me to pay into the business.

He considered that for a few moments and then he asked me if I thought six pounds would be too much.

I told him that I thought it was quite reasonable, and so I gave him the money and he insisted on giving me a receipt on which he stated that I was now a full partner in the business. He always liked to have things in writing, he said, if it were in any way connected with business. You knew where you stood then. And he asked me whether I was satisfied with the receipt. He was looking at me questioningly.

I told him I was and I suggested that as I would be doing the baling we ought to store the paper in my room and the miscellaneous stuff in his. I think he was glad I suggested that, because while I was speaking I noticed he was eyeing the busts as though he feared I were going to suggest that he should part with them. But when I was returning to my own room he insisted that I should take one of the busts with me because he had noticed my room was pretty bare. A man likes an ornament, he said.

I thanked him and said that I would begin the baling next day.

In the morning, one of the first things which gradually took shape in the growing light was the bust of the nameless man, one of whose ears was broken off and whose vacant eyes were toward me as I fell into sleep.

In the days that followed, I spent part of my time baling paper.

It was not long before I realized that it was not a flourishing business, that the stock upstairs in Peter's room was the accumulation of many months' work, and that day by day he added very little to what was already there. At first I suspected he was no longer bringing back all he collected and that he was disposing of the greater part of it without my knowledge, and before he returned home in the evening. As he had told me he kept accounts, I asked to see those for the past six months, thinking that the sudden decline in the business would show and that when I pointed it out to him he would realize that I wasn't a person to be trifled with. I expected him to be reluctant to show me his books and if he were, or if he refused outright to do so, I would know immediately that my suspicions were correct.

But it didn't happen like that. He was actually pleased when I asked him. He confided in me that he had been wondering, over the past few days, if he had made a mistake in accepting as a partner a man who was so foolish as to put up capital without wanting to see the books of the business in which he was investing. That had not seemed very businesslike to him.

I was taken back by his directness and admitted that I had been guilty of an oversight when I made my original investment. I hastened to add that I was not usually like that and was so on that occasion only because he was my friend and because I had trusted him implicitly.

He looked at the floor while I said this, and when he saw that I hadn't anything further to say he said that it was very kind of me to trust him in that way on such a short acquaintance, that that thought – and he felt ashamed of himself – had not occurred to him, which only went to show that his first impression of me had been correct, that I was a man of feeling.

I thanked him for saying so.

He said that on the contrary I had every right to be angry with him. He felt thoroughly ashamed of himself. It was unpardonable of him to have judged me at all, and it was criminal of him to have overlooked the most important factor in the situation. He hoped I would forgive him, that he hadn't lost my friendship because of it.

I assured him there was no danger of that, that to turn away from him on such a flimsy pretext would be to commit a much greater impetuosity of judgment than he had been guilty of.

He looked at me for a few moments without speaking and then he said that I was very young to speak so wisely, that it had taken him much longer to learn that lesson, and that even now, as I had seen, he was sometimes guilty of falling into his old ways.

We didn't speak for some time after that. Neither of us felt there was anything to be added. And then, suddenly, he remembered that I had asked to see the books of the business. He hoped that I would not find them too untidy and that, if there were any mistakes, I would not be too embarrassed to point them out. He found close work very difficult with only one eye and that not as good as it used to be. He limped over to the wardrobe and brought three massive ledgers out from the interior. They were half-bound in faded red leather with the numbers, 1, 2, and 3 inscribed in gold on their spines. It was only then that it occurred to me that he must have been a very old man.

I don't suppose you'll want much more than a glance at the first two, he said. There's not much of interest for you there. Two of the busts, I think, and some odd bits and pieces and a few of the books that didn't get sold the last time I had a clearance.

I asked him what period the three ledgers covered.

He didn't remember exactly, he said, but we could soon look and see because he had always taken great care to enter the correct dates.

We opened the first ledger. The pages were yellow with age and the ink had faded to an anonymous, neutral, sepia colour. The date at the top of the first page was '15th August, 1901'.

Ascension Day, he said. I should have remembered. I bought very little as you can see for yourself.

Under the date was the following inventory:

One clock (broken)	3d.
Rags (various)	1d.
One etching of a castle (unknown) signed 'E. Prout' and dated 1872 (interesting)	¾d.
Total	4¾d.

That etching, he said. I almost decided to specialize in art works, etchings, and busts, you know. You'll notice I didn't buy anything for two days after that. I had to think. He drew a half-smoked cigarette from his vest pocket and lit it. I decided against it, he went on after he had lit it, yes, I decided against it. He turned over the pages of the first ledger away from his decision and then he said I could look through the first two at my leisure the following day, that it was the third one which concerned us. The first entry was dated '28th October, 1940'.

Hallowe'en, he said. The war was on.

It didn't take me long to notice that on many days he didn't appear to have bought anything at all. I questioned him about it. He mumbled something about having enough, about not wanting to overstock himself. I turned quickly to recent business. The articles bought consisted mostly of old paper and rags, but even those he appeared to buy in ludicrously small quantities. It occurred to me that it was strange, considering the present limited business, that he should have decided to take on a partner, especially one like myself who was willing only to bale and pack what he collected, and I could think of no earthly reason why he should want more capital for a business which had not only begun to dry up over the last few years but which he didn't appear to have any intention of expanding.

He was watching me apprehensively, his head tilted like a bird's, his elbows stuck to his thin knees as he leaned forward in his chair and followed my progress from page to page; occasionally he made a vague reference to how he had disposed of this item or that, pointing to where it was recorded with the forefinger of his right hand. He apologized more than once for his handwriting, which was most exact and copperplate. He appeared, in spite of his modesty, to be the perfect clerk. What struck me as absurd was the inordinate care which he lavished on the most trivial transactions.

I asked him as casually as I could in what direction he intended to expand the business with the capital which I had invested. He considered the question for a moment before answering, and then he said that of course there were a number of possibilities, but that the main thing for any business, especially of this nature, was to possess an adequate reserve of floating capital. You never knew, he said, when you would require it.

I admitted that that seemed reasonable enough but pointed out that if we could judge from the records over the last few years we were hardly likely to be called upon to produce so much money at one time.

He said that that was as it might be but that it didn't prove anything. The very next day he might go out and find that he needed not six pounds but seven. He was obstinate in his refusal to draw any conclusions from the fact that during the past few years he had never bought more than three shillings' worth of goods in one day, and he gradually became more irritable when he realized that I wasn't satisfied with his explanations. I could feel his resentment as I turned back idly over the pages of the third volume, and, not wanting to quarrel with him, I suggested that there would be plenty of time in the future for us to discuss the business and that for the moment I was quite satisfied and felt like going to bed. His irritation left him immediately I said this, and he suggested that I should have a cup of cocoa before I went downstairs.

He boiled water on a little alcohol burner whose flame was blue and almost transparent, as though there were no density of heat there to raise the temperature of the uncovered water. The little pot was perched precariously on three flame-blackened tin spokes and it steamed gently, for a long time, below boiling point. The light in the room was a poor one. The wallpaper, dark during the day – heavy fawn anastomosed by tendrils of flowers, berries, leaves, all brown – was darker now, dark at the corners to the point of extinction; and as Peter stood watching the flame and the pot of water as though he knew what to expect, yet inquisitive – bending low to consider the flame and then peering into the pot – and nervous at the same time, I had the feeling of not belonging there . . . of being a disruptive influence in a place whose century and whole orientation were not mine, stared at by the ridiculous busts with no eyes and with three massive and indecipherable ledgers on the table in front of me which were indecipherable not because I could not add or subtract or follow the entries but because, having done so, I was unable to grasp their significance: I could see right through them, and having done so had an irresistible feeling that I had somehow missed the point. Peter still tended the flame and seemed preoccupied. He did not speak. If it had not been for a nervousness which seemed to attach to his gesture of waiting I would have thought that he had forgotten I was in the room with him. But as it was, it was obvious that he hadn't. It occurred to me that for some reason or other he did not trust himself to speak. His lips were set over the pale pink gums in which a row of brown stakelike teeth were embedded, unevenly, and in the lower jaw only. He was making cocoa. He wanted to be involved in that to be free of me. Simultaneously, he wanted to be doing something for me. I supposed it was his way of showing his disapproval and of signifying at the same time that in spite of it he still considered himself my friend, my partner. I wondered if he realised how unfamiliar everything was to me. I was aware of nothing familiar in the room. Everything – Peter himself, the miscellaneous objects – was trivial, gratuitously so, and yet, somehow, because he was so clearly involved, portentous. It was like a puppet show, but, disturbingly, the puppets moved by themselves. I could see only from the outside. I watched him grow impatient. And then, after a moment's hesitation, he stirred the brown powder into the water. While he was doing it, the realization came to me that that was not the best way to make cocoa, that cocoa tended to form into lumps if sprinkled into hot water, and I wanted to tell him about it and then found that I could not because unaccountably it came over me that I must be wrong. And yet all the time that I didn't speak I knew that I was not.

Here it is, he said at last, removing it from the flame. He went on stirring it as he carried it steaming and still unboiled to the table. You can put the books on the floor, he said. I'll put them away afterward.

I put the ledgers, one on top of the other, at my feet, and he placed two cups in front of us and filled them with the cocoa which was thin and watery like tea, on the surface of which the pinheads of undissolved powder which I had predicted when I watched his ineffectual efforts to stir it in, floated like minute balls of dark wet sand. He spilled a little on the table and wiped it away with a crumpled red handkerchief which he found in the side pocket of his jacket.

Bad pourer, he said apologetically.

I nodded.

It's not sweetened, he said then. I haven't got any sugar.

I said that it didn't matter, that that was the way I liked it, and we sat opposite one another waiting for it to cool a little, before we drank. He said that he liked cocoa because it made him sleep well, that sometimes in the middle of the night because of his insomnia – his mother too had been troubled by insomnia – he would work a bit on the ledgers.

There's always something to do, you know, he said.

He liked to make all the entries with a soft pencil first, a 3b, because it rubbed out easily, and then only afterward, when he had rechecked his figures and studied the inventory, to go over it in ink. For this latter operation he liked to use a penholder and a steel nib selected from an old lozenge box in which he kept many nibs of various thicknesses, shapes, and pliabilities, each of which, after it had been used, was wiped carefully on a penwiper which he had made himself out of four absorbent pieces of rag, circular in shape, and sewn together at the centre with a trouser button at either side. He wanted to show me his nibs, he said, and he got up with his cocoa untouched and went over to the wardrobe. He returned with a cardboard shoe box which he placed on the table in front of him as he sat down again. From the shoe box he took the lozenge box and from the interior of that, which had been lined with tissue paper, he poured a small heap of pen nibs onto the table. As they tinkled onto the wood his eyes lit up. The nibs were gold and silver and blue and brown. He selected one of the gold ones, which had two tubes on its underside, and passed it over to me, smiling.

It's a new-fangled one, he said. His tone was deprecatory. It's supposed to hold enough ink for five hundred words. It always blots.

He said that it was a good thing that he made a practice of testing all new nibs before he risked using them on the ledgers, and I agreed with him.

It always blots, he said again. I don't know why I keep it. I've been meaning to throw it away ever since I got it.

But he took it back from me, nevertheless, and dropped it back into the lozenge box. He went on to explain the merits of each nib, holding them up in turn for me to look at them, but without allowing me to touch them. This reluctance to let me look at them for myself annoyed me slightly. I don't know why, unless it was because it seemed to prohibit my becoming as interested as he was. Whenever I made a gesture to accept whatever nib he was holding up to the light for me to examine, the spear or spade-shaped point, the contour of the slit or hole, he moved it hastily back toward the lozenge box and dropped it in. I became more and more exasperated and finally, having had enough of it, I said rather rudely that his cocoa was getting cold.

He pricked back his ears momentarily, as though he hadn't caught what I said, and then all of a sudden he smiled and thanked me for reminding him. He didn't like it too hot but he didn't like it too cold either, he said. And then, after taking two or three tentative sips and showing his toothless upper gum, he confided that he always selected the nib he was going to use on a particular occasion with great care. It was more exact that way, he said. Although I couldn't quite follow what he meant, I said that I supposed it was and he said again, Oh yes, it's more exact.

After that, we drank for a while without speaking.

He closed the lozenge box and returned it to the shoe box whose other contents he had taken great care to hide from me, and then, as though he had forgotten that he had asked me before, he asked me what I thought about the ledgers. He hoped I was satisfied with them, he said, and when I said I was, he nodded his head and said that he had known all along that I would be, but that it was a relief to have my personal assurance on the point. Apart altogether from the fact that I was his partner and that naturally he wanted me to be satisfied, he was glad to have had an opportunity to hear a second opinion. He had always considered that important although, up till then, he had not had sufficient confidence in anyone to show the ledgers. One had to be careful.

I agreed. I asked him what reason he had for trusting me.

It was hard to say, he said. But he had felt quite sure from the beginning.

I thanked him without enthusiasm. I was tired. I had finished my cocoa, which I hadn't enjoyed. As I stood up to go, I wondered what his attitude toward me would be if he knew that I was wanted by the police. I was no longer surprised by his lack of comment on the fact some men were supposed to be looking for me. He accepted it, believed it, and there the matter ended for him. He was not interested.

Nothing could have suited me better.

When we said good night he shook my hand warmly and said that he would be going out as usual the next day. And then, looking round and scratching his head, he said something about having a clearance soon.

I said that I trusted his judgement, that he had had more experience after all, and that seemed to please him. He leaned over the bannister solicitously as I went downstairs to my room.

I was bored and restless. I read a book for a while and afterward fried an egg. I wasn't hungry. But to prepare it and then to eat it gave me something to do. When I had finished I spent five minutes cleaning the frying pan with old newspapers. They were more than ten years old, yellow, and the urgency of the print seemed futile, like poses in an old snapshot.

I had been over three weeks in the house, and I had already decided that it would be safe to leave the town by train the next day. I had said nothing of my intentions to Peter. Somehow, I felt, he wouldn't be convinced. During three weeks I had come to realise that the world of police and petty criminals like myself, indeed the entire world, did not exist for him, or only in a strange, oblique way. It was not that he would have worried about my safety. He was hardly conscious of my danger. I felt merely that my decision to leave him and our partnership would be beyond his comprehension. At the same time, I was inquisitive to know what he did during the long hours he was supposed to be out collecting rags and papers. It was that which decided me to follow him.

It was after ten o'clock on the following morning when I heard him come downstairs past my landing and go out. My own bag was already packed, and I had left a short letter for him thanking him for his kindness and apologizing for my sudden departure. I was able to watch him from the window. He hesitated on the street outside and then, as though something had just occurred to him, he made off to the left up the street. He was carrying a small brown paper bag and he was not walking quickly.

A few moments later I was following him at a distance of about twenty yards. The first thing that struck me was that he didn't appear to be going anywhere in particular. He frequently turned off at right angles, almost recrossing his path, and he hesitated for a long time at each major crossing. From behind, his thick gray trousers had a corrugated appearance. They were too long in the legs for him. His feet made a shuffling sound as they walked, clad in warped brown shoes whose uppers were broken and split. He wore a navy-blue serge jacket, which was gone at the cuffs and elbows, and a ridiculously wide-brimmed gray fedora hat. I wondered what was in the paper bag. I trailed him closely. In that way, I felt, the people would notice him rather than me – the hat, the paper bag, the shambling, corrugated walk.

It was a fine morning and the streets were quite crowded. Sometimes, momentarily, I lost sight of him, and once I nearly lost him altogether when he turned a corner suddenly without my noticing him. I hesitated at the crossroads and was about to go off in the wrong direction when I saw him coming back along the pavement toward me. I stepped back out of sight into a shop doorway, and a moment later he was hesitating at the corner a few yards away. Finally, he crossed the street and followed the main thoroughfare toward the park.

As I followed him into the park, I wondered what possible motive he could have for going there. The park was almost empty. Most men of my age were at work, and those who weren't were conspicuous. I was rather annoyed with myself for following him there. Two young men and a girl passed me on the footpath – students, I supposed, because they were carrying books. When they saw me they stopped laughing, and for a moment I thought they had recognised me. But then they were past me and laughing again, the voice of one of the men coming back to me, high, artificial, and excited, as though he were mimicking someone, and then the girl's laughter again. I turned to watch her. She was walking between them, swinging a pot-shaped handbag on a long leather strap, in flat shoes and summer dress, and strikingly blond, her hair rising gracefully from her neck in a ribboned horsetail. She was slim-hipped and desired obviously by both of them. It struck me suddenly how foolish I had been to be alarmed. Apart from some policemen, there was no possibility of anyone's recognising me.

Peter was climbing a patch which led uphill, more like a windmill than a man. There was something unsettling about him. I was not able to put my finger on it until later. What was familiar was the familiarity of limbs out of control, of something missing which should have been there, the absence of which, more telling than what remains, strikes at one deeply, almost personally, making one feel that one is face to face with the subhuman. The dead are like that, and the maimed, and Peter was. As he moved upward toward the skyline, a triangle of white morning light dangled between the raking black legs, and the hoop of his back and his arms twisted horizontally like a tuberous root above them, and the head, a nob under the broad hat rim, looked in no direction as though direction were irrelevant now, and the park and the traffic beyond on the road and the people who walked there were irrelevant too, all except the gratuitous movement in which he was involved and which was not his own because the man was absent from it.

When I came to the crest of the hill I looked down on the duck-pond. He was there, leaning forward across the railing, in one of his hands the brown paper bag from which he extracted bread which he fed gently to four squawking ducks. He was too engrossed in what he was doing to notice me. I watched for a few minutes without moving, and then, as I did not wish him to recognise me, I turned and walked slowly away. It was nearly noon. The train left from the Central Station in fifty minutes. I would be able to catch it. My last sight of Peter sticks in my memory. He had removed his wide-brimmed hat and was mopping with his red handkerchief his forehead beneath his thin wind-blown hair.

Part Two

'Sometimes, wandering about the city during the summer, I would catch a glimpse of myself in a shop window; a long-haired ill-clad creature, unshaven, an anonymous member of the army of foreign shufflers who walk Paris streets. I could detect it too in the faces of the tourists. Women, unless I was introduced to them, ignored me.'

October 1950

Letter to Jack

Dear Jack and Marjorie,

We travelled Newhaven–Dieppe because it was cheaper. The sea was calm, the sun shining and the deck was crowded with a merry band of pilgrims to Rome for the Holy Year – some Celtic society or other, each member with an immense buttonhole of green and yellow ribbon. They sang in Gaelic.

On the steamer we tasted French bread for the first time – like our Vienna loaves only longer, tastier, with a thicker crust. The meal consisted mainly of bread and various highly seasoned cooked meats.

Dieppe still shows its scars. Rubble, gutted buildings, fallen masonry. The railway line is unfenced. The train runs out of Dieppe at the level of the street beside vans, loaded bicycles and costermongers' carts.

By the time I'd got the registered luggage through the customs at the Gare St Lazare it was after 8 p.m., nearly twelve hours since we left London. Betty and little Jacqueline were naturally very tired. We ate a ham sandwich and drank Cinzano. Then Jacqueline disappeared. We found her a few minutes afterwards playing with a beautiful white cat which was attached to a disapproving lady by a lead of red patent leather! Apologies in our hesitant French, bows, and we retreated to our own table. In search of a hotel . . .

We had very little ready money and were reluctant to deliver ourselves into the hands of a French taxi driver. I left Betty and J. in the station cafe and went down the steps into the street. The night air was aglow with multi-coloured neon. There was a cafe, with tables on the pavement, at every corner. Vendors of roasted chestnuts, peanuts, shrimps, crabs, mussels, oysters. A conscious surrealism in all the posters. The traffic frantic, uncontrolled. In Paris one doesn't halt at crossroads. One slips subtly forward driving on the brake and on the horn.

It was ten o'clock when I returned to St Lazare. I had found a small hotel in the 10th Arrondissement, near the Place de la Republique. A week later, in the same district, we got a furnished room where we could cook, a small room on the fourth floor of a dilapidated hotel. For this room – its condition is appalling – we pay more than ten pounds a month. This is one of the anomalies of present-day Paris. The Parisian, as a rule, pays a ridiculously low rent. The foreigner pays about ten times as much. Restaurant meals for all are very expensive. It is much cheaper 'doing for oneself'. The shops are stacked with exciting kinds of food but prices are far higher than at home.

A violinist lives in the next room. I began to despair of my French because I couldn't understand a word he said. Laboriously I tried to follow him. Politely, he spoke more slowly, stressing the infinitive of the verb and waving his hands about in the air. It was only after a week that I found out he was a Brazilian and couldn't speak French. He knew about ten words of the language and flung them about with a vicious Latin-American fluency that seemed to proclaim him a master of the tongue.

The 'intellectual elite' – if one is to believe the management of the cafe 'Deux Magots' – is at St Germain des Prés. It is here that the nightclubs offer one 'Les soirées existentialistes'. It is all this long hair, the talk, the obvious tourist traps, that lead me to think (I may change my mind) that the creative centre is in the process of moving on.

For the time being, I prefer Montmartre. If it is one big tourist trap at least it is a professional one, whereas the set-up in the Boulevarde St Michel and St Germain strikes one as amateurish, a superstudents' union where the students are not necessarily superior. They make a lot of money, anyway, in Montmartre. I'm sure there must be some virtue in making money. I never seem to make any myself.

We had been in the furnished room for less than a week when we became aware that we were not alone. We were infested with 'peen'eads', a breed of bug that grows red on bloodfeasts. I had read about them – in Miller, in Celine, in Elliot Paul. But although I granted their existence, I had previously looked upon them (qua dramatis personae in autobiographies) as a sort of poetic license, an appendix of the garret dweller in post-Dostoyevskian fiction. I had been wandering about Montmartre one night and returned to the room rather late. I fell asleep quickly. Then I was aware that the light was on and Betty, clutching her nightclothes about her, was telling me to waken up – bedbugs! Gorgeous fat creatures glutted with our blood, minute ones spumed hungry from the walls. We spent an hour searching every crevice in the sheets, blankets, mattress. We found a spent match beneath the mattress. Doubtless a bugtrap of a previous tenant. The Brazilian next door tells me he has fought the advance of 'la peste' for three months. An extremely dapper little man, he is frantic but helpless. And for the moment we are helpless too. But we will move as soon as possible.

Yours always, Alex.

A Meeting

Remembering all manner of things, faces, voices, smells, situations, which he knew but which he had forgotten – almost, he thought, as though he had tricked himself into forgetting them, marks of fear or shame erased from his memory as from a diary, a bed, or a room, because he no longer wanted them, because they were irrelevant, because they threatened his present identity – he was aware of his own rejection of them, but he was aware of it only indirectly in the vague irritation which he felt at the sight of his colleagues who had scarcely existed for him the day before, or at the sight of the blot which clung to the tail of the last figure in the column of figures in front of him.

He would have liked to take off his jacket and the tie which was knotted in a tiny red knot, close, at his throat, but he put the thought away from him again because it was impossible with old Beakin sitting there and one of the partners, Mr Alan Curtis or young Mr Fenton, likely to come in at any moment.

Since ten o'clock in the morning the heat had been unbearable. His lunch in the smokeroom of the restaurant across the street had been hot, colourless, tasteless. Stewed rabbit at one and ninepence, all bones. Susie, the waitress, agreed with him, strongly enough to suggest that she considered the affront a personal one. *And us girls* (the waitresses) *doin' our best to keep you regular gentlemen satisfied.* It was the new cook, she said. She couldn't boil water without singeing it. He could still see the fork lying in cold gravy, little beads of solidified fat on the prongs. Susie removed the plate with her red hand. Afterward, he had walked about the streets for a while, but it was so hot and the streets were so crowded with people going and coming from lunch that he had returned to the office early.

He found himself resenting the sun. It sprawled across the papers in front of him and glinted painfully in the lenses of his spectacles. It was a nuisance. He felt a similar vague resentment against the fat round buttocks of Miss Eileen Lanelly tightening under a shiny blue serge skirt as she bent down to pick up a pencil from the floor. She had a habit of dropping things. And today she had made a mistake in one of the ledgers.

'Really, Miss Lanelly,' Beakin had said, 'in the six years you've been with us I have learned to expect more accuracy from you. Such a trifling mistake! What would the auditors say?'

Miss Lanelly had supported from childhood an air of conscious guilt. Mr Beakin was inspired by it and fed on it like a bird.

'I can't help it, Mr Beakin, it's so terribly hot! I can't concentrate in all this heat.'

'The work must go on, Miss Lanelly,' Mr Beakin said in his thin soursweet way. 'Perhaps if you were to open the window . . .'

The window was open now and a wall of stale city-spent air moved in with the sunlight. The broad world of Miss Lanelly diminished as she straightened up and moved over to the filing cabinet.

A fly settled on the back of his hand. He became interested in its movement, in the dull veined lustre of its minute wings and its black button-like eyes, flat, built outward like two headlamps; he wondered what it would look like through a microscope, and then he became aware that Mr Beakin was watching him and he allowed his eyes to be drawn back toward the papers on his desk. The suggestion of a sex-life for Miss Lanelly intrigued him. It was, he was sure, a small sex-life, an insectal one, almost non-existent, irritant rather than active, and smothered in tweeds, blind, impotent, diminutive, sunk, like a crippled ant beneath a clod of earth, in the amorphous mass of flesh which she appeared to have bundled each morning with some difficulty into her clothes.

A moment ago, surreptitiously, she had slipped something into her mouth. A piece of chocolate, he supposed. He had seen the silver paper and the crushed wrapper in her wastepaper basket. She was fond of chocolate.

The sun fell on Mr Beakin and on the fly and on the inkpots and pens and on the two other male clerks, Riley and Wilson.

It inclined in a wedge toward the filing cabinet where Miss Lanelly pretended to be looking for something.

He brushed the fly away and looked at his thumbnail. The noise of the traffic came up from the street through the open window. A wasp landed suddenly on the ledger, crawled a few inches, and then flew out again into the sunlight.

Mr Beakin coughed and Riley whispered something to Wilson. He couldn't hear what they were saying. He looked without interest at them. James Fidler didn't like his colleagues and seldom spoke to them. He nodded to them each morning as he came in, and then he ignored them as completely as possible. The two clerks were a tiresome pair, always amused in a silly secretive way. It had always struck him as ludicrous that five people with so little in common should pass the greater part of their waking lives together, filing, indexing, keeping the ledgers in order. He supposed they all had their reasons. For Beakin, who was over sixty, it had been a career. For Fidler himself it was 'part of the routine'; he had always considered it, or avoided considering it, in those vague terms. Riley and Wilson were grown-up schoolboys. They went to football matches on Saturday afternoons. The office was a job for them. They were free at five-thirty. And Miss Lanelly, professedly, 'needed the money.' As though they all didn't. But Miss Lanelly appeared to be convinced that she needed the money in a different way; the rest of the staff worked and it was proper that they should do so, but Miss Lanelly worked because she needed the money. God's oversight perhaps. That impression he had gathered from conversations overheard.

The afternoon was nearly over. At five-thirty he would catch a bus for the suburb in which he lived and he would eat his evening meal with his mother and his sister. It was an absurdity which he accepted, another one. Each evening he stepped onto a bus which took him to where he had never decided to be.

His sister appalled him, a frail brittle orange woman in her late forties who had grown out of the gangly young woman whom he had surprised in the act of admiring herself in the long wardrobe mirror, and who, still naked and terrible, had come upon him in his room that night and wrestled with him on his bed. Neither his sister nor he had ever referred to the incident. They had always disliked each other. Looking at her now, it was difficult to believe it had ever happened.

Kate Fidler worked in a confectioner's shop; perhaps he disliked her more because of that. She was resigned. She respected 'her betters,' she was an obsequious woman who served candy and chocolate and toffees and powdered her face with a very bright pink powder which caked into ugly little islands round her nose. She wore it because it was powder; 'all ladies powdered themselves.' She never used a mirror.

There was no conversation at table. Kate disapproved of him. He had no ambition, she said, but always to the other woman, the mother; she never spoke to him directly. And his mother's conversation was limited to her chronic arthritis. It was not a pleasant meal. That was why he had been so disappointed with the rabbit at lunchtime, he looked forward to his lunch in the smokeroom. The evening meal was always the same. The grandmother clock ticked. Fidler looked at his plate, contemplating what was on it, tough little morsels of stewed meat or boiled cod, unappetisingly transparent like candles, conscious all the time of Kate's sniffing and of the low sucking noise which came from his mother as she picked at her food. The house itself was shabby, anonymous, and an old female smell pervaded it.

The fly had disappeared. Out of the corner of his eye he watched Miss Lanelly move away from the filing cabinet.

'Have you finished it, James?' Beakin was saying.

'In a moment, Mr Beakin.'

'I don't know what's come over the people in this office,' the manager said generally and glanced at the clock. 'A little sun and the whole routine goes to pot.'

Miss Lanelly was grinning at him, a knowing look now Beakin had turned his back. He felt uncomfortable and ignored her. As the 'assistant manager' – it was not his official title but he was the senior when Beakin was on holiday: ah, Fidler, of course! Mr Alan Curtis would say on those occasions – he considered it impertinent of her. He laughed at his own feelings, but it was a question of habit. Miss Lanelly was a comparative newcomer while Fidler himself had been with the firm for nearly twenty years; the miles of copperplate handwriting, the office stamps, the endless paper clips, were as much part of his past as the little scar above his right eye or as the few furtive adventures he had had with women. Eileen Lanelly's grin recalled those adventures to him; it was friendly, she was inviting him to share something with her, and he found himself resenting her offer.

He tried to concentrate on the figures in front of him, but they had become insignificant. His eye returned to the blot and stopped there. The fly was walking across the paper toward his hand. For a moment it held his attention and then he began to think of his two weeks' holiday which began the following Monday.

The sky was clouding over.

Mr Beakin put on his hat, and Riley and Wilson pretended to tidy up their desks. They were a smug pair.

'James,' Mr Beakin said, 'I wonder if you'd mind finishing that before you leave? If you're not in a hurry.'

He nodded. He felt no inclination to get home quickly.

'And you, Miss Lanelly, if you would put right that little mistake of yours in the ledger.'

'Yes, Mr Beakin.'

'Use the new eraser, Miss Lanelly. It doesn't make such an ugly mark as the old one.'

'Yes, Mr Beakin.' A singsong voice. Ten years too young for her.

Beakin ignored it. 'Good night Riley, good night Wilson,' he said. He caught Fidler's eye for a moment and then he went out, humming.

When he had gone Wilson winked at Riley.

'Don't forget to lock up, James!' Wilson said crookedly from under his little black moustache.

Riley grinned and slammed the lid of his desk. 'Looks like rain,' he said. 'Thunder.'

Fidler ignored them.

'Come, Riley,' Wilson said, and they went out together. He listened to the neat nasty voices as they died away in the corridor. Wilson was married. Four years ago Fidler had donated five shillings toward his wedding present. He couldn't remember what it was they gave him, a metal object with a fatuous inscription.

Miss Lanelly turned toward him. They were alone now. 'They think they're funny,' she said, but he didn't answer. He appeared to be engrossed in the papers in front of him.

She walked over to the window and looked out.

When he looked up she was lighting a cigarette. He noticed that one of her stockings was laddered just below and behind her knee; it disappeared under her skirt.

He felt a sudden desire to laugh.

'Don't be long with that ledger, Miss Lanelly,' he said after a few moments. 'I want to lock up.'

She was still standing at the window, looking out, with the extinguished match in her hand. Riley and Wilson called her Eileen.

'Oh, damn Beakin!' she said. 'I'll do it in the morning before he comes in. There's the rain on now, Mr Fidler. It's heavy.'

The rain spattered in little bouncing drops on the window sill. Automatically he glanced over at the coat rack. He had not brought his umbrella and he felt vaguely annoyed with himself; he seldom came out without an umbrella.

'Oh God!' Miss Lanelly said. 'What a day! First the sun and now this! I don't know why people stay in this filthy country! Were you ever in the south of France, Mr Fidler?'

'No.' He put the cap on his fountain pen and replaced it in his pocket beside his pocket handkerchief.

'I was,' she said. 'I was in Nice and Monte Carlo. I can't understand why people stay here.'

She was a heavy woman, as tall as he was, her clothes always giving the impression that she was held together by pins.

'Why do people stay anywhere or do anything?' he said. 'Why do they?'

'Four pounds a week,' she said. 'That's easy!'

He gathered the papers together. 'You could earn more elsewhere,' he said.

'Oh, I don't know, there'd always be something. Rain in June. Just look at it!'

'There always is,' he agreed. He looked at his watch.

'Just look at it!' she said again.

'It *is* heavy,' he said, 'but it won't last long.'

Heavy rain never lasted for long, fine rain lasted for days. He had known that since he was a boy, like snowdrops in January and crocuses in February. He wondered how many times in his life he had said those exact words: 'It *is* heavy but it won't last . . .' as though he were enunciating a self-evident proposition.

'No, thank goodness,' Miss Lanelly said.

Evidently it was part of her past too, part of her girlhood. It occurred to him that he did not know very much about Miss Lanelly. This is Miss Lanelly, she sings in our church choir. Miss Lanelly wears tight skirts and catches cold each March. She 'needs the money.' When she first came to the office, Riley had gone out with her once or twice – 'for a lark' – but it had not come to anything, and now they were hardly on speaking terms. She was cold, Riley said.

'Beakin says I can't take my holidays till September this year,' Miss Lanelly said. 'Can you imagine that? Sit in this lousy place all through the summer and then two weeks, *two weeks* at the tail end!' She had taken out one of her hair clips and was holding it in her mouth while she combed her hair. 'I felt like going to see old Curtis about it.'

It was mouse-coloured hair.

'You'd have a better chance with Fenton.'

She replaced the hair clip and laughed. 'Oh no, not him! You know what he said? – If you'll just speak to Mr Beakin about it, Miss Lanelly, I'm sure he will accommodate you – Can you imagine that? Fenton! He's scared to death of Beakin!'

Fidler smiled. It was the first time in six years that he had really talked to Miss Lanelly. He liked her explosiveness, it was fresh, feminine. And she wasn't old. He found himself wondering what it would be like to make love to her.

'Are you ready?' he said. 'I want to lock up now.'

'Lock up? Why? What is there to steal? A few mouldy accounts!'

'And the new eraser,' he said.

She laughed. 'Oh, I'm ready when you are, I'll do the ledger in the morning.'

'Good.'

It gave him pleasure, somehow, to be in on this defiance of Mr Beakin. It had never occurred to him to be defiant himself, any more than it had ever occurred to him to lodge apart from his mother and sister. It was not that he had Kate's resignation, which was indulgent; he accepted Mr Beakin and the order he represented from habit, without committing himself, because his desire to rebel was no stronger than his desire to submit; he could find no motive in himself to do either. Kate's abject triumph, the certainty that spoke through thin old-woman's lips, sickened him. It was unhealthy. Miss Lanelly's bubbling impertinence was refreshing.

She put away her powder compact, arranged the white bow at her neck, and they walked down the stairs together to the street door. The rain was still coming down heavily, ringing whitely on the pavements. It occurred to him that it had been raining for precisely ten minutes.

'It can't last,' she said, glancing up the street.

Except for the traffic it was almost deserted. A few people with umbrellas were still walking about, leaning forward against the rain. Others crowded in shop doorways. He heard his lips saying 'tuttut' in vexation.

Miss Lanelly giggled. 'It's like a shower bath,' she said.

'A monsoon.'

'What did you say?'

'A monsoon,' he said.

'Oh, I thought you said it would stop soon . . .'

'I like the rain,' he said.

She didn't answer him. Perhaps she hadn't heard him. The rain continued to fall in front of them like a sparkling bead curtain. Little gushers of water rose from under the wheels of passing tramcars.

It occurred to him to invite her for a drink.

'We might as well,' Miss Lanelly said. 'It'd be better than standing here anyway. It's got cold suddenly.'

'It'll be warm again after the rain,' he said. 'It won't do any harm.'

'Oh, I like the rain,' she said, 'but let's go now. There's a bar opposite, isn't there?'

'Yes, the *Royal*.'

'We'll make a dash for it,' she said. 'Here, come under this.' She held her thin plastic waterproof over their heads. 'You hold the other end of it.'

He did so, and when he had turned up his collar with his free hand they ran across the street together and through the revolving doorway.

'Oh, my God!' she said, breathless and laughing, 'I'm soaked!' She looked down at herself. 'Damn! I've laddered my stocking!'

Miss Lanelly, sipping her sherry, felt comfortable for the first time that day.

The bar was crowded, hot and damp from the damp garments of the customers. It was nearly six o'clock. Fidler was drinking whisky and listening absently for the rain to stop. He was conscious of himself in the wall mirror, a thin man in spectacles, unprepossessing, with a permanent stoop and still wearing his discoloured soft hat; and the profile of the woman beside him – he could feel the heat of her body close to his own – soft-jowled, the lips big, and the soft gray eyes embedded like humorous buttons in her fleshy face, excited him. She smelled of wet clothes and make-up and woman.

'Do you live far?' Miss Lanelly asked.

'Not far, about twenty minutes in the bus, a few stops after East Park.'

'Oh.'

She was looking at him almost conspiratorially and he felt attracted and repelled at the same time; big and soft and clumsy. 'Our elephant,' Riley called her once with that prurient little snigger of his. Riley had the face of a fox, red and pointed.

Fidler was thoughtful. The 'oh' had been noncommittal. He wondered whether she had asked merely out of politeness.

'And you?'

'There's the thunder again,' she said.

It was a loud clap, it broke slowly into the crowded bar. For a moment everyone was silent, and then the glasses clinked and laughter broke out again.

'Ominous, isn't it?'

It was a stupid thing to say, he felt, because it wasn't at all ominous. That was not what he had meant to say. The word had sprung to his lips, simply because he had wanted to be the first to break the silence; it was as though any word would have done.

'When I was a girl I used to be afraid of it,' she said. 'I thought it was a kind of earthquake. I knew a man once who was struck by lightning.'

He supposed she was lying, making it up, but he didn't care because most conversation appeared to him in that light, false, artificial, a game of adjustment within the world of another in which what was said was insignificant, the end being to intrude oneself, ineffaceably, to make the other recognize one's existence.

'Was he killed?'

'The man? Oh yes, he was killed all right, *instantaneously*. But I was only a girl at the time. I wasn't allowed to see him.'

'Did you want to?' Fidler was wondering what a man struck by lightning would look like. Electrocuted. Like they did to murderers in America.

'I really don't know whether I did or not,' Miss Lanelly said. 'I don't remember. It's funny but I don't remember. All I know is my father went to his funeral.'

'Do you live with your parents now?'

'Oh no. They're both dead. I've got a furnished room.'

'You're lucky,' he said. 'I live with my mother and sister.'

Kate would be home now and they would be preparing the meal. They would be annoyed at his being late.

'Oh, I don't know,' she said. 'It gets a bit lonely at times with only Mrs Whelan to talk to. She's my landlady. She's Irish. And I don't get out much because I don't know many people here. Except those at the choir. They're funny. You should see them.'

'Then it's true, you do sing in a choir? I thought Riley was making it up.'

She was no longer smiling.

'Yes,' she said. 'I sing in a choir. I like singing. I don't like Riley. I think he's a fool.'

Fidler nodded. 'What do you sing? I mean what are you?'

'Alto,' she said. 'We sing hymns and anthems mostly.'

'In church?'

'Twice on Sundays. Practice once a week. Tonight, as a matter of fact. Tuesdays.'

For some reason or other, Fidler felt uncomfortable. People who practiced religion always made him feel that way. He considered them insane.

'What's wrong?' Miss Lanelly said.

'Oh nothing,' he said. 'It seems funny, that's all. You believing in God and all that.'

'Who said anything about God?' Miss Lanelly said. 'I sing in church. I like singing and they pay me a guinea a week for it.'

'Then you don't believe in God?'

She laughed. 'I think if He existed it would be necessary to murder Him! No, I don't believe. I believe in precious little. In myself, in people sometimes . . .'

'Yes,' Fidler said. He was interrupted by the waitress who arrived with new drinks. He paid for them and went on: 'But it's difficult with other people. There's a kind of 'as-if' quality about their actions. I mean, one acts oneself, but other people only act 'as-if'; one never really knows.'

She laughed. 'I know what you mean,' she said. 'It's true. But it's the same for everyone.'

'Only some people don't recognize it,' Fidler said. 'They take it for granted that they can know other people.'

'Yes,' Miss Lanelly said. 'You know I went out twice with Riley when I first came to the office. He said he didn't think there was any problem of communication in the twentieth century. He said we had cinema, radio, and television. He couldn't understand why I wouldn't let him sleep with me.'

She held her sherry up to the light, looked at it closely, and then drank.

'I'll be drunk for choir-practice!' she laughed.

She had put another cigarette in her mouth. He lit it for her.

The noise of the rain had diminished, some of the people were moving toward the door.

'Why don't you move?' she said suddenly, blowing the first breath of smoke upward from the fat part of her lower lip. 'If you don't like staying with your family you can surely move?'

'I'd have to want to first, I suppose. I don't know. I never really thought about it.'

'You can't want to move very badly,' Miss Lanelly said. 'It's up to you, after all.'

He had the impression that she was drifting away from him. The neon lighting in the bar was hurting his eyes. One of the long helio globes was flickering, something wrong with the connection.

'I don't want anything very badly,' Fidler said. 'It's rather pointless,' and, saying it, he felt false.

'If that's true it's you that's lucky,' Miss Lanelly said. 'My God, I want so many things badly!'

'Perhaps it's not true,' he said quickly. He found himself alarmed at the thought of losing abruptly the vague sense of physical intimacy he derived from sitting close to her in the hot crowded room. 'I mean, it may be just that I don't know, and meanwhile it's as though I were living in abeyance.'

'The rain's off,' a voice said.

Two men squeezed past Fidler's chair. He moved forward to facilitate their exit.

'I thought it would be different after the war,' Miss Lanelly said suddenly. 'But it's not, it's the same. Worse if anything.'

'How do you mean?'

'Oh, I don't know. It should have been different somehow.'

Fidler said nothing. It was as though whatever he said would be false.

She looked at her watch and said that Mrs Whelan would be wondering where she was.

'Yes, the rain seems to be off.' He finished his whisky and stood up.

He asked her what church she sang in.

'Limepark Congregational,' she said. 'And for goodness' sake, stop calling me Miss Lanelly. You've known me for six years now!'

He smiled and took her arm to lead her through the crowd. He was about to tell her to call him James, then didn't. He was going to put the matchbox in his pocket, but it was empty so he threw it away.

The Rum and the Pelican

James Fidler had a varicose constellation behind the knee of his left leg. That, and his feet, caused him some pain when he walked. For this reason he did not normally walk far, and since he was born and bred in a large city whose arteries were fed by a never-ending stream of often stationary tramcars this debility caused him little concern. When he contemplated the gradual decay of his various members, his dismay was a formless one, uncoloured by its object; it was in all respects the same dismay which took hold of him as in the morning papers he read of wars and rumours of wars. That things in general, his leg, his feet, the world into which he had been born, untimelily, were going from bad to worse he never doubted, often saying indeed, and perhaps twice in one week, to the postman, to the woman in the diary, the one with the ulcer (or birthmark, he couldn't decide which), to a man in a bar, to a bar of men. *It's always the same, things are going from bad to worse*, or alternatively, *Times are changing*, or, more simply if more ambiguously. *I know.*

As he grew, so did the world, older, whatever that implied, and at night as he stepped into his pyjamas, looking, his legs trailing haired and whitely, down, then sat on the edge of the bed, the flat tyre of his belly convex in the droop of his spine, to rub one yellow-soled foot and then the other and examine precisely and individually the toes, he was aware of the carpet, thin now, of the bedspread, of the door, and of the hall and the street after that, and he was aware of no transition; for the sound of the late tramcar was there with his foot and the voice of the morning with the hair of his belly straightening, saying *Raining again, eh?* as though *he* too required confirmation of a fact, indubitably there, as all theres are there, but coming after four days of rain which like most things was . . . excessive. And the tiredness then in his limbs, turning, with a vague lumbar pain and heart beating, all theres there, the out light, the bed under, and that, touching, still, tentative always, colder than the rest of the body – a medical reason – not, not that he couldn't have, remembering the rain had not in fact rained that morning, perhaps touched notwithstanding the other people in the bar her under-table part, the clue to whose sex was discretion, and talking galahadly, perched out at his voice, until she, there-ing him as he had her, was morely there, an unguent to the fatigue of his body, rinsing his drains. To experience that was to feel younger, back to the days when without embarrassment on a beach or in the public baths he could remove in a cubicle and with an agreeable sense of peeling himself his trousers, was moreover to desire again the experience, place-time confederate, of cohabitation, for a night or a week's holiday of nights, born in the *Palais de Danse*, lived along the fairy-lighted dusk of the resort's promenade, deceased on the one dim flight of carpeted stairs between their rooms. The first time, minutely conscious of time, was always, with the skirt loose only and in partial collusion – until the elastic at his fingers was wet, quite wet – the best time, most gradual, moving on the gradient of his will athwart hers, brave against lack, obvious but for his scepticism, and hers, of resistance. To experience that, even in imagination, the sight, the feel, the smell – he considered them initially in isolation and then more voluptuously in a cognate form – was, touching, to become for the future anyway resolved. And yet resolution was foreign to him, such decisions as he made being, as he had noticed on more than one occasion – tilted backwards on a dentist's chair in the shadow of the appalling crane, standing in the palmstrewn foyer of a cinema with a ticket between his forefinger and thumb – somehow already there, as the present resolution was already if ambiguously there when Miss Lanelly stooped to pick up from between splayed legs the dropped pencil. *Oh, Mr Fidler!* The voice – derisively singsong, the squarish teeth arranging words under her big lips and the work of all present momentarily at hangfire until she had repeated her absurd request for a 2 ½ d. stamp – no longer signified, was even pleasant if one considered not the words but the lips and the peculiar damp breathlessness with which the words were articulated. *Oh, Mr Fidler!*

Undoubtedly, in ebb, in flow, in procession and recession, in inoculation and pollution, his life was fortuitous: go out, go in, a bus, a shop, opening and closing his umbrella, his yellow face close to the yellow face of the barometer, somewhat of a meteorologist, *Cirrus, cumulus, stratus*, he said and added, *Cirro-cumulus, strato-cumulus*, before, lowering his eyes to the level of the streets, he turned, caught a glimpse of a wasp-waisted red-buttocked nearly-woman with the tremor of jelly in her kilted tightness, and thought himself to be something of a morphologist. He might, he supposed, have been a painter. But as for decision, that was something else.

It might have been a cold morning in the earlier part of January and his breath sprouted longly and whitely from his nostrils. His nose nipped, and his toes, vegetable almost from forty shodden years, were cold, a band of pain at his extremities. Inside his gloved hand he held his nose, not for thought although he hoped to give that impression, but for heat. He was scarved against the wind to the tips of his ears and his gaze, recessed under his bowlerbrim like a caved animal, moved bleakly outwards over his tilted hand towards the frost-blackened hedges. It occurred to him that the situation was not new or that if in particular it was – he had cut himself that morning in shaving and his skin was minutely painful where his scarf chafed – it was at least familiar. Of that he was certain. And there for the moment, overtaken by a vague sense of the familiar, his mind ceased to function. And that too was no novelty. His thought processes were frequently stricken in this way, atrophied indeed before he could properly have been said to have thought anything at all, this or that line or (more exactly) point of speculation simply did not happen, or, if it did, happened in a most exasperating way, collapsing abruptly a moment later, its object, often anyway merely verbal, puttering surely and suddenly downwards like a cake of soap in a deep bath. After a few feeble attempts to retrieve it Fidler consistently gave up. At this point and on this particular morning it was the bus stop to his left and the frost-daggered hedges at the other side of the street which gently in the ensuing vacuum were there. And when it occurred to him that the hedges, similarly black and similarly frosted, had previously been there, he was almost and effortlessly in repossession of the train of thought which had eluded him. But then in a familiarly defensive manner he coughed and was distracted by the sound of the approaching bus.

He boarded the bus and climbed upstairs. He could not remember ever having sat downstairs, except when his mother accompanied him, and sometimes not even then, his desire to smoke – prohibited on the lower deck by a penalty of five pounds – furnishing him with a good enough reason to desert her temporarily and to escape the heightened ordeal of fifteen public and immobile minutes in her company. But in the morning on his way to the office he seldom smoked a cigarette and thus his habitual ascent was difficult to explain. Often as he clumped up the metal stairs, his umbrella clasped firmly in a perpendicular position in front of him and his shoulders hunched under his rough grey overcoat to avoid denting his hat on various metal protruberances, the purposelessness of that ascent occurred to him, the more so because it caused his bad leg to ache, and he would be critical of himself. But before he reached the top deck he was conscious of the familiar cognitive shrinkage, of the familiar sclerosis in his mental processes, and as soon as his eyes were level with the top deck he found himself more or less exclusively occupied in finding if possible a window seat.

The purpose of a window seat was two-fold. In the first place, irrespective of the width of a man on sitting down – broader no doubt than in standing up – there was never room for two on one seat, and thus, while the man at the window was often constricted, he was never overbalanced, and he was not prey to the vigorous passage movements of others fighting to get off or on. Secondly, to sit on one buttock, without either newspaper or window to distract one from one's predicament, was more than Fidler's dignity would allow. And each morning he was compelled to board the bus without a newspaper. This came about because since the war the local newsagent had discontinued the practice of delivering the morning paper. The shop was a pre-war wooden structure of temporary intention situated more than three hundred yards away from Fidler's house. To walk there so early in the morning, to pass from one dismal bungalowed street into another and into another beyond that, was depressing, so depressing that four years ago he had ceased to do it. Thus he had no newspaper. He might have taken a book instead, but while the journey was too long to be without a newspaper it was too short to get into a book. Each morning therefore, bookless and without a newspaper, he travelled on the bus to work, and the journey even in a window seat would have been unbearable had it not been for a particular landmark mercifully there about halfway towards the office along the bus route. As it was, except on those luckless mornings when, no window seat – left-hand window seat – being available, he was perched precariously on the slipping fulcrum of one buttock, he passed the first half of the journey in pleasing anticipation and the second half in somewhat indelicate speculation.

For the thighs of the negress were at least four feet long, turned and lustrous as gunmetal. Her yard-wide abdomen – Fidler contemplated it with a ringing in his ears – rose smoothly and massively from the red silk hangings at her curved loins which, thrusting forwards from the hips, were disclosed voluptuously. Above, twisting backwards in a supple line, the upper part of her torso spread nakedly except for the brassière into the sleekness of arms stretched out above her head to grasp or nearly grasp, for her body was all the more beautifully flexed if it evaded her, the rum bottle in the pelican's beak.

Fidler was able to discount the bird, and the bottle too, as he had always been able to discount, by some species of selective vision, the ulterior motive in the dentifrice smile.

Unhappily, the duration of his vision depended entirely upon the state of the traffic lights. As best, the bus would be brought to a halt at the red lights exactly opposite the huge billboards; at worst, his vision would be fragmentary or totally obstructed. This could come about in three separate ways, which Fidler, with his habitual precision, was pleased to call *acceleration*, *procession*, and *occlusion*. For the signals might be green and the locomotion speedy. Or the signals might be red but because of traffic unapproachable. Finally, too frequently, the bus on which Fidler travelled might at the critical moment slide relentlessly on to the blind side of a second double-decker, and that was occlusion. In these ways, and in their various permutations and combinations, Fidler was often deprived of the sight of that magnificent torso which from the moment he was installed in a left-hand window seat occupied his thoughts and caused in his solar plexus an anticipatory prickle like a minutely electrified wire. That that feeling, a kind of faint nausea at his roots, might at least in part have been caused by his hurriedly-eaten and ill-digested breakfast did not escape him, but the transformation of mere weight at his midriff into the heavy magnetic potential which lay not so much on his stomach as at his throat and thighs was not, he knew, caused either by porridge or by stewed tea. And as the double-decker lumbered on to where the poster was situated James Fidler polished the window with the sleeve of his overcoat.

From the moment almost at which he had obtained a seat, his favourite one, he had been pressed heavily and warmly against the window by a rather broad man who was reading a copy of the *Daily Express*. With his eye for figures and his small capacity for amazement, he noted that its daily circulation had increased to 3,986,401, held the nebulous figure for a moment in his mind's eye, and then, enjoying to the full the sense of fortification he derived from the pressing nearness of the man, he allowed his mind to become blank, jelloid, receptive.

Then the billboards came in sight. Out of the front window he could see them in the distance at the turn of the road. The signals were red. Now had arrived that nerve-wracking period during which he would have liked, if he could have driven a vehicle, to have piloted the bus himself. A careless approach could ruin everything. At the present speed, Fidler calculated, if no one got on or off at the last remaining stop between bus and lights, the signals would be nastily green by the time the bus drew opposite the poster, and the bus would career onwards like a blind rhinocerous past the dynamic negress, on, to the unexciting assortment of posters advertising *Hovis*, *Bovril*, and the razorblades of the moustachoied Gillette. Fidler was tense. His soul, in point of fact a morass of trepidation, was patient only in its upper layers for the bell which would order the bus to stop. He perceived on looking out of the front window that the amber caution signal was already there beside the red, and then, before he took his eyes away, the green light appeared. At that moment the bell rang and the bus, which had seemed about to lurch out towards the crossing to catch the green light, shuddered into a slow crawl and came to a halt beside the kerb at the request bus stop. An old lady descended and appeared before Fidler, glancing this way and that along the pavement. The bus moved slowly forwards, relented as the gears changed, and cruised at middling speed towards the changing lights. There was no procession of traffic in front of them and Fiddler experienced a small flicker of triumph as the bus, seemingly guided by his own silent and powerful will, glided to a halt exactly opposite the lustrous immensity of the negress from Martinique. Without haste, he inclined slightly forwards and sideways and trained his eyes through the glass on his nose through the glass of the window to bring into existence the tilted breasts, more than eighteen inches in diameter (circumference eighteen inches times pi), their lower lobes peerless and dusky where they protruded from the miniature brassière. He breathed more deeply, relaxed in his seat, and allowed his eyes to move over her body, taking in the thighs, the navel, the arms, in their separate sinuosities. And then the lights had changed again and the bus was moving, and, having seen almost to excess, he was able to resist a backward glance. His eyes, unseeing, drew level with the beginning of tenements.

Gradually, the image faded, even from behind eyelids shut covetously behind his spectacles, until his consciousness, vacant of image, veered irresolutely towards thought. His first thought, a mere eidolon of what had passed so smoothly before, was that it was a pity; his second, that it was familiar; for images, however much he sought to preserve them, because they excited him or because they limited thought, were without exception subject to the same drastic dissolutions as his thought processes, to correlative drainages in clarity and definition, until, without reference to his will, the flesh – for James Fidler had a predilection for flesh which informed a disproportionate percentge of the fleeting images which came and went during his waking day – came first to resemble a tadpole's tail in transparency and then . . . nothing, for even that was gone. He lamented the fact that the process was beyond his control. His mental drains, indeed, he had on more than one occasion compared to a faulty lavatory cistern, he wist not when it sluiced. And so the fillings up and emptyings went on, thoughts displaced by images, images by thoughts, unpredictably, in aggravating, in bogus succession.

Had this experience been peculiar to the northern winter, when every breath of air attacked his organism with the paralytic effect of a preservative, to whose fogs, rains and sleets he attributed the murmur of his marrow-fats, he might have put it down to the cold. Indeed, if a thought pointed to tiresomely complex implications, he frequently employed such a procedure, saying to himself, *It is impossible to think clearly under such conditions.* But in general, particularly with images, that line of approach was impossible, because now it was June; in general, particularly with images, courted, courted, lusted after, it was impossible, because the sun was hot and a short while ago Miss Lanelly, straddled downwards to retrieve the pencil, should have left and did not leave an indelible impression which should have endured and did not endure long after dinner during which he fought to bring the amorphous white blob into focus that he might recognise it as female. That image, like its innumerable precursors, he had been unable to recreate. With that, Fidler thought, as with this, and in winter and in summer the second half of the journey was the antithesis of the first. His mind, formerly receptive, was strung by inner lesions. The magnetic load which yard by yard along the route had built itself up inside him began to dissipate from the moment at which the bus drew away from the traffic signals, and the world, hitherto excluded by the image of the negress, reasserted itself in all particulars, the greaseladen hat of the man in front, the amputated thumb of the man beside him, 3,986,401 copies of the *Daily Express*, and the memory of a hundred and one facts gleaned from a curious reading of geographical magazines.

Yes, it might have been winter but it was not, for it was summer, and what season can be both winter and summer and in the same hemisphere? And although for all the difference it made, it might have been that cold morning in the earlier part of January when his breath sprouted longly and whitely from his nostrils, when the toothless combs of his bony feet impelled his scarved body forward under his bowlerbrim into a new day which was old except in particular, it was not, for it was evening now and the rain was off and Miss Lanelly with a ladder in her stocking and wearing a bright yellow oilskin had shaken hands – for the first time – and was walking away with the knowledge of his knowledge of her knowledge that he desired her, walking away, the oiled garment a second and rippling epidermis, quickly, taking her decision beyond traffic out of reach.

Background again. Like the war. Soon be over, Fidler remembered thinking. But business, as Beakin had said, went on. Gasmasks, the blackout, compulsory firewatching. *Whatever you do, don't throw water over them*, the instructor said. *Lie on your belly, crawl forward and dowse them with sand. Sand. That's what you've got it for, four buckets on each landing. Remember, the main danger to the civilian populace is incendiaries. Fire. The answer is sand.* Fidler stepped to one side to avoid a puddle. He had stubbed his cigarettes on Tuesday and Thursday nights in four ridiculous buckets of sand, and one morning as he awoke to a hangman's noose of braces dangling at the level of his eyes – he had been very drunk the night before, having gone out to a bar in St Vincent Street for a nightcap to relieve the boredom of his long watch – he stretched forth his arm to remove from the bucket which served as an ashtray the four lipsticked butts.

One . . . two . . . three . . . four . . .

Lay them gently on the floor.

7.15 a.m. Following Beakin's injunction, he opened the office window to allow the inward sag of dank winter air. Sniff. *See the place is aired, James. We are at war but at least we can observe the elementary rules of hygiene.* He turned to dismantle the altar of love, folding its prongs within the canvas and shaking the fetid memory out of the blankets. He remembered then, at that moment and before he drew on his trousers, thinking it was fortunate that the nocturnal equipment of firewatchers did not run to sheets. To *Ross's* for two buttered rolls and a cup of tea.

The war was over. It ended falsely, with fairground music as he crossed Argyle Street to catch the bus home. It sank into a lost winter, a lost series of winters as he hesitated before the impudent onward rush of a mail van whose skirling wheels splashed his trouser legs. It (the war) and the vague image of sex on an army blanket was quite defunct as he rounded St Enoch's subway station in search of his transport. He joined the queue.

The journey back, like the journey to, was by way of the hoarding. But he climbed aboard without eagerness. For this time there was an obvious explanation. The very possibilities were parched for they were but two. To follow his own nomenclature, they were *obliquity* and *rapidity*, the latter term being admittedly redundant since it was indistinguishable from *acceleration*. Vision was oblique when the lights were at red. The crossing was between, the femininity flat. Alternatively, and anyway successively, the bus ran through the lights and on the other side of the street the billboard sprang and diminished, a short-thrown stone, fragmented by traffic in its trajectory.

When he thought of Eileen Lanelly, he closed his eyes to isolate the thought which, in the damp and smoke-hung human atmosphere of the bus's upper box, burgeoned and fled to whiteness, fats, white slats of flesh, strung nervously. The close humidity of the bus contributed to the phase. At three fingers his hat-peak was gripped, wet upon his knees, and felt, ambiguously, as flesh would, wood might, if it were wet and sodden.

The bus arrived.

Stairs descended and road crossed, he put his key in the door, his coat on the rack, his hat on top. He sniffed and grimaced at the odour of fish.

Eileen Lanelly

For some reason or other she had wanted to get away from Mrs Whelan as quickly as possible. She had eaten her kippers quickly, thinking, Oh God, she wants to talk!

Ordinarily Mrs Whelan amused her. She talked about her dead relatives most of the time. Her family of fifteen brothers and one sister besides herself withered, and in season grew, between Glasgow and County Cork and was ravaged persistently by the twin sweats of birth and death.

She had not wanted to hurt her feelings and so she had told her she had a headache.

Once in her room she kicked off her shoes and rolled down her stockings. She stood at the window for a moment trying to make things out in the dusk and then she closed the curtains and walked over to the dressing table where with a piece of cotton-wool and some cream she removed her make-up. For a moment she studied the lines of her face and then, throwing the cotton-wool on the dressing table, she moved still in her bare feet across to the bed where she *collapsed*. It was the word which she would have used herself. She stretched out, very conscious of the pleasant tiredness of her body after the hot day. With her left arm she reached for her cigarettes and lighting one she stared at the ceiling. How pleasant it was just to drop like that! A tightness at her waist annoyed her. She twisted her body and undid the buttons of her skirt. Relieved, she moved her hand under the elastic of her knickers and felt with the tips of her fingers its indentations. She was relaxed with the cigarette in her other hand and her eyes lazily on the white expanse of the ceiling. The alarmclock at her bedside ticked. It was familiar but for the moment she did not resent it.

She had said with such conviction, My God, I want so many things badly! and yet she had never really been able to say what it was she wanted. Beneath a hundred and one specific desires for this and that she felt the presence of something more final, a hunger which remained unappeased afterwards and inevitably. Last summer, for instance, she had desired that man in Bournemouth, Bournemouth! – and had given herself to him, what a way to put it! – on a quiet part of the beach with a sense of finality that was excruciating; but it had not been final, nothing ever was. He called himself Brown, Browne? – and smelled of pipe and haircream and Harris tweed and likened the sea's saying oh ooh oooh in distancing to a symphony, of life and death, he said. Awe-inspiring. She was not convinced by Browne. Space, depth, sound, Beethoven, and the sea glimmering quietly at run's reach, but he couldn't with her because of his leg. She had noticed that first and had been attracted. Shot up. Tank landing craft. His feet squelched unevenly beside her as they walked out round the rock to reach the promenade, for him another beach-head. It's very quiet, he said. Somehow I've come to appreciate things more. But he had talked too long. And made too much of it. Well, he had landed that time alright in spite of his game leg. And there I was flattened under him like a starfish waiting for the world to end! Beethoven! The symphony of the sea! After three martinis and a short glide in his MG. And then she had shaken hands with him on the promenade. You're sure you don't want . . . Sure you won't come? And saying *no* she stepped away from him and walked for a long time by the sea. At one point she stopped and leaning over the sea wall said to the sea and to the sand and to anyone who was listening below in the shadows, How could I? *How could I?* But no one replied. Indeed she would have been surprised if someone had! Some little peeping Tom in the shadows! She had taken a bath when she got back to the boarding house; somehow with nothing final – what did she mean by that! – coming of it she had the sensation of being, well, unclean. Like a towel which has fallen and which has become dirty before being used. Not a – *real* towel; *that* was what she had wanted.

Indolently she stubbed her cigarette and lay back on the bed with her arms stretched out on either side. Should she undress or just lie there for a while?

She had not known Fidler was an intelligent man. Before today he had been the person in the office whom she was least conscious of. She supposed that was why she never actively disliked him. The rest were unbearable, heavens! Sometimes of course she could have screamed at him. He appeared to be tied body and soul to his work. For what? For perhaps nine pounds a week. Twice what she earned. It was damned unfair. Of course he had been in the damn place an unheard of number of years! He must have gone there straight from school. He lived with his mother and sister, he said, and seemed to envy her living alone. And yet he did not appear to be touched by it all, so it appeared anyway from the way he had talked about not wanting anything very badly. I'll bet he made that one up, she thought, and then she smiled when she remembered telling him about the man she knew who was struck by lightning. *Instantaneously*, she had said. She read it in the paper. Death was instantaneous. A drink does one good, she thought. One talked. A thin man of forty-five rode at the head of the column. She imagined the small sound of the bullet in the pass and the man, Major Lanelly, toppling. The Lives of a Bengal Lancer. Did Fidler believe her? She would have to remember to put on another stocking tomorrow, find one that matched. She had worn it with the ladder for three days.

She was tired, pleasantly, but tired. She wished she could pull a string and have her clothes fall off. Like they unveiled a monument. That was about it, she thought, a monument! It wouldn't have been so bad if she had had money. She would like to have travelled. Genoa, Cairo, Calcutta. A slow boat to China!

Oh hell! She said it aloud, slipping off the bed to a sitting position at the edge.

She undressed slowly, not bothering to arrange her clothes as she took them off. They lay in a little heap at her feet on the floor. She moved them with her foot, warm clothes, still warm from her body. She was naked.

I'm fat, she thought. *You're fat*, she said aloud. This is me, she thought, the me beneath it all, and looked down at herself, at the heavy mould of her abdomen, at the thick white forward jut of her thighs and the roundness of her knees; hairs on my body like Aunt Milly said I would. Excite men. It was funny how men wanted to mate with a woman, even fat women. Aunt Milly was fat. Look at all the men *she* had, heavens! She giggled. Must have been hundreds.

Raising her thighs like the smooth necks of horses she rolled back on to the bed and lit another cigarette.

A little girl with rosepink flesh and growing up to be a better bigger girl, hotter in places, and finally not from contrariety drawing corsets on.

It was as though when he came he carried with him the caution of the forest. The trees which were the curtains parted to reveal his face.

At the kitchen sink in his shirt sleeves – his bare arms were black not as coaldust or soot but smoothly and ambiguously black as the black skin of an eggplant – he stirred blue powder into a bowl of water and filled little bottles with the mixture. When the bowl was empty he carried the bottles over to the kitchen table, corked them one by one, and packed them neatly away in his black leather bag. When the meal of thickly cut bacon and bread was over he rolled a cigarette, slowly, exactly, in palms that were almost white but on which the lines were dark and sharply defined as the skeleton of a rotting leaf; he seemed not to see or be aware of her at all until, finally, when he had smoked the cigarette down so far it seemed to burn his lip, he removed it quickly, ground it in his saucer and turned to her and said, *Where's your aunt?* but she knew that he knew as well as she did where her aunt was and that he would stand up and go to her presently, so she didn't say anything. After a few moments during which he had again thought his own thoughts, and she not quite sure of hers, he got up, wiped his mouth on the back of his hand, scraping his chair back along the wooden floor, and without a word went into the next room. Later she heard a noise like the sudden cry of an alley cat but she didn't think anything about it because it happened often.

Now about an hour later the woman came stumbling through the bedroom door in her faded pink petticoat and padded in her bare feet across to the sink. She hoisted herself onto it backwards and urinated. There was a communal privy at the foot of the stairs but her aunt seldom went to it because she seldom went out of the house. Eileen was cutting strips of paper with the scissors.

The woman watching her slid softly off the sink and raced the tap behind her. *Put them things away and go to bed*, she said. *It's time you were in bed.*

Awake beneath the black spars which made a cage of the kitchen, occasional noises of the other inhabitants coming to her through the walls, a pulley going up to hang above like those, a door slammed, a shout, the noise of feet on stairs, she wondered why her aunt had bled, for there was blood in the sink, and she waited into a gradual sleep for screams or laughter.

Another day she said: Aunt Milly, what was my mother called?

The woman was sitting up in bed with her breasts bare and a woollen shawl over her shoulders. In her hand a half-empty glass of port tilted and glowed. Through the slow red bead of diaphanous glass a mote of dying light thrust its image, a coin or a bubble, flickering at the skin of her abdomen. She started, altering her gaze which had been fixed on the wallpaper opposite.

What did you say, dearie?

Aunt Milly had henna-treated hair which contrasted strongly with the muddy whiteness of her two heavy breasts: she was white and at twenty-four already plump and she didn't get out of bed much except to get biscuits or port wine or to urinate. Aunt Milly sometimes called her Tilly, saying, *Milly and Tilly, howzat sound Eileen*? and Eileen laughed and said she thought it sounded fine, and Milly, her laugh like current at her flatulence, shook in amusement. *What'll it be then? a sweet one or a digestive? how many holes is in a digestive biscuit?*

What she had said was for Aunt Milly to tell her her mother's name, not because she didn't know it because she did – it was Beryl – but so that she would tell her that though her mother died when she was having her she was nevertheless born lucky with a real caul. But Aunt Milly must have been tired or thinking of something else because she merely said that Eileen's mother was called Beryl, and then she said, *Pass me a biscuit, there's a good girl.*

Eileen passed over the box of sweet biscuits and her aunt took one, crunched it, and examined the filling closely. *Praline*, she said, pronouncing it to rhyme with mine and sucking the stickiness off her fingers.

Was she like you, Aunt Milly?

Who?

My mother.

She was a jewel your mother was. And very pretty.

She finished the wine in her glass and reached for the bottle.

Why have you got hair under your arm, Aunt Milly?

You'll have hair too, dearie, when you're older.

Aunt Milly?

Yes dearie? She had filled her glass, smelt it and drunk, and now her tongue protruded from between her lips, licking them at their edges. Her attention was wandering. Her fingers, scissorlike, held the nipple of her left breast, considering.

Why did my mother die when she was havin me?

Them's God's ways, dearie. None can tell.

Dusk was falling. The coinlike reflection had lost its intensity. The pink wallpaper became less vivid. Shadows growing upwards from the floor set the woman apart from the girl. Eileen knew better than to switch on the light. It would have been to make everything, the shadowy objects with which her aunt was surrounded, the empty parrotcage by the window – Aunt Milly insisted that Ludo (the parrot) was poisoned, she blamed the man who read the gasmeter – the dressing table and the bed with which her aunt's reclining figure seemed to merge, sharp and painful, to disperse the torpescent shadow in and through which her aunt's body seemed to exist and to bring everything suddenly into hardness in the naked light of the illumined bulb. With the light out the stale atmosphere was innocuous and warm. And her aunt's voice from somewhere in the pillows was already saying, *Time you went to bed, dearie, I don't think your Uncle Sam'll be in the night.*

Although the room was dark she could see when she opened her eyes the mass of a chair and of the settee beyond that as inscrutable as the face of the man who had married her aunt and whose face appeared to her as the curtains parted. Tomorrow would be another day and have to get to work earlier to make that correction. And find a stocking without a ladder. The last time she had seen him had been night too only it had been snowing outside and in the distance she could hear the wavering music of the Salvation Army brass band because it was Christmastime and they were in the street playing carols. When the outside door opened and shut she couldn't think who it could be and then all of a sudden Uncle Sam was in the kitchen and the light was on and he was carrying the little black bag he kept his bottles in. He put the bag down on the table and then without glancing at Eileen who watched him from the kitchen bed he moved towards the bedroom door through which voices laughing came.

The Holy Man

The hotel was located in a short impasse near the Bal des Anglais. The street face bulged outward and upward from street level, receding again after the first storey like a long narrow forehead until it was cut short by the skyline. Back from the ridge of the roof, out of view from the street, there was a single attic window and above it an uneven row of dilapidated chimney pots, yellow and black, and tilted in oblique postures. There was no break in the tenement structure of the street, and the hotel was distinguishable from the buildings on either side only by its more pronounced bulge and by the peeling yellow paint which covered its outside wall.

It was not a light street. The sun seldom percolated downward beyond the second storeys and, except for a month or so during the summer, the street at ground level was in shadow. There was life in the street, and an occasional outraged cat; but more than anything else it was a street to die in.

The ground floor of the hotel had at one time been a bar, frequented by North Africans and by the prostitutes of the quarter, and it remained shopfronted. Above, the windows, tilting at various angles from the perpendicular, looked out through absence of sun and through grime like the mucous eyes of some of the blind or half-blind men who in latter days came to stay there. Access to the passage which led to the staircase was by a single narrow door. A man entering from the sunless street into a darker corridor which smelt of dampness and urine and decaying ordure was in a passage twenty feet long; on his left immediately was the yellow slit of light which came from under the door, the former back door, of what used to be the bar. Through that door, often, and especially at night, came female laughter. The room was inhabited by three German women who had come to France with the victorious army and who, like other odds, ends, and chevrons of the defeated army, had been ambiguously left there. Their names were Liza, Greta, and Lili.

The staircase at the end of the corridor was a wooden one. Its steps, worn smooth and concave by centuries of climbing feet, had absorbed grease, dust, sputum and spilt water until their surface was like soft graphite. What fell soaked in and remained. Halfway between landings at the turn of flights, the water spouts dripped into iron bowls inadequately gridded against garbage which sank to the drains and caused each bowl to overflow its contents onto the stairs below. The rooms were small. Except for those which gave onto the street, their windows opened onto an airwell which was their only source of light. One of the rooms on the second storey was inhabited by a thin Hungarian. All night he stood near his uncurtained window, old and stark naked, and a candle flame ranged across the skin and hairs of his little abdomen as he picked over and examined the rags he had collected the previous day. His room was full of old clothes, but except when going abroad into the streets he did not use them. Sometimes he spat through a broken pane and his spittle descended down the airshaft to its bottom below street level where broken boxes, discarded bed-springs, and other debris were piled. When he did so, he leaned forward slightly, with an air of attention, as he listened for the sound of its break . . .

Opposite him on the second storey, with a window that gave directly onto his, lived a one-legged woman nearly as old as himself, a native of the city. Her muffled curses rose to the other inhabitants up the airwell. Sometimes the Hungarian paused in his task of inspection and gazed with his one good eye – the other had receded into what was now a pink rim of hair – across to the lightless window where she cursed. Each morning before seven she hobbled downstairs with her crutch close at her left armpit and the thong of her amputated leg in a gray woollen stole just visible below the hem of her skirt. Her face was twisted in a fixed red sneer, and her free hand against the wall prised her torso into balance as it descended. In the roadway she looked this way and that before she set off, like a bent hinge, always in the same direction.

Apart from the German women, and they were all over thirty, no young people lived there, and as the old died off, or moved to the almshouse, or to the sanatorium, or to prison for petty theft or chronic alcoholism, no young people presented themselves to occupy the rooms. Always another old man or another old woman, younger or older than the previous tenant, but old, and often emaciated. Already there lived in the rabbit warren of five storeys one hunchback, one dwarf too old for the circus, one strong man too weak to break chains, two blind men whose white probes brushed walls and stairs to the side or in front of them like antennae of insects, one dumb man, and the woman already mentioned with the amputated foot. For the rest, they came and they went, on foot and sometimes on a stretcher. And not long ago a man died on the stairs.

But above all, and of a power that was intact because it was undivined, there was the holy man.

Why this man was holy, or what holy was, none of the other tenants was quite clear. That they were one and all willing to concede his holiness was quite clear from the fact that all referred to him – and without a trace of humour – as the holy man.

He was above all the others, not only in the sense that he suffered from no physical disability – at least if he did, no one knew about it – nor because he neither had, nor appeared to require, means of subsistence, nor even because he was admittedly holy, but also in the sense that he was above them in space, for it was he who inhabited the tiny attic room at the apex of the house, a room which, were it not for the fact that he had shuttered the dormer window with boards painted black, alone of the rooms in the hotel commanded an uninterrupted view of the sun and of the blue heavens.

The holy man had shut out the sun and the blue heavens from his room. He came years before, almost beyond living memory, clad in a dark mantle against recognition. Accepting the key from Mme Kronis, proprietress, he had mounted the stairs for the first and for the last time. He had carried with him a black blind of wood of the exact dimensions of the attic window, and with a hammer and nails he had boarded himself into darkness like a vegetable. From that day onward he had never set foot on stairs, nor for all they knew on ground or floor, but had lain in a prone position beneath a gray blanket on a narrow bed like a long cocoon.

It was known, or if not known suspected, that he had occupied this horizontal position for more than ten years in his black box at the apex of the hotel.

Now, none of the tenants loved the sun, unless it was the German women who, during the short period of the year when the sun struck down to street level, sprawled untidily on their doorstep (that of what had once been the bar) and scratched the pendulous deathly-white flesh of their thighs which, in their reclining position with knees up, called out, like jaws, at the sun. But evidently no one hated the sun as much as the holy man, not the thin Hungarian nor any of the tenants who went abroad daily to beg in those parts of the city frequented by tourists during the summer. For a beggar in summer must sweat, and those who laid down their truncated limbs near the bridges where the tourists congregated did so in full sunlight, that the sweat might aggravate the emaciation, and the horror the charity.

And so at the beginning this strange hibernation, in spite of its occurrence in the twilit catacomb where all flesh was white from lack of sun, caused a great deal of comment, and various theories were advanced throughout the years to make it less foreign to the general comprehension.

The first was the obvious one: the man was dead.

Such an explanation would have occasioned less dismay than any other. To live, to grow old, and to die: the process excited little interest. Those acquaintances who were not already dead were dying, or were preparing to die in the near future or in the winter, for most of them felt that they could hold out at least until the winter and the frost. It was true that few died in the hotel. The man who died on the stairs, a vast man from Lille with a mountain of weight to carry up five flights of stairs, had been taken by a spasm during his climb. That had been unexpected, the sudden thump around midnight as his body toppled backward down the narrow staircase, but he had been drinking heavily and he had a bad heart – usually he had climbed very slowly, taking a few steps at a time. For the most part they went away to die, to the almshouse or to the sanatorium, and if somebody came round to inquire about a vacant room Mme Kronis would say she was expecting a key in a few days' time. For each dead man, a key; it was usually returned to her by a policeman who climbed up the stairs behind her to make an inventory of the effects of the deceased. Later she would say if questioned: His key came back today. There's a key if you want it.

But it was not unnatural for a man who was about to die to make a crypt of his room. The sun was an irrelevance. If the holy man had died it was as well he had died in darkness. A man wanted to die with a little dignity. Dark made that easier. It shut out the world.

Yes, it would have been easy to believe that the holy man was dead, had it not been for the stubborn recurrence of the symptoms of life. A hundred little facts combined to make the theory untenable.

In the first place, and perhaps most significantly of all, there was no key. Secondly, there was the direct evidence of the German women. For a number of years past, Liza, Greta and Lili, in strict rotation and in complete submission to some unknown authority, had borne his food and later removed his excrement. It was true, or so they said, that they had never seen the holy man. The room was in total darkness. Sometimes they had tried to make conversation, but the mass on the bed – their only experience of that mass was the sound of heavy breathing – remained inert and voiceless; nevertheless, they were aware of him. There was something there, they said, you could feel it on your skin, and the fetor of the place was suffocating. All the air that got in must have been with their exits and entrances, so the stench aroused neither disgust nor disbelief in the other tenants. It was interesting but not important.

Of course, the German women might have been lying. But that they should lie over a number of years, climbing daily to the attic with food for a dead man (or a nonexistent man) to relieve themselves up there in order to be able to return with the chamber pot, seemed unlikely. It was laughable – unless they had murdered him and were trying to cover up for themselves. That theory was suggested and caused so much indignation among the tenants that a few of them got together and, without consulting Mme Kronis, brought a policeman to the hotel. In spite of her protests, the policeman insisted on going to the room to see for himself. She allowed him to do so only on the condition that the rest of the tenants would remain below, and they heard her bicker about interference and lying thieves as she climbed slowly and painfully upward ahead of the policeman.

It did not take long. A few moments later, the policeman descended and without a word went off into the night. A short while afterward Mme Kronis herself came down, still muttering under her breath, and disappeared into her room, locking the door behind her.

The procession of days continued uninterrupted during which, as usual, Liza, Greta, and Lili bore food and carried refuse to and from the holy man. Some said Mme Kronis had bribed the policeman. That was quite possible. Mme Kronis was rich and policemen were human. Was it not so? But, generally speaking, the tenants were convinced. The holy man was alive, even if his life were not what one would expect of a man – it was more like the life of a slug or of a bedbug – what did it matter? Perhaps he had gone up there to die and had not died after all, or was dying but was taking a long time over it. That would have been commendable. They were all of the opinion that a man should take a long time over his dying.

And perhaps that was what it was: he was merely taking a long time over his dying. He had boxed himself into his death chamber in anticipation of his immediate death, and then, finding each time he woke up that he still lived, he had concluded he would die on the morrow, and therefore had not troubled to take down the shutter that shut him off from the sun and from the blue sky. That would have been proper. After having outlived for so long his expectations it would have been a shame to be caught napping with the shutter down. He might even have had a stroke if he had made the great effort that would have been required to tear down a shutter so firmly fixed with long nails. He was presumably no jackass or half-wit who wanted to die before it was strictly necessary to do so.

On the other hand – it was the thin Hungarian who suggested this – it was quite possible that the holy man thought he was dead. That would have accounted too for his passivity. If he thought he were dead he would also think, and logically, that there was no need to act, neither to act nor to decide to act, for he would most certainly be of the opinion that the will – the personal will as distinct from the all-embracing will of God – ceased to be effective after death. And the fact that he had existed in darkness over a period of so many years would naturally conduce to the belief that he was suspended in Purgatory to await God's final judgement. That, the thin Hungarian thought, would explain everything, including the deaf ear he turned to the husky-voiced conversation of the German women which, as he was now dead and beyond the failings of the flesh, he would most certainly interpret as the hallucinatory temptation of that part of his soul on whose account he was condemned to Limbo. He would be afraid to be taken in by his hallucinations, because if he were so taken in it would prove his basic carnality beyond a doubt and that proven beyond the grave even, he would feel himself in imminent danger of being toppled right out of Limbo into something much worse. The holy man, the Hungarian concluded, was wise as well as holy.

The theory of the woman who had her foot amputated was less subtle, and, on those rare occasions when she ventured beyond her monotonous blasphemies to express an opinion, hers was expressed with hard and brittle conviction. The holy man was no more or less than the Devil himself, right on top of us, God knew; the German women, all three of them, were witches as well as Germans and should have been burned.

The German women, indeed, were not popular, never had been since ambiguously they had come to be there. In relation to the holy man, they were suspected of withholding information. That itself was exasperating and grounds enough for dislike. But that was not all. Their full bodies and their thick loud laughter was out of place. It was the laughter of the living against the condemned; it seemed highly unlikely that they would be dying soon, and probable that they would outlive the rest by half a century. A female tenant could not be expected to forgive that insult. A male tenant might and, when alone, did more often than not, for was he not a man before he was old?

The summers passed, and after the autumns, the winters and the springs. No one again sent for the police on the holy man's behalf. Indeed, in the course of the years he was seldom referred to. During the winters more keys became available. The percentage was always higher during the winters. Among others were the keys of the hunchback, of the dwarf too old for the circus, of the strong man too weak to break chains, and of one of the blind men who, crossing a boulevard, got accidentally run over by a bus. Tenants came, tenants went, some to die, others to linger on. During the summers, Liza, Greta, and Lili lounged on their doorstep, their fat thighs exposed and their broad haunches warm from the warm stone under them. They joked with the North Africans, winked or guffawed at a stray tourist, and amused themselves by scratching and comparing their knees. At one point each day, one of them did the chores for the holy man, Liza or Greta or Lili, climbing up stairs which, in former days and with a strange man's eyes following the slow swing of her haunches, she had climbed for other purposes. All the year round, discreetly, they received visitors in their room which used to be the bar or, alternatively, went with them to the hotel round the corner, for some men, sometimes, prefer privacy in lovemaking. The thin Hungarian continued to exhibit his nakedness to those who faced him across the airwell, to pick at his rags, to spit and wait as a bird might, and to elaborate his theory of the holy man. Daily he pushed a small tublike pram around the neighbourhood and beyond, in search of rags. The female citizen continued to mingle curses with the dank odours of the airwell and to break startlingly out of the hotel at dawn into the quiet street. The rest of the tenants prostrated themselves before their old habits, or, if they were new tenants, brought new or old habits to the hotel. And then, quite abruptly, it was the early spring of a certain year.

The end came quickly. One day all was as usual. And on the next day it happened.

Lili, in the midst of her chore, had the sudden ungovernable impression that the holy man was dead. The atmosphere in his little black box contained a new and frightening element. She sniffed and her skin prickled. Taking the chamber pot to a light part of the staircase, she found that it was empty. She returned at once to the room and spoke quietly and urgently at what she believed to be the holy man. It had apparently stopped breathing. There was, as usual no response. But this time, with an irrepressible sense that something had changed, she put her hand forward and touched. She drew it back quickly. What she had touched she did not understand. With trembling hands she lit a match. At this point she uttered one long bloodcurdling scream and hurtled downstairs as fast as her short fat legs would carry her. She reached the room which used to be the bar before anyone had time to intercept her. Locked fast there, and in spite of the loud knocking that came sporadically to her from the outside, she was able to slip out of the hotel at dusk, having spoken to no one of her experience.

Liza ran off that same night with a sailor from Marseilles, and Greta, the biggest but most buxomly beautiful of the three, moved up to Pigalle where (in nights that followed) under myriad coruscations of colour her flesh gleamed whitely and naked in a darkened nightclub. She left barely an hour after Liza.

Mme Kronis had taken control of the tenants. There was an uncanny power in the woman. None of the other tenants was allowed to see the attic where, according to Mme Kronis, the holy man, poor soul, lay dead.

The following day there was the funeral. Mme Kronis, the thin Hungarian, one blind man, and the woman with one foot missing, turned out to follow the coffin.

Mme Kronis, now that the German women were gone, decided to reopen the bar. Meanwhile, she let it be known that there was one key available.

Foreword to Vol. 5 of Frank Harris' *Memoirs*

Those who have read M. Girodias's comments on Harris in *The Olympia Reader* will know that the famous Volume 5 consisted in fact of a sheaf of unrelated notes, about one hundred badly typed pages bound together, if I remember rightly, with a short length of faded blue ribbon. M. Girodias writes that I was 'madly excited at the very idea' of undertaking the rewrite. This assertion requires some qualification. By the time I had laboured through the first two volumes of the famous (or notorious) work, I had conceived an acute dislike for the bombastic little fellow who was responsible for them. And any excitement I felt at 'faking' a fifth volume derived from the excellent opportunity it would afford me to commit an act of literary sabotage and, if I may be excused the expression, to 'take the piss out of him', using his own execrable style in the grafting operation. This I proceeded to do.

For some years, this literary confidence trick was a well-kept secret. And readers will be able to imagine my amusement when that best selling book *Pornography and the Law* first appeared. In the section dealing with the character of Frank Harris, the largest percentage of quotations were taken from the fifth volume and from that part of it for which I myself was responsible!

About this time, some friends of mine from the Kinsey Library at the University of Indiana visited me in New York. They were seeking information on Olympia Press works in general . . . this would be about 1959, five years after the appearance of Volume 5 . . . and because they *were* friends of mine, and because they were engaged in work which I considered to be serious, I decided that at last it was time to let the cat out of the bag. Whether I was the first to do so, or whether Girodias himself had done so earlier I don't know. Two years later I had the pleasure of meeting the authors of *Pornography and the Law*, and I must say they took our jest in very good part. Anyway, we became friends.

I don't suppose I am the one best qualified to judge the rights and wrongs of this piece of literary 'fraud'; but I believed then and I believe now that some scholars are far from happy at being fooled and point-blank fail to view this act of literary deception as something well and funnily done. Those who now come forward to say that of course Volume 5 was evidently spurious, were, if I may say so, rather slow in saying so. For at least five years the whole world was taken in, and I am aware of no one's exposing the 'obviously spurious text' until some time after I myself had spoken to my friends from the Kinsey Library. Here therefore is another example of just how easy it is in the cultural field to confound the 'experts'. The 'spurious' volume five is now published again. Again I must disagree with M. Girodias in so far as I never regarded it as my job to produce a really 'sumptuous work of art'. That would have taken far longer than the ten days I actually spent on the writing of it, and even if it might have been accomplished in ten days, one would certainly have to have ditched Harris's own notes altogether to have any chance of success. For, candidly, those pages for which Girodias paid so much[4], were some of the worst writing it has ever been my misfortune to read.

That the book appears again now is not my decision, though I do think it is probably worthwhile. Naturally, for fear of censorship, we have had to lop off some of the more extravagant scenes. Enough may remain however to show the reader acquainted with the first four volumes just what it was I was about when I came to satirize Harris in Volume 5.

London 1966

---

4. Maurice Girodias had purchased manuscript notes on 2 April 1954 from Frank Harris' widow for 1,050,000 francs – a considerable sum – to overcome her pangs of conscience, since a 5th volume had not been intended for publication.

Letter to Samuel Beckett

30 August 1954

Dear Mr Beckett,

I'm not quite sure what kind of answer you want or expect from me. The cool tone of your last letter makes it difficult for me to say anything at all.

As far as your text in the current issue of *Merlin* is concerned, the decision to use it here and not in the next number *was* a sudden one, and I had Seaver's assurance that the text in manuscript had been passed by you. Let me say at once that I am fully satisfied that Seaver told the truth on this point. He has far too much respect for you to try to circumvent your wishes. As for the proofs themselves, the circumstances under which *Merlin* was printed this time made it almost impossible to send them to you, and our own check against the manuscript was so thorough that we were confident you would be well-satisfied. I'm very sorry you're not. There's not much more I can say.

The question of our debt to you I have explained before. The whole complication arose over the fact that you were in Ireland and had left no specific instructions. As you know, it has been Girodias of Olympia Press who has handled the sale and accounts of *Watt*. When I received your last letter, he was going through a lean period and it was rather difficult to fix a precise date for payment. Now, fortunately, his situation is better and I can give you my assurance that 85,000 francs will be paid into your Paris account by the end of this week.

That you were able to get so many recriminations directly and by innuendo on one small page does credit to your literary ability but says little for what I believed was our friendship. I really am more sorry than I can say that you felt obliged to adopt the tone you did in your letter.

Had you been here in Paris, I hope you would change your mind on your MS. Really, I don't think you have much to complain about in our treatment of you. The whole group has worked hard and loyally for a long time looking after your interests, and whenever there has been a possibility of friction, we have subordinated our other interests to your wishes.

Extract from *Young Adam*

These are times when what is to be said looks out of the past at you – looks out like someone at a window and you in the street as you walk along. Past hours, past acts, take on an uncanny isolation; between them and you who look back on them now there is no continuity.

This morning, the first thing after I got out of bed, I looked in the mirror. It is of chromium-plated steel and I always carry it with me. It is unbreakable. My beard had grown imperceptibly during the night and now my cheeks and chin were covered with a short stubble. My eyes were less bloodshot than they had been during the previous fortnight. I must have slept well. I looked at my image for a few moments and I could see nothing strange about it. It was the same nose and the same mouth, and the little scar above and thrusting down into my left eyebrow was no more obvious than it had been the day before. Nothing out of place and yet everything was, because there existed between the mirror and myself the same distance, the same break in continuity which I have always felt to exist between acts which I committed yesterday and my present consciousness of them.

But there is no problem.

I don't ask whether I am the 'I' who looked or the image which was seen, the man who acted or the man who thought about the act. For I know now that it is the structure of language itself which is treacherous. The problem comes into being as soon as I begin to use the word 'I'. There is no contradiction in things, only in the words we invent to refer to things. It is the word 'I' which is arbitrary and which contains within it its own inadequacy and its own contradiction.

No problem. Somewhere from beyond the dark edge of the universe a hyena's laugh. I turned away from the face in the mirror then. Between then and now I have smoked nine cigarettes.

* * * * *

It had come floating downstream, willowy, like a tangle of weeds. She was beautiful in a pale way – not her face, although that wasn't bad, but the way her body seemed to have given itself to the water, its whole gesture abandoned, the long white legs apart and trailing, sucked downwards slightly at the feet.

As I leaned over the edge of the barge with a boathook I didn't think of her as a dead woman, not even when I looked at the face. She was like some beautiful white water-fungus, a strange shining thing come up from the depths, and her limbs and her flesh had the ripeness and maturity of a large mushroom. But it was the hair more than anything; it stranded away from the head like long grasses. Only it was alive, and because the body was slow, heavy, torpid, it had become a forest of antennae, caressing, feeding on the water, intricately.

It was not until Leslie swore at me for being so handless with the boathook that I drew her alongside. We reached down with our hands. When I felt the chilled flesh under my fingertips I moved more quickly. It was sagging away from us and it slopped softly and obscenely against the bilges. It was touching it that made me realize how bloated it was.

Leslie said: 'For Christ's sake get a bloody grip on it!'

I leaned down until my face was nearly touching the water and with my right hand got hold of one of the ankles. She turned over smoothly then, like the fat underbelly of a fish. Together we pulled her to the surface and, dripping a curtain of river-water, over the gunwale. Her weight settled with a flat, splashing sound on the wooden boards of the deck. Puddles of water formed quickly at the knees and where the chin lay.

We looked at her and then at each other but neither of us said anything. It was obscene, the way death usually is, frightening and obscene at the same time.

'A hundred and thirty at elevenpence a pound': an irrelevant thought . . . I didn't know how it came to me, and for more than one reason, partly because I knew Leslie would be shocked, I didn't utter it. Later you will see what I mean.

The ambulance didn't arrive until after breakfast. I don't suppose they were in a hurry because I told them she was dead on the telephone. We threw a couple of potato sacks over her so that she wouldn't frighten the kid and then I went over and telephoned and went back and joined Leslie and his wife and the kid at breakfast.

'No egg this morning?' I said.

Ella said no, that she'd forgotten to buy them the previous day when she went to get the stores. But I knew that wasn't true because I'd seen her take them from her basket when she returned. That made me angry, that she didn't take the trouble to remember how she'd examined the shells because she thought she might have broken one of them, and me there in the cabin at the time. It was a kind of insult.

'Salt?' I said, the monosyllable carrying the cynical weight of my disbelief.

'Starin' you in the face,' she said.

It was damp. I had to scrape it from the side of the dish with my knife. Ella ignored the scratching sound and Leslie, his face twitching as it sometimes did, went on reading the paper.

It was only when I had begun to eat my bacon that it occurred to me they'd had an egg. I could see the traces on the prongs of their forks. And after I'd gone all the way across the dock to the telephone . . . Leslie got up noisily, without his second cup of tea. He was embarrassed. Ella had her back to me and I swore at her under my breath. A moment later she too went up on deck, taking the kid with her, and I was left alone to finish my breakfast.

We were all on deck when the ambulance arrived. It was one of those new ambulances, streamlined, and the men were very smart. Two policemen arrived at the same time, one of them a sergeant, and Leslie went ashore to talk to them. Jim, the kid, was sitting on an upturned pail near the bows so that he would get a good view. He was eating an apple. I was still annoyed and I sat down on a hatch and waited. I looked out across the water at the black buffalo-like silhouette of a tug which crept upstream near the far shore. Beyond it on the far bank, a network of cranes and girders closed in about a ship. 'To sail away on a ship like that,' I thought, 'away. Montevideo, Macao, anywhere. What the hell am I doing here? The pale North.' It was still early and the light was still thin but already a saucer of tenuous smoke was gathering at the level of the roofs.

Then the ambulance men came across the quay and on to the barge and I pointed to where we had put the body under the sacks. I left them to it. I was thinking again of the dead woman and the egg and the salt and I was bored by the fact that it was the beginning of the day and not the end of it, days being each the same as the other as they were then, alike as beads on a string, with only the work on the barge, and Leslie to talk to. For I seldom talked to Ella, who appeared to dislike me and who gave the impression she only put up with me because of him: a necessary evil, the hired hand.

And then I noticed Ella pegging out some clothes at the stern.

I had often seen her do it before but it had never struck me in the same way. I had always thought of her as Leslie's wife – she was screaming at him about something or calling him Mister High-and-Mighty in a thick sarcastic voice – and not as a woman who could attract another man. That had never occurred to me.

But there she was, trying very hard not to look round, pretending she wasn't interested in what was going on, in the ambulance men and all that, and I found myself looking at her in a new way.

She was one of those heavy women, not more than thirty-five, with strong buttocks and big thighs, and she was wearing a tight green cotton dress which had pulled up above the backs of her knees as she stretched up to put the clothes on the line, and I could see the pink flesh of her ankles growing over the rim at the back of her shoes. She was heavy all right, but her waist was small and her legs weren't bad and I found myself suddenly liking the strong look of her. I watched her, and I could see her walk through a park at night, her heels clacking, just a little bit hurriedly, and her heavy white calves were moving just ahead of me, like glow-worms in the dark. And I could imagine the soft sound of her thighs as their surfaces grazed.

As she reached up her buttocks tightened, the cotton dress fitting itself to their thrust, and then she alighted on her heels, bent down, and shook the excess water out of the next garment.

A moment later she looked round. Her curiosity had got too much for her, and she caught me looking at her. Her look was uncertain. She flushed slightly, maybe remembering the egg, and then, very quickly, she returned to her chore.

The police sergeant was making notes in a little black notebook, occasionally licking the stub of his pencil, and the other cop was standing with his mouth open watching the stretcher-bearers who seemed to be taking their time. They had laid down the stretcher on the quay and were looking enquiringly at the police sergeant, who went over and looked under the sheet which they had thrown over her when they put her on the stretcher. One of them spat. I glanced away again.

Out of the corner of my eye I saw Ella's legs move.

Four kids from somewhere or other, the kind of kids who hang about vacant lots, funeral processions, or street accidents, stood about five yards away and gaped. They had been there almost since the beginning. Now the other policeman went over to them and told them to go away.

Reluctantly, they moved farther away and lingered. They grinned and whispered to each other. Then they whooped at the gesticulating cop and ran away. But they didn't go far, just round the corner of the shed across the quay, and I could see them poking their heads out round the corner, climbing over each other into sight. I remember one of them had flaming red hair.

The ambulance men had lifted the stretcher again but one of them stumbled. A very naked white leg slipped from under the sheet and trailed along the ground like a parsnip. I glanced at Ella. She was watching it. She was horrified but it seemed to fascinate her. She couldn't tear her eyes away.

'Woah!' the man at the back said.

They lowered the stretcher again and the front man turned round and arranged the leg out of sight. He handled it as though he were ashamed of it.

And then they hoisted the stretcher into the back of the ambulance and slammed the doors. At that moment Jim finished his apple and threw the core at the cat, which was crouched on its belly at the edge of the quay. The cat jumped, ran a bit, and then walked away with its tail in the air. Jim took out a tin whistle and began to play on it.

The sergeant closed his notebook, looped elastic round it, and went over to speak to the driver of the ambulance. Leslie was lighting his pipe.

Leslie had been a big man when he was younger, and he was still big at the time, but his muscles were running to flesh and his face was heavy round the chin so that his head had the appearance of a square pink jube-jube sucked away drastically at the top, and, as he didn't shave very often, the rough pinkness of his cheeks was covered by a colourless spreading bristle. He had small light blue eyes sunk like buttons in soft wax, and they could be kind or angry. When he was drunk they were pink and threatening. The way he was standing, running forwards and outwards from his razor-scraped Adam's apple to the square brass buckle of his belt, you could see he wasn't a young man; in his middle fifties, I suppose.

The ambulance was driving away and the sergeant was going over to talk to Leslie again. I remember it struck me as funny at the time that he should address all his remarks to Leslie. I watched the cat sniffing at something which looked like the backbone of a herring near the quay wall. It tried to turn it over with its paw. Then I heard Ella yelling at Jim. It seemed she hadn't noticed him before.

'I thought I told you to stay down below! I'll get your father to you!'

And then she turned on me and said I ought to be ashamed of myself for not keeping the boy out of the way. Did I think it was good for him to see a corpse? She said she thought I put the sacks over the body so as not to frighten him. I was about to say he didn't seem very frightened to me – sitting there playing 'Thou art lost and gone forever, oh my darling, Clementine' on his tin whistle – but I could see she wasn't very angry. I could see she was in some way trying to get her own back for the long look I had at her backside, and that amused me and I didn't say anything. She turned away, lifted the basin which had contained the wet clothes, and I heard her clump down through the companionway into the cabin. Then, suddenly, I laughed. The kid was looking at me. But I went on laughing.

Part Three

'The bright and crowded days of my first long stay in Paris had come to an end. Suddenly it was as though I had nothing anymore, no wife, no love, no Merlin, not one shared certainty; I was alone and . . . out of Paris . . . unknown. Young Adam, written in 1952 and the first of a new genre of book, had been rejected by virtually every publishing house in England and the manuscript was growing daily yellower in the drawer of a publisher in New York . . . would I have to follow my friend Beckett's example, and take to writing in French?'

A Being of Distances

It was behind now, the station, the yellow steam. The train moved slowly out of the terminus, sidled against signal boxes, abandoned trucks, and then, incongruously, where a wall fell away, against palely lit windows in a tenement. Glimpses of rusted gutters, of garish wallpaper, but there was life there, or it was curtained off and not to be seen; hoardings, *Gordon's Gin, Aspro, Sandeman's Fine Old* . . . until he felt the train pulled away again by the rails into a new direction.

It was nearly dark, and the old man whose face had aged in the last half hour and with whom he had walked along the platform was in the past, beyond him.

Soon then the spokes of the city rotated and fell away from the carriage window, and gradually, an uneasiness in his own body, the rhythm of the wheels on the rails came to him – his mind on his father without image – and then from somewhere ahead, like a hound straining at a leash the thin scream of the engine as it thrust more quickly into open country.

He stretched his legs and noticed the mud in the crevices of his shoes. The girl sitting opposite was wearing a red coat. He noticed that first, and then the dull turnip-like sheen of her heavy legs and the self-conscious feet in shoes of worn black suede. Tired feet, arched whitely, awkward. A spent match lay beside her left foot. He did not look up – he was conscious that he was pretending to look at the carriage floor – and soon the legs became merely a lustre on which he was aware of the fine sensitive antennal quality of hairs. He was sorry then that he had stepped onto the train.

For his father would be alone now. And soon he would turn on the light in his room and be alone. But in the end – her legs were crossed at the knees, her black skirt where the coat fell apart was drawn tightly above the kneecap against the flesh – in the end, it would always be like that; no intrusion of his own would alter it. To get to a man it was necessary to accept his premises, and with his father that had been impossible. He had been unable to say: 'It won't be long' because he was sick of his own voice, of dissimulation, and anyway both he and his father had known – 'Next time it will be for me' – when they glanced at each other that afternoon at the grave of the uncle.

The coffin had brass fittings and smelt of varnish. It had been supported by scrubbed deal-wood trestles in the middle of the room, the 'blue' room, and had dominated the room as an altar dominates a small church, blue pillars, and over it all was the smell of flowers and death and varnish – like the smell of cider-apples, he had thought – which set the mourners at a distance from the dead man far more utterly than his mere dying had. The smell pervaded the whole house, met one at the door, and as the mourners arrived in their white collars and black ties, shaking their hands, talking in hushed tones, nodding to others distantly known, it had descended on them, crystallizing their emotion, and drawn them inexorably toward the room given over to death.

In the room he had glanced from the waxlike face of the dead man upward at the tall blue curtains with their faded silver flowers, trying to recognize again the familiarity of ten years before, when, down from the university, he had sat there on one of the blue chairs and told his uncle that he would no longer be interested in accepting an appointment with the firm. The uncle – a man nearing sixty at the time – showed no surprise; like father like son, Philip's child; said shortly he was disappointed: '... thought you'd turn out more like *our* side of the family,' and when Christopher did not reply, 'but you seem to have made up your mind ...'

'Yes,' Christopher said, 'it's quite definite.'

'I'm sorry about that,' his uncle said, 'and in spite of our differences I think your father will be disappointed too.'

He had felt like saying then that it was not for his father that he was doing it, not even for the *other* side of the family, but at that moment for his father who had felt bitter against the uncle and against Jack and Harry ... Harry who brought to everything his soul of a piano-accordian.

Now, in the room beside the dead man, and his gaze falling from the long blue curtains, he had felt no bitterness, only perhaps a vague sense of disgust and a strong desire to be outside in the open street and away from the cloying sacramental odour of flowers and death in the suburban room.

Neither he nor his father had been invited to be pall-bearers. They had watched from a distance as the coffin was lowered into the grave, tilting, from silk cords, and then, following the example of others, they had each thrown a handful of dirt and cut grass on the lid of the coffin – a flat hollow sound from distended fingers, rain on canvas; did the dead man hear? Afterward, the group of mourners stood back and the clergyman led a prayer: a small man with a bald head who had donned his trappings at the graveside, and when, without music, he had broken nervously with his small voice into the 121st psalm and the mourners had taken it up, their voices ineffectually suspended like a wind-thinned pennant between earth and sky. Christopher glanced directly at his father and for a second they had understood one another.

His father dropped his gaze first, almost involuntarily, and Christopher looked beyond the mourners across the green slope where the gray and white gravestones jutted upward like broken teeth.

After the prayers and the singing, the two workmen moved forward self-consciously and threw the earth back into the grave, and the long block of raised earth was covered with wreaths. The clergyman shook hands with the family, muttered an apology, and went with his little leather case alone down the path without looking back.

Harry was there, puffy and self-important as usual, and Jack, as though, now that their father was buried, they had noticed him for the first time, and there was talking and questions: how was he? were things going well? lucky devil to live abroad these days! Overhearty, evasive. Was it not funny how everything had turned out differently, not as one expected? And he supposed they were referring to his clothes, informal and beginning to be threadbare – poor old Chris, gone the way of his father – his general air of anonymity.

'Come and see us before you go,' Jack had said vaguely, but he was already signalling to his wife that he would join her in a moment. 'Don't forget now, old man, Catherine would *love* to hear all about your travels, always talking about you. See you soon then – before you go, Marco Polo, eh? – sure, and give my regards to your father, do.'

'You should have told him to keep them,' and Christopher looked round and his father was standing at his elbow, small, gray, inconspicuous, and he said again: 'You should have told him to keep them, Christopher. Why should I accept his regards through you?'

'Forget it, Dad. They're not worth thinking about.'

'The last time any of them spoke to me was fifteen years ago, nine years after your mother died. It was on Armistice Day. I remember, because I bought a poppy . . .'

'Don't worry about it.'

'There's a reception,' his father said. 'We were not invited.'

'Would you have wanted to go anyway?'

'Not really, no.'

'Well then.'

'Next time,' his father said when they were alone, 'it will be for me.'

'I'll be back soon. I promise.'

He had thought then that it was hardly a lie; there was no way of knowing.

They lingered after the other mourners were gone, walking along the gravel footpaths between the graves, and the grave of the uncle with its covering of bright wreaths was nearly out of sight.

'Your mother was buried here,' his father said. 'Would you like to see the grave?'

'Not particularly,' he said after a moment's hesitation.

'You've never visited it.'

'No. I never have. Would you like a drink?'

'It's just as you wish,' his father said without looking at him, 'but I thought as we were here anyway . . .'

'No, Dad. I don't want to.'

Springtime, he was thinking. To be in England. Casually he

stooped to pick up a broken flower which had fallen on the path. It was quite fresh.

'From a wreath,' his father said.

'Probably.'

They walked slowly, in silence, and the sky was low and white-gray, like milk which has stood for a long time in a cat's saucer collecting dust, and as he looked up he felt a raindrop on his face. 'Looks as though it's going to rain,' he said.

'I come here every month,' his father was saying. 'Sometimes I miss a month but not often. It's the least I can do.'

In Christopher the impulse to say something died. He glanced at him but his father avoided his eye and there was a faint flush on his cheeks. It was as though his father had said: 'I'm old now, Chris, you must understand,' said that, and not the other thing, which was not important and which was not really what he had wanted to say. And Christopher wanted to put his arm round him and to say 'We're like one another, Dad,' – does he expect me to? – but he could not make the gesture.

His father was looking at him uncertainly.

'I've sometimes wondered, Chris, why you didn't go into the business, your uncle's I mean.'

'Have you?'

'You'd have been independent today. Take Jack and Harry.'

'I *am* independent.'

A gust of wind then – how naked the cemetery was!

'Of course. I know,' his father said. 'But you know what I mean.'

'Money?'

Coughing, 'And position, you know. Your cousins are both in good positions now.'

'Do you envy them?'

'Who? Me?'

His father's laugh sounded false and forced. Christopher looked away at an urn on a pillar of white marble; the inscription was in Latin . . . *in vitam aeternam*, he read.

'You know that's not true, son.'

'Why bring it up then?' He added more quietly: 'I don't like them and I don't like talking about them.'

'It's just as you wish,' his father said. 'I didn't mean to upset you, Chris, you know that. It's just that sometimes, well, I think it was your birthright. Your mother was his sister after all.'

'And you're my father.'

He had meant it to be a statement of fact only but his father had crumpled and his mouth had fallen open. Then he had had an impulse to explain himself to his father – he would not have had it otherwise, at no point would he gladly have gone back on the past, didn't he see? – but he would not have understood. 'We're alike, son, you and I.' He might have said that. His son, after all. The second generation.

'I realize, of course,' his father said at last, 'that I've stood in your way. You shouldn't have let me, Chris.'

He would always believe that; my son, my world; holding on to them like men held on to their dead, with words and memories of words. *Perducat nos in vitam aeternam.*

He found himself saying: 'You needn't blame yourself, Dad. You didn't really stand in my way,' and he was going to add: 'It wasn't you who decided me, not at all,' but the smile of disbelief was already there, like a vizor over the eyes.

They walked on.

And now he noticed that his father's hat looked too big for him. It did not fit him. And he took his father's arm.

'Your hat's too big for you, Dad!'

The old man laughed. 'Can't afford another, Chris! D'you know, when I bought my first hat, they cost 12/6 d. – the best, mind you. The same hat costs 62/6 d. today. The cheap ones are no good, no good at all – *This* is a Borsalino.'

A Borsalino. His father had halted, removed his hat and pointed with his forefinger at the discoloured silk lining (pomade, a little jar of green stuff in the bathroom cabinet). 'Borsalino. Made in Italy. You see?'

'Must be a good one.'

'The best,' his father said.

They were walking toward the main gate of the cemetery. The cortege had already broken up and the last of the cars was gone. The gate porter nodded to them as they walked out onto the street.

'I suppose those shops do good business?' Christopher said to his father, referring to the row of shops which sold graveside ornaments and flowers. 'Like bookstalls in railway stations.' A point of departure.

'Capital,' his father said. 'I bought a vase there once for your mother's grave, but one day when I went back somebody had broken it. That's over two years ago now, yes, must be that at least.'

'And shells,' Christopher said.

'Yes. You can buy shells with inscriptions.'

'Pink ones,' Christopher said, and he smiled but his father was looking straight ahead and walking quickly as he always did on the street, and he seemed to have forgotten what they were talking about.

'Will you go abroad again immediately?'

'I suppose so,' Christopher said. 'There's nothing for me here, you know that, Dad.'

'I know.'

'I may spend a day or two in London.'

'And then where? France?'

'North Africa, perhaps.'

'Was there during the first war,' his father said. 'Alex.'

'Yes.'

'I know! It was the day before your Aunt Eleanor died.'

'What was?'

'The day I found the vase broken. Sheer vandalism.'

'Yes, it was a pity.'

'I paid 17/6 d. for it. It wasn't cheap. Come on, we'll get a drink across the road there.' And they crossed the street toward the green-painted public house.

It had been easy there, with a glass of whisky in front of them, to recreate the surface intimacy which, ten years before, he had assented to during a game of billiards – 'never pot your opponent's ball' – their having even then little to talk about, and their inexpertness at the game causing them to smile, to laugh, to be together, until, in the sun again, they had taken leave of one another before they grew apart, Christopher to go to a class at the university, his father to drink coffee in some smokeroom or other, and to read and reread the local paper.

His father had talked and lived again memories of Cairo, Jaffa – the oranges were tremendous, like small melons – and Suez, spoken of a head wound he had received, shrapnel – fingering his scalp tenderly – and which had resulted in his being 'sent down the line' to the base hospital and thence home to 'Blighty,' and as his father uttered the word lovingly, Christopher wondered how he could have failed to relate that homecoming to those things to which he *came* home – or did he come home? – for it seemed to Christopher that those years and those vague memories were the only positive thing in his father's life – he invariably returned to them after a few drinks – and that from the day he had set foot again in England he had known nothing but humiliation. The successful brother-in-law, the dead wife, the son (Christopher) who was brought up in a world in which one could refer to his father only in a discreet whisper and never in the presence of guests, his father's debts, his pride, his humiliation before the brother of his dead wife, and his gradual and, in practice, final exclusion from the world into which he had married: those were the things to which his father returned and to which, sitting there in the bar, he could refer incongruously as 'Blighty.'

'Those were the days, Chris! You were too young, of course. Good Scotch, what was it? 7/6 d. a bottle, yes . . .'

Jaffa oranges, pick them off the trees, get a native to do it for you ackers, the price of secondhand furniture, '. . . too bad you're not setting up house, know where you could get some cheap,' a dealer, Silverstein, good business in the East End, trust the Jews, '. . . see a man was convicted at the Old Bailey, *fif*teen thousand gold watches, that's smuggling!' no wonder income tax, bloody robbers – conversation which always in the end returned to the same theme, the *deaths* column in the local paper, as though the printed notices informed him, quietly bringing desolation to his eyes, that time was running out.

'Did you know old Macarthy, Chris? The one who left three hundred thousand? The widow, Hargreave's girl, 'sgone to the

Riviera, didn't do so bad for herself. Can't be more than thirty-nine.'

His father didn't talk much during dinner – 'the doctor says to cut down on eats,' dabbing with the napkin at his shrunken potato-like mouth and chin — and later, at the railway station, he did not look round. He was still carrying the local paper with its columns of births and deaths, carrying the living and the dead, and he walked quickly across the main hall of the station past the bookstall. His head momentarily in profile, his hat *was* too big for him, and then his back walking away. His son watched him go and returned along the platform to the waiting train. The guard had already whistled, and as Christopher boarded the train he became aware that some soldiers were singing in the next compartment. Song, not words, the umbilical chord. Poor old man . . .

The train lurched over points and steadied against the flickering ribbon of another train which flared past in the opposite direction. Their noises merged and separated. And then the countryside was dark.

After everything, the unexpected arrival, the funeral, the departure just as unexpected – because he felt 'impelled' to go – he was the same man. The noise of the wheels on the rails moved in on him and treacherously his thoughts crystallized. He had not the faintest idea why or where he was going.

Going to the past, remembering places he had gone to and come away from, and the passage of time, he felt very cut off, and more unsure of himself, now he was approching middle age, than he had ever been before. He had stepped aboard because the momentary impulse to run after the retreating figure of his father had seemed silly. Tomorrow or the next day he would have been at the station again.

The smoke from the girl's cigarette made him look at her face. She was not much more than twenty, fair, with a rather heavy face and unexpressive gray eyes. She was looking out of the window and pretending to be unaware of him. There was no one else in the carriage. Ten years ago he would have tried to seduce her.

That made him think that she reminded him of something, a gramophone in a hotel bedroom in Oslo and a woman with heavy limbs, a melody which cried out in a little boxy voice; and the red neon sign at the opposite side of the street was visible, confederate, at the small window.

From a brown paper bag on her knee the girl had taken an orange and was peeling it. She dropped the bits on the floor and pushed them with her heel out of sight under the seat, carefully. He noticed now that she had thick ankles and that the straps of her shoes bit into the flesh which bulged over them like fungus over the edge of wood. She opened up a newspaper between herself and him before she ate the orange.

And his uncle too had been pink and somehow angry when he was living (an undertaker's colour in his coffin) and he had said in his serious unsurprised voice, 'I'm sorry about that', and looked for the only reason he understood to explain the attitude of the young man who faced him in the 'blue' room without explanation. And so for the world of his uncle he was his father's son, a chip off the old block, and everything was simple and understandable and in no way implied criticism of that world.

The girl opposite was still pretending to be unaware of him, and yet she was aware, and there it was, as effective as words, a decision, an act, which he had rejected before and which he would continue to reject wherever it met up with him, which had driven him out of the world of the cousins and the uncle into his own isolation.

In the morning he would be in London. Nothing isolated him more than Victoria Station, especially in the morning when the local trains came and thousands of office workers moved across the hall to the various exits. He had stood not more than a week before drinking tea in the railbar and watched until the stragglers had left the station. Afterward, he had decided over again.

He could not remember making the decision. It had been there all the time. He found himself not part of and therefore driven to reject the world into which he had been born. His father could say: 'Most of the old gang are gone now', because he had need of the words, now he was growing old, and because he was part of a generation in society which was dying, a few each month in the *deaths* column of the local paper. But if his father were alone it was not because his contemporaries were dead.

Neither of us had contemporaries.

Like father like son, even unto the third and fourth, the dead man knew.

Christopher rested his head against the back of the seat and lit a cigarette. His own wound, knife, his own decision. He rejected the women who would have married him and borne his children, he rejected the men who would have employed him and those who would have been employed under him. He rejected war and peace, and the artificial truss of all opposites which men died for or fought against. There could never be a retraction because whatever he looked at was false. 'Most of the old gang' were not dead for him because they had never existed. Sometimes he watched men or women or traffic in the streets, but always from the outside, and with the same feelings with which he would have listened to a story which had no point; and yet there they were, everything, everyone, each under his umbrella, each under his own lie of significance.

A man came in out of the corridor through the sliding door. Christopher glanced away from him and rubbed the window with his sleeve. The train had halted at a station. When he looked back into the carriage the man nodded to him, smiled to the girl, and put a briefcase on the rack. He had a red face which had the appearance of being too much soaped in hot water. He sat down near the girl.

Christopher turned back to the window. He thought that now his father would have turned on the electric fire and would be poring over the *deaths* column like a speculator over a stock-market bulletin. Later he would make tea for himself and drink it, looking at the two bars of the electric fire – 'Damn chilly just now' – and then he would get up, wash the cup and saucer, and prepare in detail, reluctantly, to go to bed. If I hadn't gotten onto the train, Christopher thought, I could have stayed a few more days with him.

'– for holidays,' the girl was saying.
'Not very good weather,' the man said.
'You're telling me!' She glanced at Christopher and, as though he had caught her at something, flushed.
He looked out of the window but it was too dark to see anything, sometimes, only, a patch of cinders from the engine, lambent, isolated.
Later, all three occupants dozed.
The train ran over rails with a monotonous voice into minutes and hours between night in two towns. In the compartment, the windows were misted and the air was cold with the coldness of the unsheathed electric-light bulb. On one seat the girl dozed uneasily with her head on the shoulder of the redfaced man. On the other seat, the man who had left his father for no reason was carried with his absurd thought of a window perspiring on the Riviera into distances from which he would always – until one day, perhaps with words, and because he feared death – be excluded.

(A revised version of this story appears in part in the novel, *Cain's Book*.)

Wolfie

It was New York, 1958 or '59, I don't remember, and Lyn and I were living in the loft in West 23rd Street, between Sixth and Seventh. We inherited it from Johnnie Welsh and Al Avakian when they split up, a superb big place which could have been palatial if we'd had some money to spend on it. Even as it was with some of our own artefacts it was quite impressive. The only thing: it took a helluva lot of heating in winter. And it was November. Late November and the beginning of a very cold winter such as New Yorkers from time to time experience.

I took the subway up to the Bronx. At that time of night, long after the rush hour, it was grey, bleak, cold, and lonely, especially at a station like 23rd Street. I was the only passenger to get on. But there was no alternative. I had to go to cop some heroin from our connection, Wolfie. A long journey it seemed in that all but empty carriage, only two others, an old lady in faded black who muttered constantly to herself, the bow of her lips startlingly red, bright as a cherry, twitching. Or was she nibbling something? The other passenger who sat on the same side as she only farther along the car was a near dwarf in a huge greasy grey fedora, a shiny brown suit, and extremely pointed, biscuit-coloured shoes. He sat unmoving with his hands on his knees and stared straight in front of him. God, I used to hate that journey, even when I remembered to take a book which, for some reason or other, this evening I hadn't. At 42nd Street a few more people got on. But they were all muffled up, nipped by the cold, and in that garish but still dim light of the old subway carriage their pitiful look contributed to my own low spirits. Who would be out on a night like this if he could help it? And where I was going I had no real wish to be. I never felt relaxed in that chromium-plated nightmare that was Wolfie's pad. Wait, I'm not there yet, I'm not even off the train!

A very cold winter, late November. I came off that train onto the platform of God knows what hundredth street in the Bronx. What a journey that had been, a long long one, sitting there, looking at those other people and wishing to hell I would arrive! Finally I did get off at that deserted station away up in the Bronx, the streets black and wet with traces of snow still on the ground. I walked out of that bleak empty station into a deserted street. Wet, wet and cold, my shoes were soon sodden, a cold wind flattening my trouserlegs against my shins. Cold steam at my lips and nostrils; God, how my nose was cold! Slush and snow, the snow turning to water everywhere, but with that wind it would probably be ice by morning. And my toes! I stamped my feet as I walked to keep the blood circulating. My God, what a district Wolfie lived in! Endless empty streets of vast high-rise buildings with not a yard of defensible space in sight! The night air dark, ink-black, the streetlights garish, the streets wet and glistening where the snow had already melted and slush on the footpaths which led off the street amongst the vast oblong shadows of the buildings of the estate. The Mondrian effect of the pattern of lighted windows did nothing to dispel the overwhelming sense of desolation I felt as I took the path towards the building where Wolfie's flat was. No friendly neighbours here to look on if you were slugged, mugged and neatly butchered in these baleful shadows. A man might not be found until morning. Of course everything contributed to my uneasy state of mind; not only the cold impersonality of this north Bronx housing estate, but the subway journey there and the winter weather itself, the fact that my shoes leaked, and, perhaps most significantly, the knowledge that there was always an element of risk in visiting a known pusher at his home. I never felt particularly good going up to Wolfie's place. But on this particular night . . . whether or not I had some kind of premonition . . . I felt distinctly ill at ease. Moreover, the simple thought of living in a place like this brought me down, down, down. Those architects who put a thousand boxes together and called them homes for men I have never understood; indeed, I have always felt they should be indicted. Set a bourgeois architect to design homes for the working class and without fail he will design homes for sardines! To tell the truth, that night I was not particularly socially conscious; nevertheless, that kind of highrise multibox architecture made me very uncomfortable. Sleet had begun to fall again and the wind had sprung up, so I was very glad when I pushed my way through those swing-doors into the buildings.

I was after all where I had to be . . . the place where I could cop the shit. So you could say I was glad to be there at last, relieved anyway. I had arrived. The hall was empty. The lift was over there. Press the button. I was lucky. The door slid open immediately. God is good. Inside. What floor? Fourth. No Jack the Ripper anyway. Lucky me! Press number four and I am on my way up. That whine a lift makes in rising. I can't find the onomatopoeic equivalent. Click and the door opens. I step out into a long long corridor. It is well-enough lit but deserted. On either side in front of me, door after door after door. I am looking for number 479, some distance along the corridor. Yes! There it is! Thank God, it's still there! Press the buzzer. Footsteps. A short delay during which time I felt myself examined through the little spyhole exactly in the centreline of the door. The sound of the chain being released and the door swung open and there was my friend, Wolfie. Yes, in a limited way Wolfie was my friend. There was no doubt about that. On the other hand, my being who I am and his being a Puerto Rican with his particular attitude towards women, for example, I was aware of a real cultural gap. He cherished his wife as he would have cherished and groomed his horse if he had had one, but when there was something serious to be discussed his pretty fat little wife appeared to me to have been trained to withdraw. Frankly, I found this aspect of their relationship disconcerting. Sometimes I felt that pretty little woman was just some kind of cow for him.

Wolfie. My connection. Five feet seven inches tall, inclined to be stout, with a large round head, black hair cut neatly around the ears, soft brown eyes, and full red lips which often smiled exposing excellent white teeth. He had one of those hairline Latin-American moustaches fringing his upper lip. In Spain he would have been a lawyer or a pimp. Sharp blue suit, tasteful black shoes, hands well manicured. He was never without a tie and wore an expensive Rolex on a brown and rather hairy wrist. A man of much *machismo*. Nothing of the beatnik about him even when visiting clients in the Village or the lower East Side. One of his most likeable traits was his readiness to learn. He wanted to know all about art and literature, to better himself, he said, and he would listen politely with an expression of rapt and grave humility on his smooth olive face. 'Each time I see you, Joseph,' he used to say, 'I *learn*. I find out things that are important!' I was often embarrassed.[5]

5. While in Wolfie's apartment, Trocchi was arrested during a Police raid and was arraigned in the Bronx. Luckily he was able to persuade the Police that he was merely an innocent visitor and was freed – for the time being.

Letter to Terry Southern

New York
December 1956

Dear Tertullian,

I have been wandering about the streets all night, stalking cats and lying in wait for unwary dogs, with my gimlet eye alert for the fuzz. What final corruption, what last ditch pollution 'fore dawn breaks? thought I. And then to Jim Atkins where I drank a cup before I returned to my lair. One cup or two. Does it make any difference? Small payment for the night's good work! Three cups. I drank three cups, then. A man must have sustenance.

I rolled over in my straw and looked at your communication. And a most false and inventive document it was if I am not mistaken! Bringing as it did together men of divers persuasion who even for the foul purpose of execrating my memory would not be seen dead together in one café, far less at the same table, and in the shadow of a church! That Hadj AND Midhou AND Austryn AND Sinbad AND Mason AND Debord AND hot Iris[6] should exist all at one time on this poor earth of ours, and in their infinite and vicious variegation, is God (certainly) knows blasphemy enough, but that you, a Priest of the Faith, and sworn to the veneration of the True Word, should confound and confuse and commit buggary with the facts, smearing them with that heinous creative talent of yours, that wordlust, that poetic diarrhoea, is.

---

6. These were members of Trocchi's 'set' in Paris. Mr Hadj was the owner of the Hotel De Ville, Midhou was an Arab dope-dealer, Austryn Wainhouse was an American writer and translator of De Sade, Sinbad Vail was the editor of *Points* magazine, Mason Hoffenberg was an American writer, as was Iris Owens, Guy Debord was one of the founders of the Situationist International.

Miss Linkel was pleased to hear that her meat was selling well. She is willing to sell her meat at any time, raw or braised, suck or fuck, so long as she does not end up on 14th Street, Manhattan. Convey this to Master Girodias.[7]

Miss Linkel would also like your uncreative opinion upon how much she might demand for a choice piece of tenderloin some time in 1957.

New York? There are not three good men unhung in this accursed city and one of them is lean and murders cats and dogs.

John Welsh? A short while ago he came creeping down from the south citadel at 23rd Street, to the Village, for a peep at the dirt, and a sly fix. He brought with him three spikes of various dimensions as though he would outjunk the worst of us. Naturally – a worker he – it was Saturday night. At six a.m. on the Sabbath morning, surrounded by myself and two of my female cronies, all three of us bung full of shit and horizontal, he took fright and cast us on the street in foul weather and threatened by fuzz and this in spite of all my entreaties, the hellish act carried out with a square jaw and the light of righteousness in his eyes. Indeed, dear friend, there was much that was surprising about that night, and not at all in accord with the previous testimonies concerning the past life of John Welsh, to wit, Luciano to you and me and Lucky to him, and dope-peddling in the Bronx, much, I say, or mean to say, that led me to pose the following horrendous questions:

(1) Was John who professed to hate bullshit a bullshitter?
(2) In those historic years was he after all no pedlar but simply a paddler?
(3) Would it be necessary to strike him off the Social Register?

The first two questions I was forced to answer in the affirmative. The weight of evidence, believe me, etc. The third question I was able to answer in the negative. John is after all a Welshman and loved by both God and your correspondent. Even he is trying to ruin my literary career by pointing me to those with whom I wish to curry favour as a 'lost cause' and a junkie to boot. (In

---

7. Miss Linkel; a reference to Trocchi's nom-de-plume of Frances Lengel, whose novels were published by Maurice Girodias' Olympia Press.

this connection I admit that some people think me careless. Some people, for example, are not amused by the fact that I gave George P . . . n[8] a mainline a few moments before he sat down and wrote me a cheque for $50. – The dose was weak. He left at once for the White Horse where he cried: *I've taken junk! He gave me junk!* and he bared his brave arm that the damsels might see his wound. He has not been down to the Village since, but if I know George . . . ha! ha! . . .)

Sabre, Mel? I have removed that man's name from the Social Register and for the following reasons:

(1) He's a perfume salesman!
(2) He has a copy of Colin Wilson's *The Outsider* on his shelf.
(3) Vilely hypocritical, he has encased it in newspaper that it may pass unnoticed.
(4) It is a well thumbed copy.
(5) He refused to lend me his spike. (I swear, by God, I lent him mine five times!
 Donating shit
  To go with it.)
(6) He keeps his spike in the jacket of a suit of mine which hangs in his wardrobe!
(7) I overheard (a great strain!) the following 'business conversation';

Scene: Mel's pad. Mel is on the telephone.
Hello? Ah, oui, âllo Monsieur X! . . . oui . . . oui . . . oui . . . ah oui? OUI! Certainement . . . je suis tout à fait d'accord . . . t'as raison . . . oui . . . oui . . . oui . . . pour dire la verité j'avais l'intention de le suggérer moi-même . . . oui . . . oui . . . tu as fait les arrangements . . . oui . . . oui . . . mais si je ne suis pas invité . . . ah oui, avec toi . . . oui . . . je suis d'accord . . . il nous faut presenter notre cas . . . oui . . . oui . . . oui, c'est clair . . . quoi! ni toi! . . . mais Monsieur X, si nous sommes pas invités . . . ah non! . . . oui . . . oui . . . mais . . . non . . . mais . . . écoute, Monsieur X, je t'en prie! . . . non . . . non . . . pas ça . . . je n'ai pas peur mais . . . oui

---

8. George Plimpton, founder-editor of the *Paris Review*.

... oui ... mais ... non, Monsieur X, après tout, c'est ton affaire ... je suis assez content ... je n'ai pas dit ça ... ah oui mais ... non Monsieur X, je regrette mais ... non ... non ... non ... non ...! La justice, oui, mais ... je ne peux pas ... non, non!

You will no doubt agree that I had no alternative. I shall consider his application for readmission at the time of his child's birth, and solely, I assure you, for the sake of the infant. (Anyway, I am inquisitive to see how Mel will bear up under the deluge of piss and shit which at that time will visit his pad.) Dorothy is well. She loves him.

John[9] and Sue Marquand: living at present in Stockbridge, Mass, near the site of what John cleverly calls the *Sedgewick Pie*. I spent last weekend with them in what they called the 'chicken-coop', a large mansion of enormous proportions (three rooms and kitchen and bathroom!) in the grounds of the main Sedgewick dwelling, a beautiful eighteenth century country house. John does his writing in one of the rooms of the big house, and, thinking psychogeographically in the manner of Guy Debord, I suggested that the difference between our writings was that his was permitted in the mansion and mine was committed in the public lavatory (hee, hee). Before I forget let me tell you about the Pie. It had snowed the day before and Stockbridge (pretty village!) was covered with snow as white ... as the belly of a dead Jewess (Come out of the lavatory, you swine!) ... John and I, muffled and booted against the weather, (Al Avak gave me the ugliest pair of big brown dressy boots you ever saw and I wear them only on those rare occasions when I am not interested in making an impression or when, together with a pair of yellow and red Argyle socks, they form, with my spike-tipped umbrella, part of my impenetrable disguise as I walk along after dark on my missions of mercy amongst dumb animals) walked beyond the village to the graveyard. We turned in at the gate and judging distances from the gravestones which jutted up about us like broken teeth we moved with great care through the boneyard.

9. John P. Marquand, American author, a friend of Trocchi from the Paris scene.

Beyond the mingy little stones of hoi polloi we came upon a number of large plots fenced off by rails of iron. These evidently belonged to various important families of the district who were naturally concerned not to mix their dust with dust of an inferior nature. You and I, Tertullian, having worked for the NY Trap Rock Corporation are cognizant of the fact that dusts differ, varying in quality and no doubt in quantity too, and so we can understand these subterfuges. In one of these surely, thought I, the Sedgewicks are laid. But no! we walked on until in the very centre of the graveyard we came upon a kind of grove. Here John struck bravely across country into the thicket, and lo and behold at the centre of the thicket was a clearing, circular in shape, and lit by the wintry sun. All around us snow dripped silently from the trees. Imagine our joy to discover there at the centre the tombstone of John's great progenitor, Jason Sedgewick let us call him, his grave on a raised mound in the dead centre of the clearing and marked by an obelisk or prick, while at his left hand his sweet wife lay, Maud let us call her, her grave marked by a noble urn! Next, at the feet of this grand couple, the bones of a slave bearing a tablet with the following inscription:

> (I quote from memory, of course, and cannot vouch etc.)
> Here lies Bella Blackbum, dead in her fifty-fourth year (approx). Born a slave, she was granted her freedom by Jason Sedgewick whom she lived to serve faithfully for the rest of her glorious life. Although she could neither read nor write she knew much that is not contained in any book (Naturally, Jason Sedgewick, or whoever composed this elegy, was not acquainted with the works of Miss Linkel.) and this knowledge she brought generously to her life's task. Known and loved by all.

And then all about, buried feet inwards, like spokes radiating from the hub of a bicycle wheel, Jason's dead progeny. Thus, on the Day of Judgement, the Sedgewicks will rise and face into the history of their family, their backs protected on all sides by the thicket of trees. One of God's smaller explosive turds should do the trick, eh?

As we left that holy place, our minds ennobled by thoughts of eternity, we came, ah sweet Jesus save us! on the footprints of a ghoul! Four footprints only and none that led thereto or therefrom . . . therefore!

One last anecdote of my visit to Stockbridge, Mass. Rigg's Sanatorium is located there (retreat of Judy Garland and S. Higginson, from time to time). All strangers are presumed to emanate from Rigg's. As the train drew out of the station and I waved goodbye to John and Sue the conductor* . . . Funny thing, Dup or Pud, your ex-wife, stops Burn on street, shoots ogling glance raising his self-esteem who had affected not to notice her scintillating approach. – Burn, says she, with sobbing urgency, the father of Terence has passed away, and goodness knows I'm sure I cannot think how to break the news to him! Burn, dear, continues she orchidaceously, you will do it for me, won't you! Burn's bright brain in awe of all the implications is unable for one second to speak and so she sinks three long green talons in the upper arm, says: I'm counting on you, Burn! and leaves him flopping like a fish in protest on the pavement. But she is archly gone. So Burn, having nothing better to do, comes to the Horse and tells me. Hee, hee, hee! How to tell Terence that his father has died? Work indeed for two keen minds! Hey, yer old man's died (proncd: *deed*, with accent on the consonants: anc. Scots, with the black regard of an Eyetalian) . . . Hey, terrie, yer auld man's died! Ye droaped yir fickin typewriter onim! (Speaking of typewriters, mine was stole, darkly from 72 Bank Street, and when Davie and me'd got enuf courage to face them detectives at the precinct, said one fat keen one in a bantering tone: *Probably one of those moronic junkies.* I made a thing of being Scotch then, and we dropped red herrings until we were safely esconced at the Riv.) A postcard framed in black? We, Burn and Trok, regret to announce that yer faither's deed. *Auld Nickie-dé,/Has taken him away.* Organmusic tonite. Burn emphasized the delicacy of the matter. My dear Terry, I'm sorry to be the one to tell you that yer faither's fuckin deed. My heart goes out to you in sympathy at this most trying time. Praise the

---

* Original page of letter missing.

Lord and pass the ammunition. Or a PS: By the way, (old) man, yer faither's deed. Of course it wasn't the news that paralyzed Burn. It was the self-esteem quenched at its spring, corked at its fart, as Dup or Pud was off without hearing one bright remark from him. Hee, hee, hee! One thing about our Davie, a topic is seldom sustained unless he has the telling of it! But the genius, the genius, the beautiful genius! Rather this great subjective frog than the dull wits, the titless bastards, eh? Yes, I thank you for Mr Burnett. And then borrowing money from Al Avak we found out you knew already, aye, even as David was painting a little wooden corpse and I was building a fine coffin to put it in. Bloodlessly, in our wraithlike way, we lay aside the work and visit for a mainline. (Supposing Al is mistaken? says Burn . . .)

Dear Alec . . . Happened by . . . Couldn't help noticing the above. Forgive me summat didactic attitude, but in the interest of pure rhetoric, felt some stylistic deletion in your last sentence might not be inappropriate, and took the liberty. I mean, you mufficker, watch how you use people's names. The man does.)

Yours for discretion,
Paul the Perfumer

(Dear Terry . . . Happened on further correspondence (filed hereabouts under cryptic sub-classifications in mammoth Scottish (sperm-stained) steel-and-barley-candy-wrapper files. A strangely opprobrius reference, by the recondite Troc, to my own behavior. For the record, sir, and because I will not have your own insights sullied, that paper-wrapped copy of *The Outsider* held, (gummed to the centerfold) a quaint Tibetan treatise (in translation) on tantric procedure for efficacy in the market-place (not for the impure heart) which same has aided vastly in the Schiaparelli epoch. Suggested to zoon that certain formulae remain yet a bit obscure, and ask him if a prayer-wheel *really* amplifies effects.

Your letters are, even vicariously, a solace. Ah, ceux de la plume . . . s.

Extract from *Cain's Book*: 'Jody'

There is no story to tell.

I am unfortunately not concerned with the events which led up to this or that. If I were, my task would be simpler. Details would take their meaning from their relation to the end and could be expanded or contracted, chosen or rejected, in terms of how they contributed to it. In all this, there is no it, and there is no startling fact or sensational event to which the mass of detail in which I find myself from day to day wallowing can be related. Thus I must go on from day to day accumulating, blindly following this or that train of thought, each in itself possessed of no more implication than a flower or a spring breeze or a molehill or a falling star or the cackle of geese. No beginning, no middle, and no end. This is the impasse which a serious man must enter and from which only the simple-minded can retreat. Perhaps there is no harm in telling a few stories, dropping a few turds along the way, but they can only be tidbits to hook the unsuspecting with as I coax them into the endless tundra which is all there is to be explored. God knows it's a big enough confidence trick to make someone listen to you as you gabble on without pretending to explain how Bella got her bum burnt. I said to myself: 'Well now, here's a nice barren wilderness for you to sport and gamble in, with no premises and no conclusions, with no way in and no way out, and with nary a trail for the eye to see. What more can a man want to fill his obscene horizons?' Drainage trouble in your home? Drainage trouble? A stopped-up sewer may be to blame. I drank a bottle of cough syrup (4 fluid oz., morphine content $\frac{1}{6}$ grain per fluid oz.) and took a couple of dexies and felt better. Nothing like a short snifter to buck you up when you find yourself near Perth Amboy, New Jersey, sitting on the handpump on the port quarter of your scow whose starboard side is swinging just free of the docks, and the dung-coloured water sliding away smoothly, horizontally, before your eye. On it, a tanker. Beyond it, and to either side of it, low brown and green countryside, low bridges, concrete piles, elevated roads with automobiles like little ladybirds running across them, and squat and strutted things, trucks, gas-tanks, telegraph poles, scows, gravel, endless concrete, low, flat, dispersed, representing, dear reader, man's functional rape of unenviable countryside, marginal flat and bogland. As the afternoon wore on the sky was becoming thin and milky-white and the water gleamed blankly in reflection. To walk beyond it all would have taken how long, one pillbox after another through the skeleton factory, mile after mile flat and deserted? The nearest bar, I was told by the last dockhand before they knocked off, was just over a mile away beyond that underpass; that the first evidence that man was not only a working animal, and yet really not much more than a filling station between there and the next bar a mile farther on, and so on. It reminded me of the North Sea in a fog, of Hull or Sheerness, places like that on the east coast of England.

I left my scow after dark around 10:30 and walked through a brickyard to reach the path leading up to the road. I walked slowly along a single railway track overgrown with weeds and found myself amongst brick kilns like the kind of sandcastles you make by inverting a child's sandpail. The furnaces of two of the kilns were going full blast, casting a red glow which threw my shadow in black on the wet gravel. – I am walking through hell or Auschwitz, I thought. And then the dreary climb up beyond the underpass. It was spitting rain.

It took me an hour and a half by bus, ferry, and subway to reach the Village. I bumped into Jody in MacDougal Street. We walked towards Sheridan Square. Jody was wearing blue jeans and a cheap, imitation-leather jacket, powder blue in colour. Someone gave it to her. She disliked it but it was at least warm and all her own clothes, so she had told me, were locked away in two suitcases, impounded by some landlady uptown to whom she owed rent.

As we approached the lights of the intersection her hand went automatically to her hair. It was fine brown hair, cut short and close at the ears, and cut short like that it made her finely chiselled features look hard and sculpted. This impression was intensified by the wide sweep of her plucked eyebrows and by the mockery which came often into her beautiful pale brown eyes.

She lived with a girl called Pat who loved her and paid the rent. That was Jody's way. Jody's share of the rent, if she could have brought herself to pay anything, would have been less than the price of staying high for a day. But for some reason or other Jody never paid. She invented excuses. She had lost it. It had been stolen. She had been burned. Pat was a square, a lush . . . why pay her anything? And if it wasn't Pat it was someone else, even myself at times, and Jody could always find a word to cap her victim and justify the unseemly executions. There was the time she took $20 from me to cop and didn't return until the following evening high out of her mind with a full-blown story of a big bust and shit flushed down toilets and arm inspections and Malayan elephants and she had been lucky to get away at all. (Not just one little taste for me, Jody? *The iris closing.* You hang me up for twenty-four hours waiting for shit, you come back zonked and expect me to think it's lucky you get back without it? Aw, Joe, I couldn't help it, honest. Let's blow some pot, Joe, just you and me . . . I didn't burn you, Joe, honest . . . I told you it was a bust, honest . . .)

I met her first through Geo. I was staying at Moira's place. Moira had gone away for a fortnight. The blinds were drawn all the time. I scarcely left the apartment. It was a time of fixing and waiting and being and fixing and waiting. Jody made all the runs. She had a good contact. She came with Geo and when he left she stayed, like some object he found too heavy to carry away. How do you do, Jody? It seems you're living with me. The atmosphere became much less tense the morning Geo left to return to his scow. Jody asked me if I would like a cup of coffee. And she went out and brought back some milk and a few cakes. Jody loved cakes. She loved cakes and horse and all the varieties of soda pop. I knew what she meant. Some things surprised me at first, the way for example she stood for hours like a bird in the middle of the room with her head tucked in at her breast and her arms like drooping wings. At first this grated on me, for it meant the presence of an element unresolved in the absolute stability created by the heroin. She swayed as she stood, dangerous as Pisa. But she never fell and I soon got used to it and even found it attractive. One time she turned blue and I carried her over to the bed and massaged her scalp. She came round almost at once. It might have been the increase of circulation in her head. Or it might have been the fact that Jody didn't like anyone to touch her hair, or indeed, any other part of her. She was always at the mirror, arranging her hair. It had to be perfect, that and her makeup. Sometimes when she was high she would spend as much as an hour in front of the bathroom mirror.

'Does it never occur to you that you spend a helluva time each day in front of a mirror?'

She was immediately, you might say understandably, on the defensive. A shadow crossed her face, the secret closing of the iris.

Her skin and her colour suggested delicate, fragile china. The clearly marked eyebrows, the finely curved cheek, and the dark, accentuated beauty of the eyes, heightened this masklike effect. Her lips were dull, soft, red, hard, full; the nose aquiline, curved smoothly and sharply, like all the other aspects of her face. Her pupils were often pinned and shadowy, her delicate nostrils tense.

In a way she was always abstracted. I have described a beautiful face, but the beauty was not at all conventional. In fact there were moments . . . when she was stoned in the flesh and tired by the use of too many drugs, by too little sleep, by a hard coil of inner desperation which caused a certain latent vulgarity that was hers to come to the surface . . . when she looked cheap and ugly. Below the mask then a stupid confusion was evident. It showed in her whole manner, particularly in the nervous movement of her hand arranging her hair, a movement which was indistinguishable from the fatuous gesture a cheap whore might make as she stood up, caught sight of herself in a wall mirror, and prepared a face to leave the bar with.

Like many part-time hustlers she had had many affairs with other women. They always ended in the same way. The other woman did the hustling. When Pat had an accident and was taken to hospital Jody didn't budge from the apartment. 'I hate sick people,' she said. Pat sent Jody money from the hospital. When Pat came out she was confined to bed. 'She thought I'd take care of her, Jesus! I'd be readin and she'd *want* somethin! She always *wanted* somethin!'

We crossed Seventh Avenue and went into Jim Moore's.

'She comes on with this baby stuff,' Jody said. 'Jo-dee! It makes me sick. Always buggin me!'

'What did you do?'

'I ignored her. Then she got mad and said she paid the rent. I asked her what that had to do with it. She thought she'd *bought* me! Can you imagine that? You broke your leg, I said. I didn't. If you didn't get so damned lushed it wouldn't've happened. I wouldn't take the blame for anythin, nothin!' Jody said. She pulled her coffee to her and drank some as soon as it arrived. She put sugar into it and asked for some more jelly with her English muffin. 'She screamed herself sick all day and next day she moved out. She went to stay with a friend till her leg was better.'

I burst out laughing.

The way Jody said it was funny. But that wasn't what I was laughing at although she was under the impression it was and burst out laughing in delight at my response. And her delight was no less affecting because it was, in a logical sense, mistakenly triggered. Spontaneous laughter is infectious and draws people together. And I had laughed first and found myself effectively delighting in her delight. The words, even their meanings, were in a sense superfluous. I remember wondering at that, how the fact of laughing together nullified the inauthenticity. Even now it is with a feeling of generosity that I remember what I laughed at then, which was the memory of her own pathetic indignation when someone up in Harlem burned her – 'The bastard! After all I've done for him! When he had no bread I used to turn him on!' – about that, and the self-criticism her hard talk about Pat implied, for like people generally, Jody, no matter what she was talking about, talked exclusively about herself. I used to wonder whether she knew it.

When we had finished our coffee and when no one we knew had come along . . . we were looking for loot to score with . . . we crossed West 4th to the Côte d'Or. We pushed in through the swing doors. The place was crowded, dark as usual, the bar on the left and the single row of tables on the right. The first thing you noticed was the exhibition of paintings along two walls just below the ceiling. At that time they changed them every so often, but soon it was just a bar again with a mixed clientele. I didn't go there much by that time because it was one of the few places I was fingered. I had been waiting for Fay, drinking a beer, and I had been spotted by the barmen as one who was more interested in dope than in drink. That's a bad thing in any bar, and barmen are quick to notice. Most barmen are very indignant about drugs. Still, one of the barmen had been in Paris and most of his customers were very friendly towards me. It's true that Fay was as loud as a white feather in wartime; if anyone ever looked like a junkie, she did. With her unkempt hair, her fur coat, and her blue face, she moved ferret-like into a noisy barcrowd and out again. I have seen many a drunken face frozen, the lower jaw dropping, to follow Fay with the eyes out of the bar. Fay and I left together and hadn't gone much more than a block when we were suddenly grasped from behind and thrust roughly into the entrance hall of a small block of flats. A strange coolness descended on me as soon as I felt the hands; in my imagination I was already saying to the policeman: 'And now be on your way, sir. You have no business with me.' And then I was looking at them. Middle-sized, they were dressed in leather lumber-jackets and looked like competitors in the *Tour de France*. They were flashing some kind of identity cards which evidently convinced me. It hadn't occurred to me that they could be anybody else. They were straight out of Kafka. And yet I knew they were real beer. I don't know whether they were members of the Federal Bureau of Investigation or of the Internal Revenue Service, but they were very ugly in their anonymity and very impatient. Fay seemed to know them well and immediately adopted a dog-like attitude towards them. She wagged her tail. Tongue and saliva drooled from her mouth in friendly effervescence. I found myself against the wall with one of the bicyclists ordering me to turn out my pockets. My passport would stop him for a bit. Ten years of border crossing had furnished me with impressive documents. I was carrying some bennies, but I wasn't worried about my vulnerability. I was worried about Fay's. In fact she knew far more about these men than I did, having met them before. But I was a foreigner and might be deported very easily. Fay could expose more with less danger than I. As I slowly and absent-mindedly emptied my pockets, I ignored the man who was examining me and kept interrupting Fay's interrogator.

'You stay outa this!'

'Look. I kicked. I'm clean, I tell yah!' Fay repeated.

'Can't you see she's telling the truth?'

'Look, who are you, mister? Didn't I tell you to stay outa this?'

They didn't find anything on us and Fay was shooting in her hand and not in her arm at that time. They didn't look at her hand and fortunately they didn't look at my arms either.

'It was that bar fink in the Côte d'Or,' Fay said when they let us go.

So I wasn't going much to the Côte d'Or. I thought twice about going there.

Jody was past caring. *Sometimes.* I found it difficult to distinguish between her and my own projections and caught myself from time to time accepting her mask of bravado at its face value. And yet I knew that she, like the rest of us, was not always impregnable. I suppose there was a contradiction in my own desire. I found myself attracted by her pose of outrageous independence. At the same time I did not anticipate she would expect me to take it seriously all of the time.

I wanted to say: 'Look, Jody, I understand. I too have a mirror.' But somehow I couldn't get through to her. I said instead: 'You're beautiful, Jody. I don't know how you can be with those stinking innards of yours, but you are.'

Someone said she was a whore.

'Me too,' I said. 'I couldn't have anything to do with a woman who didn't know she was a whore. I couldn't connect for long with a woman who wasn't conscious of having been, at one time or another, a whore.'

The fact that Jody did turn a trick now and again, when it was necessary, and that at the same time she didn't think of opening a shop, endeared her to me.

At hustling her fats she was the best and the worst.

She drew young Jewish businessmen like a magnet iron-filings, but they soon found out she was a sleepwalking whore, and they got uneasy and often indignant when they found out she used heroin. 'Man,' Jody said, 'can you imagine me lettin them screw me if I wasn't high on somethin?' In itself heroin doesn't lead to prostitution. But for many women it does make tolerable the nightly outrage inflicted on them by what are for the most part spiritually thwarted men.

Moreover, Jody didn't always turn up for a date. This unreliability was attributed to the fact that she was a drug fiend by her indignant customers. And, of course, if she had been hung up without bread and with no junk she would probably have turned up to get the money for a fix. Which confirmed for those gentlemen that the best things in life cost money.

Men were always asking Jody to marry them. They wanted to protect her, to save her from herself. Many of them were rich and at least one was very rich. But what she wanted was a john who would send his check each week from the North Pole, one she could love at a distance for being so generous, while she got down to the business of loving one of her own (un)troubled kind. At all times I sensed a great capacity for love in Jody. As, I suppose, her (other) johns did.

For us to be together was difficult, at least until I went on the scows again. I met her during a period when I had quit, when I was sleeping wherever I could find a bed. By the time I went back on the scows it was too late. She was too strung out. I no longer cared enough to make the effort. I wanted a woman who could sometimes be casual, even about heroin.

During those few months there were several ways we might have made it together. We could have stopped using junk. She could have hustled for us. Or we could have boosted from department stores. Or pushed.

Most male addicts are eventually pimps, boosters, or pushers. We made the motions of kicking. Jody couldn't bring herself to get out of bed. That was the scene that inspired Moira to say: 'Jody! She just uses you! She's like a bird, a fat, greedy little bird waiting for you to come back to the nest to feed her. How much do you want this time?' I couldn't get through to Moira either so I returned to the room where Jody lay nursing her general outrage, compounding her spite, in the single bed which she hogged. As soon as I entered she accused me of forgetting the cakes.

'What cakes?'

'The cakes I asked you to get for me! The Twinkies!' she screamed. 'I told you to bring two packages of Twinkies!'

'Two packages of Twinkies . . .' Repeating it to control my exasperation.

It lasted four days and then Jody turned a trick and we got high. A couple of times and I got fed up hanging around all night diners, waiting.

We could have boosted. Most junkies we knew did that eventually. They had to keep up their habit. But at the point at which one decides to make it as a booster one has already faced up to the probability of spending a large part of one's life in an iron cage. No doubt a man can adapt, even to periodic incarcerations. And the world will certainly look doubly beautiful each time one returns to the street. But for myself I couldn't have chosen that life any more than I could have chosen to live out most of my existence in Greenland. There is infinite possibility everywhere, up until the moment of dying, even in the skin of a leper wielding the power of his bell, but the extremity, the violence, and the sudden nature of the transitions in the existence of the inveterate convict, a life, as it were, of continual shock therapy, of brutalization, the daily endurance of machine-like discipline imposed from without, the mob and lynch-law of the numbered men, guarded by men vaguely resembling themselves in whatever 'big house' of men, the daily insults, the small indignities, the constant clang of steel and glare of artificial light, eat, sleep, defecate, the daily struggle to escape the limit of one's perceptions – the Baron de Charlus, chained naked to the iron bed in Room 14A at Jupien's, was still master of his destiny in a sense in which no convict is – it would have been improbable for me to choose all that.

As for pushing the stuff, we never seriously considered that. To do it properly you have to make it your profession, and as a profession, with the vague, arbitrary, and ambiguous alliances along the boring way, it stinks.

Jody and I stayed together a few days longer until that moment we had both anticipated when we parted somewhere near Sheridan Square, she to return to Pat's, I . . . I don't remember.

Jody moved ahead into the bar. Moe, Trixie catatonic under goofballs, Sasha, the White Russian, lushed, at the brink of tears; avoid them.

'Jody!' A small woman, nearing fifty, with brown hair leaned out from between two men at a table in the rear. It was Edna.

Jody nodded to her uncertainly.

'I wonder if she's got any bread?' she whispered to me.

I shook my head.

The woman made a sign gesticulating with her fingers. It might have meant anything. Jody shook her head to show she hadn't understood and when Edna began to gesticulate more vigorously Jody turned away with a short sharp shake of the head. 'Let's get out of here,' she said.

Outside again we hesitated in the drizzling rain.

We crossed the avenue and went into the drugstore which sells the paperbacks. 'We gotta get some loot!' Jody whispered urgently when she saw I was about to examine the books.

'Sure,' I said. 'But I don't know how yet.'

'There must be someone . . .'

'There he is! Wait here,' I said to her.

Alan Dunn, a man I had known in Paris and who owed me a favour, had just entered the drugstore. It was a break. I knew he would lend me some money.

'Hullo, Alan.'

'Hi, Joe! It's good to see you, man! I heard you were here and tried to look you up. I saw Moira the other day and she said you were working on the river. Getting much writing done?'

'A fair amount,' I said cautiously. But I knew Dunn too well to feel obliged to mention it again. I brightened at the thought and said: 'Listen, Alan, I need some money, now, tonight . . .'

'Sure, Joe . . . how much do you need?'

'Twenty dollars would do.'

He already had his wallet out. He handed me two tens.

'How about a coffee?' he said as I accepted the money.

'Let's,' I said. 'And thanks for the loot, Alan. I appreciate it.'

'OK boy, any time,' he said.

'Excuse me a moment,' I said to him. I walked over to Jody. 'I'll meet you in a quarter of an hour in Jim Moore's. See if you can get something up.'

'How much?'

'Depends what it is. I got twenty.'

Her smile was beatific. 'We could go round to Lou's. I'll phone him now.'

'OK See you.' I returned to Alan who was sitting at the counter.

'Who's the girl?' he said when I sat down beside him.

'Her name's Jody.'

'She's got beautiful eyes. But she looks beat. Are you living with her?'

'No. I once thought it might be nice to fall in love with her. But it wouldn't. It'd be like loving Goneril.' I sipped my coffee. 'When did you get back?'

'Just a week ago.'

I was glad to see him. I liked to talk about France. Soon we were laughing about how *l'Histoire d'Ô* had been banned in Paris at the same time as it was awarded a literary prize. In Paris the corruption of literary censorship is a war the wise have waged against the foolish for centuries.

'It's good to see you, Alan! Where are you staying?'

He gave me his address.

'Have you heard from that Arab friend of yours? . . . what was his name? . . .'

'Midhou,' I said. We had taken Alan by bus to Aubervilliers where we knew a Spanish place. It was hidden away in the Spanish slum of Paris near a canal. It was to this district that those who were not poets came over the Pyrenees after the Spanish Civil War.

Midhou was a great smoker of hashish, a troubadour, an Algerian in Paris who ate with his hands. Seated cross-legged on the floor, the snarl of his lips emphasized by his Mexican moustache, he made his hands upwards into claws and spoke of flesh. The heavy brow, the receding forehead, the small, pointed ears, the black eyes of a bird of prey, the foreign words spat from clenched teeth, the claw becoming a fist, becoming a knife, becoming a hand.

'Yeah, I heard he went to Algeria,' Alan said.

'I got one postcard,' I said. 'But I heard indirectly he lost half his face driving a truck into a brick wall in Algiers. There was a police road block. I don't know whether he was carrying guns or hashish.'

'Poor guy,' Alan said. 'Is he alright now?'

'I heard he was. I heard he was back in Paris for a while and was the same as ever. Do you remember his guitar?'

We were talking excitedly when Jody came back.

'You comin, Joe?'

'Sure. This is Alan Dunn . . . Jody Mann.'

Jody nodded and Alan smiled at her.

'I won't keep you,' Alan said, standing up.

'Yeah, Joe, come on,' Jody said.

'I'll give you a ring,' I said to him.

'And finish that book,' he said.

When we were outside Jody said: 'What kept you so long?'

'Fuck you,' I said.

'Lou's waitin!' she said.

'Did you hear what he said to me?'

'No. Who? Lou?'

'No, not Lou. The guy we just robbed.'

'Oh, him? No. What did he say?'

'He said to me: "Get that book written."'

'What book?' Jody said.

'Man, *any* book!' I said.

'Yeah!'

'As though that were my fucking *raison d'être*!'

'Your what?'

'I mean I didn't say to him: "Get that soap sold," did I?'

'Yeah man, he was too much! Lou said to hurry.'

'What happened?' I said, exasperated.

'Fay's making the run. She'll be back by the time we get there.'

'Who put up the loot?'

'Lou. He's puttin up ten for us.'

The count we got for the dime wasn't much. Lou had poured out the shit onto a mirror and was dividing it with a razorblade when we arrived. There was Fay, and Harriet, Lou's wife, who was making a bottle for the baby, Willie, everybody's parasite, who when his personal needs were met was a man of good will, thirty-five, with bad brown teeth and thick-lensed spectacles, Lou, Jody, and myself. Geo arrived almost immediately with Mona. He was looking hot and red in the face above his white collar. He usually wore a white collar when he was with Mona. She was wearing a hat and had had her hair permed and looked like someone's maiden aunt, incongruous in her tweed costume beside Fay who had taken off her fur coat and was rolling up the sleeve of her shapeless green dress, and Harriet, her hair in rats' tails, wearing her shirt and jeans, and dangling her baby on one arm. When Geo went out with Mona he adopted a mock sanctimonious air which was to tell the rest of us he knew she was fattish, with newly permed hair and a hat she wore indoors. He explained her saying she had an ass he could get a good grip of. But his apologies embarrassed us and only tended to make Mona exaggerate her air of respectability. Mona was alright. It was sad to see Geo turn her into an awkward plagiarism of herself.

'Where's that nickel you owe me, Geo?' Lou said from where he stood at the draining board of the sink. With Lou looking at Geo the razorblade was immobile over the little heaps of powder on the mirror.

I saw a flash of annoyance come into Fay's yellow eyes.

'Lou, put enough in that spoon for a fix for me. You can take it out of mine later,' she said to him.

'Why you motherfucker!' Geo said to Lou. 'I made the run. I was entitled to a third. How many fixes have I laid on you?'

'Fuck that,' Fay said, nudging Lou. 'The spoon. Put some in. Would you shut up for a minute, Geo?'

Lou stood at the sink, not even looking at Geo now, but down at nowhere, smiling his private smile.

'Hello Harriet, hello Joe,' Mona said. We were all bunched up at the end of the room (a kind of groundfloor passage or long cellar) which was the kitchen, near the stove, near the sink. Then, as she herself wasn't going to fix, she turned her perplexed attention to some ad or other which Lou had pinned to the wall. A girl was saying to her mother: 'Mom . . . couldn't you get Daddy to stay upstairs when John comes?'

'Look baby,' Geo said to Fay, 'you still owe me a ten dollar bag. And what about the three bucks I laid on you last night?'

'Everything he says is irrelevant,' Lou said from behind his smile.

Fay grunted as she heated the spoon over the gas flame.

'All this arithmetic,' Willie said, choosing sides.

'Gimme some more, Lou,' Fay said. 'I won't even feel this.'

'Sure you will! It's a dirty spike!' Jody said.

Mona moved quietly to the other end of the room, sat down, and opened a magazine. Geo followed her unconcernedly with his eyes and then said to me: 'Will you tell these motherfuckers to get off my back?'

'Man, I told you before I don't want you all coming to turn on here,' Lou said to Geo. 'This pad's getting too hot.'

'What's that got to do with it?' Geo said, grinning.

'You talk about me being irrelevant? Anyway, you turned on often enough at my pad.'

'Shut up for a minute, Geo,' I said. 'For God's sake, Lou, if you're turning on next start cooking up.'

'Yeah,' Jody said, 'Lou'll turn on next if Fay ever stops booting it.'

'Fay's thick, dark, purplish-red blood rose and fell in the eye-dropper like a column of gory mercury in a barometer. A word that failed to materialize spluttered out of the corner of her blue mouth in an outward thrust of inarticulate indignation

– what? accuse Fay? – her eyelids drooping, mumbling, 'Not . . . sure . . . got . . . a . . . hit . . .'

'Yeah, looks bad, Fay, you're wounded,' I said.

'She's going to give Lou a transfusion,' Jody said.

'What's your blood type, Fay?' Lou said.

'Has anyone here got the time?' Mona said from her end of the room. To get him off the hooks, I told Geo I would give him a taste. Inspired by that good office he performed the same for Mona, telling her it was ten past two.

'I'll give Willie a taste,' Lou said.

'Don't give him much, Joe,' Jody said.

Harriet took the baby's bottle out of the pot of hot water and squirted a jet of milk against her wrist to test it. The baby accepted the nipple eagerly.

'Wow! dig his habit!' Willie said.

We all shot up, except Mona. – Why don't you turn her on, Geo? 'No. She doesn't *use* it,' he would answer piously, as though it were self-explanatory.

Tom Tear arrived with a hurt look and tried to find out if anyone had any shit left. Only Fay had, and she explained it in a vague and unregenerate way as some stashed away from yesterday and subsequently found. I always felt Fay's was a peculiarly unvenomous treachery though she seldom took much trouble to cover her duplicities, compensating for this impertinence with the added impertinence of a ready indignation – what? accuse Fay?

I remember Mona a few hours later. You couldn't complain about her patience. Or you could complain. You could say to her: 'Geo turned on an hour ago. Do you think it's a bloody virtue to be so patient?' But Mona smiled at you, about as (un)ambiguously as her namesake in the Louvre, her slightly cross-eyed smile, worried, with no condemnation in her attitude. She would probably have turned on if it hadn't been for Geo. He was like a man defending his wife against swearwords. *Doncherknowtheresladiespresent?*

Geo was saying to Lou in the manner of Tertullian: 'What I mean is I don't care whether you *prove* I'm an evil mother, you're lying!' and Mona said to the room at large: 'Isn't he insane?'

Harriet looked demure.

'I thought you said you didn't have any,' Tom said to Fay.

Fay didn't say anything. Working silently at the sink like Dr Jekyll brewing his potion, she had no doubt hoped to go in this her second fix unobserved. Her hand trembled as she held the match to the spoon.

'Oh man!' Tom said, seeking allies.

Fay still said nothing. She drew the liquid into the eyedropper.

'Come on, give me a taste, Fay!'

'I'll leave you a taste in the spoon,' Fay grunted.

Tom came alive in a way he sometimes did.

'Man, I knew you'd make it!' Geo jeered.

'Up yours, Geo,' Tom said.

'He's right, Geo,' Lou said, his eyelids fluttering momentarily as he stood swaying near the sink. 'You're an impertinent mother.'

'Geo, I'm going now,' Mona said. 'I can take a taxi so it's OK, you needn't come. You stay if you want.'

Geo looked pained. 'Oh baby, can't you stay a half hour longer?'

'Sure,' Mona said unhappily. 'It's just that there's nearly an hour between trains at this time of night. You know how it is.'

'OK,' Geo said, 'but I'll go with you as far as the station anyway.'

'The family that kicks together, sticks together,' Lou said elliptically swaying.

There was a knock at the door.

'Just a minute for Christ's sake, see who that is!' Lou said, going near the door. Tom removed the spike neatly from his vein, squirted a jet of water through it, and stashed it among the knives and forks.

'Who is it?' Lou said loudly, his shoulder against the door.

'He thinks he's Horatio defending the bridge,' Geo said. 'If it's the Man they'll trample him underfoot. You know the time they busted me they came in with their guns out and I'm standing there with a fucking spoon. Now, if it'd been a flame-thrower!'

'Shut your fat mouth!' Lou hissed at him in an undertone.
A voice from the outside said 'Ettie!'
'It's OK, Lou, it's Ettie,' Fay said.
'Fuck Ettie!' Lou said. 'This pad's becoming like Grand Central Station. I don't want the whole fucking world coming here!'
'Is Fay there?' the voice said in singsong.
'Let her in, man,' Fay said. 'She's probably got some shit with her.'
Ettie came in.
Ettie was a thin negress who shot up ten five dollar bags a day. One time she wanted Jody and me to move in with her. Ettie pushed everything, clothes and other valuables she'd boosted, shit, her own thin chops, and speculated with the minds and bodies of her friends. 'Last night I had a scene with the Man,' she said to Jody and me once as she opened an oilskin pouch on the bed and disclosed half an ounce of badly adulterated heroin. 'Bastid had his hand on my leg right near my own sweet self. With that I can deal. I'll show that boy!'
'She will too,' Jody said to me.
'He might bite your ass,' I said to Ettie.
Ettie wanted us to move in with her, the two of us; Jody could hustle again and I could be the man about the place. 'Then you git all the shit you want, no hassle.'
'No hustle?' Jody said drily.
'I didn't say anything about that, babydoll. What are you anyway? an idealist? You know well what you kin do, Jody. You kin manipulate those soft pink fats of yours. That's Greek.'
'No kidding?' Jody said.
'Man, it's a hassle what you do,' I said to Ettie, 'peddling around town all day with the heat breathing down your neck.'
'He kin breathe right up my vagina, dear, jist so long as he don't bust me,' Ettie said.

'What's this?' Ettie said now as she came in. 'I've never seen so much evil in one room. If my mother could see me now. Hi there, Jody! Are you straight?'
'Joe gave me a taste,' Jody said. 'But I didn't get anything. Have you got some shit on you, Ettie?'

'You think I come all the way downtown just for the ride?' Ettie turned to Lou who had locked the door behind her. 'Mind if I get straight here?'

Lou hesitated. I could see his point. He might as well have opened up a shop. Finally he said: 'OK, but I want a taste.'

'That might be arranged,' Ettie said, and, a few moments later, after a few incredibly quick motions with spoon and eye-dropper, she was probing with the needle at her thin black thigh.

Jody leaned near her.

As Ettie withdrew the needle she looked up at Jody and said: 'I know what's comin and the answer is no. First there's that nickel you owe me from last week. That's yours there, Lou.' She pointed to a small heap of powder in a spoon.

Harriet, after shrugging her shoulders at Ettie's entrance, had retired to the bed where she was now lying, playing with the baby. Willie was stretched out near her.

Fay was talking urgently with Geo. Mona, now seated stiffly in an upright chair near the door, looked on disapprovingly.

'Man, I've only got a nickel,' Geo was saying to Fay.

'Anyone wants anything, say so now,' Ettie said.

Lou, who had just fixed again, continued to sway near the sink, the dropper with the needle on it still in his right hand.

'Aw, for God's sake, Ettie!' Jody said, 'I'm gettin some bread tomorrow, honest!'

'What about her?' Fay said to Geo. She meant Mona.

Geo groaned and looked pleadingly at Mona who appeared to be at the end of her tether.

'Look, Mona, you could lay ten on me tonight, and I could give it back out of that thirty.'

'I thought you were going to buy a suit?' Mona said.

'Don't forget you owe me a nickel, Geo,' Lou said, swaying, his eyes closed.

'Who needs a suit?' Fay said to Tom.

I was looking at Mona. She had already taken a ten dollar bill from her purse. Geo took it and said to Fay in a hard voice: 'Anyway I don't see what you're getting so excited about. I didn't even say I'd give you a taste.'

'I got her down here,' Geo mimicked.

'That's correct, she did,' Ettie said and turned back to Jody. 'Honey, I jist can't understand what it is you think you've got between your legs that's valuable. It's jist lyin idle and meanwhile you ain't even got a nickel to git straight with.'

'Yeah, it's not so easy,' Jody said. 'Look, Ettie, tomorrow . . .'

'I'm going now, Geo,' Mona said.

Geo was interrupting Jody. 'For Christ's sake shut up for a minute, will you?' He turned to Ettie. 'How much for fifteen? a sixteenth?'

'I don't know about any sixteenth,' Ettie said. 'You git three five dollar bags for fifteen.'

'Oh, don't come on, man!' Geo said. 'I can go uptown later myself and get a full sixteenth!'

'I came downtown,' Ettie said.

'That's right, Geo, she did,' Fay said.

'I'm not buying any five dollar bags,' Geo said. 'I'll score later.' He turned away from Ettie and Mona said: 'I'm going now, Geo. If you want to come to the station with me you'll have to come now.'

Geo hesitated and then said: 'OK, baby. I'm coming now. See you all later,' he said to the rest of us.

'Hey, wait a minute, Geo,' Lou said, lurching out of a comatose state. 'You've got to lay that nickel on me. I need it to score.'

'You really think I owe you that nickel, don't you, Lou?'

'Man, you're not impressing anyone!' Lou said.

'Come on,' Fay said, 'you owe him a nickel. We need it. Give it to him.'

'Will you hurry up and shut that door?' Harriet called from the bed.

Mona was already outside.

Lou chuckled, his face suddenly becoming friendly. 'You know, you don't always have to argue, Geo. You never win anyway.'

With a look at Fay, Geo gave Lou a five dollar bill. 'I don't know,' he said as he went out.

'That bastid,' Fay said when he was gone.

'Fuck you, Fay,' Lou said, smiling at her.

'She's right,' Tom said. 'Sometimes Geo's too much.'

'Sure,' Lou said, 'but he's never refused you a fix.'

'He's refused me offen,' Jody said contemptuously.

'An I'm refusin you now baby,' Ettie said. 'Now, does anyone want to do business? I got to be at 125th in an hour.'

'We'll share a bag, eh Lou?' Fay said, moving at once over to the sink.

'OK,' Lou said, and paid Ettie. 'Do you want a taste, honey?' he said to Harriet.

'Yeah, leave me a taste,' she said. She was playing with the baby's fine hair. 'It's just like silk,' she said to Willie.

'Are you going to score, Joe?' Jody said to me.

'I'll get a bag and we'll split it,' I said to her.

'Half of one her bags is nothin,' Jody said sulkily.

I didn't answer. I intended to keep a nickel so that I wouldn't be stranded on the scow.

I divided the bag in two and shot up my share. Three of us were shooting up at once, each working silently and efficiently. Somehow Tom got some, and Willie. As soon as I withdrew the spike Jody accepted it from me.

'You want I should call on you Friday?' Ettie said to Lou. 'I'll be in the neighbourhood.'

'No, man,' Lou said.

'Why don't you make it across to my place?' Tom said.

'Around what time?'

'About nine.'

'See you all,' Ettie said, 'and you, baby, you take your mother's advice,' she said to Jody as she left.

Fay sat on a low chair and began to nod.

Harriet moved quietly over to the sink and Lou gave her a shot. They went back over to the bed together.

'Will you people get out of here as soon as you can?' Lou said to the rest of us.

Jody raised her hand quickly to her mouth and dropped the needle back into the waterglass.

'Where are you going now, Joe?' she said to me. 'Can I come along?'

'No baby. I'm going back to Perth Amboy.'

A Note on George Orwell

In the realm of human behaviour God has functioned primarily as a witness against whose judgements men have measured (or pretended to measure) the validity of their own. If God is evicted, the very possibility of such a comparison is annihilated, and responsibility, the phosphorescent struts of the conscious self, is, as it were, left in the void.

To whom am I responsible? To myself? And for what?

Unlike his more philosophical French contemporaries Orwell never, to my knowledge, consciously posed such questions. In a Godless world his naked and undefended plea was for 'decency, liberty, and justice,' a plea which, in his own gentle and unpolitical mind, was synonymous with a plea for Socialism.

'. . . looking back through my work,' he wrote in 1947 (*Why I Write*), 'I see that it is invariably where I lacked *political* purpose that I wrote lifeless books and was betrayed into purple passages, sentences without meaning, decorative adjectives and humbug generally.' No estimate of Orwell's work could be further from the truth. His purpose was seldom so much political as humanitarian (or moral) and where he tried to make it so, as in the present work* – it was written on assignment for the *Left Book Club* and first published in 1937 – the result is an unsuccessful medley of firsthand description, timestaled statistics, and naïve political exhortation. In spite of some fine description, I doubt if the book would ever have seen the light again if it hadn't been written by Orwell. Threadbare phrases like '. . . the real Socialist is one who . . . actively wishes – to see tyranny overthrown . . .' and 'All that is needed is to hammer two facts home into the public consciousness. One that the interests of all exploited people are the same; the other that

---

* *The Road to Wigan Pier*, by George Orwell.

Socialism is compatible with common decency,' and '. . . only Socialist nations can fight effectively,' are hard to take in 1958.

A most important essay for an understanding of Orwell is entitled *Inside the Whale*. This essay, written in 1939 before and after the declaration of war, was published as the title essay of a book in 1940, and was significantly omitted from the collection of critical essays published in 1946. Written in a moment of extremity, when it must have occurred to Orwell that all his concern for 'political issues' had availed the world nothing. It is a rather pussyfooting English assessment – because of the obscenity 'one is determined above all not to be impressed'* – of the writing of that holy Nero of American literature, Henry Miller. Orwell's fundamental honesty comes through. He admires Miller because he 'has chosen to drop the Geneva language of the ordinary novel and drag the *real-politik* of the inner mind into the open.'

'Good novels,' he continues, 'are written by people who are *not frightened*. This brings me back to Henry Miller.' Orwell argues reasonably 'that for a creative writer possession of "truth" is less important than emotional sincerity.' He draws a parallel from the First World War, feeling 'like Mr Forster that by simply standing aloof and keeping touch with pre-war emotions, Eliot was carrying on the human heritage.' (The reference is to *Prufrock*; which was published in 1947.) He concludes, 'that passive, non-cooperative attitude implied in Henry Miller's work is justified. Whether or not it is an expression of what people *ought* to feel, it probably comes somewhere near to expressing what they *do* feel.' – 'Here in my opinion is the only imaginative prose-writer of the slightest value who has appeared among the English-speaking races for some years past.'

Orwell describes his meeting with Miller:

I first met Miller at the end of 1936, when I was passing through Paris on my way to Spain. What most intrigued me about him was to find

---

* There is a curiously revelatory focus on Miller's obscenity – as though that were germane to anything but a conditional response pattern to taboo words.

that he felt no interest in the Spanish war whatever. He merely told me in forcible terms that to go to Spain at that moment was the act of an idiot. He could understand anyone going there from purely selfish motives, out of curiosity, for instance, but to mix oneself up in such things *from a sense of obligation* was sheer stupidity. In any case my ideas about combatting Fascism, defending democracy, etc., were all baloney. Our civilisation was designed to be swept away and replaced by something so different that we should scarcely regard it as human – a prospect that did not bother him . . .

The implication of this essay (and the hesitation evident in his constant qualifications contributes to the view) is that for the moment at least (1939) Orwell is sick to death of the political optimism which dominated English literature in the thirties. He himself had contributed to that optimism . . . 'the common man will win his fight sooner or later . . .' and:

> *No bomb that ever burst*
> *Shatters the crystal spirit.*

By September 1939, Orwell, always unorthodox ('No one who feels deeply about literature, or even prefers good English to bad, can accept the discipline of a political party'), has lost faith. Apart from a pamphlet (*The Lion and the Unicorn*), he publishes nothing for nearly five years, and then, in 1945, *Animal Farm* appears. And from now on his approach to politics is entirely negative. He moves from the extreme pessimism of *Animal Farm* to the even more extreme pessimism of *1984* (1949); his concern is for the spiritual integrity of the individual in a world which seems to be moving inexorably towards totalitarianism.

For all his polemical brilliance Orwell was not a profound thinker. There is something 'occasional' about most of his writing. V.S. Pritchett once called him 'the conscience of his generation' and this is appropriate insofar as we can clearly distinguish between 'conscience' and 'consciousness.' He was a moralist, a preacher, a pamphleteer, an honest man who threw himself wholeheartedly into a book or an essay in the same way as he threw himself into extreme situations in life – and into indignation. This led naturally to contradiction – I think no one would deny that his works are riddled with contradictions – and, more seriously, from my point of view, to his failure to descend into the belly of the whale, to cross the threshold unto himself. This makes him in a sense the most uncontemporary of contemporary writers. In his concern for the day to day movement of sociological currents he never seriously concerns himself with the fact that, after all, everything is filtered through the prism of self, that it is not enough to control what is coming upon one from without, and that it is precisely when men in their organizational zeal forget this that freedom dies. The notion of freedom arises when a man feels himself to be the victim of external forces – I am speaking of political freedom – and in our times, when it is totalitarianism that threatens. It is essentially a protest of the relatively apolitical against the overzealously political.

The emergence of the mass, the pressure of mass values: it is, as Orwell knew, almost meaningless to say you are against the emergence of the mass, like saying you are against molecular fission. The proliferation of vast projects in human engineering and the resultant threat to the integrity of the individual, is a direct consequence of the *sudden* emergence of the mass. Ortega y Gasset speaks of the 'vertical invaders,' referring to the hundreds of millions of men of no tradition being born into history through a trapdoor – a consequence of the Industrial Revolution. By and large, the education for these men-without-roots has been governed by the technological requirements of expanding industry. What culture they have has been acquired from the daily newspapers, pulp or slick magazines, the popular cinema, lately from television. The technician, qua technician, is essentially passive, and the structural attitude which is imposed upon him during his working hours is carried away by him into his leisure hours; he is the victim of leisure, not its master. Restless, passive, with few vital inner resources and little creative doubt, he has to be amused, and, as a consumer of amusement, he is subjected to the same batteries of techniques which have boosted production. There is no doubt that this kind of efficiency-consciousness is dangerously closed. One might say that man's idea of himself is something less than it was before God became a stuffed owl in the museum of natural history.

Orwell himself was intermittently aware of all this and overwhelmingly so in his last works. This comes out particularly in his concern for the precision of language – 'the totalitarians use language to obscure thought'; and 'Newspeak' (*1984*) – 'was designed not to extend but to *distinguish* the range of thought, and this purpose was indirectly assisted by cutting the choice of words down to a minimum.' In the world of *1984* revolt is no longer possible because skepticism is impossible: '. . . the expression of unorthodox opinions, above a very low level, was well-nigh impossible.' The only hope as far as Winston Smith was concerned was the existence of the proles. The future belonged to them.

This tremulous breath of hope (all there is in *1984*) sounds suspiciously like Orwell's earlier sentimental statement: '. . . the common man will win his fight sooner or later . . .' It is this kind of vulgar democratic unreflectiveness, this obstinate subordination of his vision to the idol of his era, that prevented him from directing his creative energies to the more vital level of insight which begins with a total revolt against all abstractions with which society traps, labels, and affixes status to the individual, and whose object is the self, here and now and unique and doomed in the end to absurdity in a strange cosmos. Insofar as Orwell stopped short of this total revolt, preferring instead to concern himself with 'socio-economic vectors,' 'class oppression,' and all the other abstractions of the 'socially conscious,' he is of little interest for those of us who come after him, but then, as I suggested at the beginning, one gets the feeling in spite of his constant references to politics that he was fundamentally unpolitical, that if he hadn't lived when he did, when it was fashionable to be 'socially conscious,' the superb, poetical element which is present in all his work would have made him one of our models. Around 1933, in a short essay entitled 'A Hanging' he wrote:

It is curious, but till that moment I had never realized what it means to destroy a healthy, conscious man. When I saw the prisoner step aside to avoid the puddle I saw the mystery, the unspeakable wrongness, of cutting a life off when it is in full tide. This man was not dying, he was alive just as we were alive. All the organs of his body were working – bowels digesting food, skin renewing itself, nails growing, tissues forming – all toiling away in solemn foolery. His nails would still be growing when he stood on the drop, when he was falling through the air with a tenth-of-a-second to live. His eyes saw the yellow gravel and the grey walls, and his brain still remembered, foresaw, reasoned – reasoned even about puddles. He and we were a party of men walking together, seeing, hearing, feeling, understanding the same world; and in two minutes, with a sudden snap, one of us would be gone – one mind less, one world less.

We shall go on reading Orwell for this kind of thing, but one cannot help regretting that Orwell didn't take time out from society to explore one such world.

Part Four

'I am cut off from every sympathetic soul, unknown, unemployed, regarded all round (if at all) with a canny suspicion, sometimes even disgust. My doctor for example fairly astounded me by announcing in great anger that he regarded my writings as "obscene and feelthie rubbish, enough to disgust the most broadminded man!"'

15 November 1961

Invisible Insurrection of a Million Minds

'And if there is still one hellish, truly accursed thing in our time, it is our artistic dallying with forms, instead of being like victims burnt at the stake, signalling through the flames.'
Antonin Artaud[10]

Revolt is understandably unpopular. As soon as it is defined it has provoked the measures for its containment. The prudent man will avoid his definition which is in effect his death-sentence. Besides, it is a limit.

We are concerned not with the *coup-d'état* of Trotsky and Lenin, but with the *coup-du-monde*, a transition of necessity more complex, more diffuse than the other, and so more gradual, less spectacular. Our methods will vary with the empirical facts pertaining here and now, there and then.

Political revolt is and must be ineffectual precisely because it must come to grips at the prevailing level of political process. Beyond the backwaters of civilisation it is an anachronism. Meanwhile, with the world at the edge of extinction, we cannot afford to wait for the mass. Nor to brawl with it.

The *coup-du-monde* must be in the broad sense cultural. With his thousand technicians Trotsky seized the viaducts and the bridges and the telephone exchanges and the power stations. The police, victims of convention, contribute to the brilliant enterprise by guarding the old men in the Kremlin. The leaders hadn't the elasticity of mind to grasp that their own presence there at the traditional seat of government was irrelevant. History outflanked them. Trotsky had the railway stations and the powerhouses, and the 'government' was effectively locked out of history by its own guards.

---

10. *The Theatre and its Double*, Grove Press, New York, 1958.

So cultural revolt must seize the grids of expression and the powerhouses of the mind. Intelligence must become self-conscious, realise its own power, and, on a global scale, transcending functions that are no longer appropriate, dare to exercise it. History will not overthrow national governments: it will outflank them. The cultural revolt is the necessary underpinning, the passionate substructure of a new order of things.

What is to be seized has no physical dimensions nor relevant temporal colour. It is not an arsenal, nor a capital city, nor an island, nor an isthmus visible from a peak in Darien. Finally, it is all these things too, of course, all that there is, but only by the way, and inevitably. What is to be seized – and I address that one million (say) here and there who are capable of perceiving at once just what it is I am about, a million potential 'technicians' – is ourselves. What must occur, now, today, tomorrow, in those widely dispersed but vital centres of experience, is a revelation. At the present time, in what is often thought of as the age of the mass, we tend to fall into the habit of regarding history and evolution as something which goes relentlessly on, quite outwith our control. The individual has a profound sense of his own impotence as he realises the immensity of the forces involved. We, the creative ones everywhere, must discard this paralytic posture and seize control of the human process by assuming control of ourselves. We must reject the conventional fiction of 'unchanging human nature.' There is in fact no such permanence anywhere. There is only *becoming*.[11]

Organisation, control, revolution: each of the million individuals to whom I speak will be wary of such concepts, will find it all but impossible with a quiet conscience to identify himself with any group whatsoever, no matter what it calls itself. That is as it should be. But it is at the same time the reason for the impotence of intelligence everywhere in the face of events, for which no one in particular can be said to be responsible, a

11. The *prise de pouvoir* by an avant-garde is obviously only an early stage in a larger, more universal movement, and it must not be forgotten that our group of originators '*ne pourra réaliser son projet qu'en se supprimant . . . ne peut effectivement exister qu'en tant que parti se dépasse lui-même*'. (Added to French version.)

yawning tide of bloody disasters, the natural outcome of that complex of processes, for the most part unconscious and uncontrolled, which constitute the history of man. Without organisation concerted action is impossible; the energy of individuals and small groups is dissipated in a hundred and one unconnected little acts of protest . . . a manifesto here, a hunger strike there. Such protests, moreover, are commonly based on the assumption that social behaviour is intelligent; the hallmark of their futility. If change is to be purposive, men must somehow function together in the social situation. And it is our contention that there already exists a nucleus of men who, if they will set themselves gradually and tentatively to the task, are capable of imposing a new and seminal idea: the world waits for them to show their hand.

We have already rejected any idea of a frontal attack. Mind cannot withstand matter (brute force) in open battle. It is rather a question of perceiving clearly and without prejudice what are the forces that are at work in the world and out of whose interaction tomorrow *must* come to be; and then, calmly, without indignation, by a kind of mental ju-jitsu that is ours by virtue of intelligence, of modifying, correcting, polluting, deflecting, corrupting, eroding, outflanking . . . inspiring what we might call *the invisible insurrection*. It will come on the mass of men, if it comes at all, not as something they have voted for, struck for, fought for, but like the changing seasons; they will find themselves in and stimulated by the *situation* consciously at last to recreate it within and without as their own.

Clearly, there is in principle no problem of production in the modern world. The urgent problem of the future is that of distribution which is presently (dis)ordered in terms of the economic system prevailing in this or that area. This problem on a global scale is an administrative one and it will not finally be solved until existing political and economic rivalries are outgrown. Nevertheless, it is becoming widely recognised that distributive problems are most efficiently and economically handled on a global scale by an international organisation like the United Nations (food, medicine, etc.) and this organisation has already relieved the various national governments of some of their functions. No great imagination is required to see in this kind of transference the beginning of the end for the nation-state. We should at all times do everything in our power to speed up the process.

Meanwhile, our anonymous million can focus their attention on the problem of 'leisure.' A great deal of what is pompously called 'juvenile delinquency' is the inarticulate response of youth incapable of coming to terms with leisure. The violence associated with it is a direct consequence of the alienation of man from himself brought about by the Industrial Revolution. Man has forgotten how to play. And if one thinks of the soulless tasks accorded each man in the industrial milieu, of the fact that education has become increasingly technological, and for the ordinary man no more than a means of fitting him for a 'job,' one can hardly be surprised that man is lost. He is almost afraid of more leisure. He demands 'overtime' and has a latent hostility towards automation. His creativity stunted, he is orientated outwards entirely. He has to be amused. The forms that dominate his working life are carried over into leisure which becomes more and more mechanised; thus he is equipped with machines to contend with leisure which machines have accorded him. And to offset all this, to alleviate the psychological wear and tear of our technological age, there is, in a word, ENTERTAINMENT.

When our man after the day's work comes twitching, tired, off the assembly-line into what are called without a shred of irony his 'leisure hours,' with what is he confronted? In the bus on the way home he reads a newspaper which is identical to yesterday's newspaper, in the sense that it is a reshake of identical elements . . . four murders, thirteen disasters, two revolutions, and 'something approaching a rape' . . . which in turn is identical to the newspaper of the day before that . . . three murders, nineteen disasters, one counter-revolution, and something approaching an abomination . . . and unless he is a very exceptional man, one of our million potential technicians, the vicarious pleasure he derives from paddling in all this violence and disorder obscures from him the fact that there is nothing new in all this 'news' and that his daily perusal of it leads not to a widening of his consciousness of reality but to a dangerous contraction of consciousness, to a species of mental process that has more in common with the salivations of Pavlov's dogs than with the subtleties of human intelligence.

Contemporary man expects to be entertained. His active participation is almost non-existent. Art, whatever it is, is something of which the majority seldom thinks, something almost derisable towards which it is sometimes even proud to flaunt an attitude of invincible ignorance. This sorry state of affairs is unconsciously sanctioned by the stubborn philistinism of our cultural institutions. Museums have approximately the same hours of business as churches, the same sanctimonious odours and silences, and a snobbish presumption in direct spiritual opposition to the vital men whose works are closeted there. What have those silent corridors to do with Rembrandt and the 'no smoking' signs to do with Van Gogh? Beyond the museum, the man in the street is effectively cut off from art's naturally tonic influence by the fashionable brokerage system which, incidentally, but of economic necessity, has more to do with the emergence and establishment of so-called 'art-forms' than is generally realised. Art can have no existential significance for a civilisation which draws a line between life and art and collects artifacts like ancestral bones for reverence. Art must inform the living; we envisage a situation in which life is continually renewed by art, a situation imaginatively and passionately constructed to inspire each individual to respond creatively, to bring to whatever act a creative comportment. We envisage . . . But it is we, now, who must create it. *For it does not exist.*

The actual situation could not be in sharper contrast. Art anaesthetises the living; we witness a situation in which life is continually devitalised by art, a situation sensationally and venally misrepresented to inspire each individual to respond in a stock and passive way, to bring to whatever act a banal and automatic consent. For the average man, dispirited, restless, with no power of concentration, a work of art to be noticed at all must compete at the level of spectacle. It must contain nothing that is in principle unfamiliar or surprising; the audience must be able easily and without reservation to identify with the protagonist, to plant itself firmly in the 'driving-seat' of the emotional roller-coaster and switch over to remote control. What takes place is empathy at a very obvious level, blind and uncritical. To the best of my knowledge it was Brecht who first drew attention to the danger of that method of acting which aims to provoke the state of empathy in an audience at the expense of judgement. It was to counter this promiscuous tendency on the part of the modern audience to identify that he formulated his 'distance-theory' of acting, a method calculated to inspire a more active and critical kind of participation. Unfortunately, Brecht's theory has had no impact whatsoever on popular entertainment. The zombies remain; the spectacle grows more spectacular. To adapt an epigram of a friend of mine: *Si nous ne voulons pas assister au spectacle de la fin du monde, il nous faut travailler à la fin du monde du spectacle.*[12]

Such art as had claim to be called serious touches popular culture today only by way of the fashion industry and advertising, and for many years it has been infected by the triviality attaching to those enterprises. For the rest, literature and art exist side by side with mechanised popular culture and except in an occasional film here and there have little effect upon it. Only in jazz, which retains the spontaneity and vitality deriving from its proximity to its beginnings, can we see an art which springs naturally out of a creative ambience. But already more adulterated forms tend to be confused with the authentic. In England, for example, we are confronted by the absurd craze for 'trad'; a rehash of what went on in New Orleans in the early twenties, simple, obvious, repetitious, overshadows almost completely the vital tradition of the post-Charlie Parker era.

For a long time now the best artists and fine minds everywhere have deplored the gulf that has come to exist between art and life. The same people have usually been in revolt during their youth and have been rendered harmless by 'success' somewhere around middle age. The individual is powerless. It is inevitable.

12. *Notes editoriales d'Internationale Situationiste*, 3 décembre, 1959. Freely adapted from the original.

And the artist has a profound sense of his own impotence. He is frustrated, even confounded. As in the writings of Kakfa, this fearful sense of alienation pervades his work. Certainly the most uncompromising attack on conventional culture was launched by Dada at the end of the First World War. But the usual defence mechanisms were soon operating: the turds of 'anti-art' were solemnly framed and hung alongside 'the School of Athens'; Dada thereby underwent the castration by card-index and was soon safely entombed in the histories as just another school of art. The fact is that while Tristan Tzara *et alii* could point deftly to the chancre on the body politic, could turn the spotlight of satire on the hypocrisies that had to be swept away, they produced no creative alternative to the existing social order. What were we to do after we had painted a moustache on the *Mona Lisa*? Did we really wish Genghis Khan to stable his horses in the Louvre? And then?

In a recent essay[13] Arnold Wesker, concerned precisely with this gulf between art and popular culture and with the possibility of reintegration, refers to the threatened strike of 1919 and to a speech of Lloyd George when the strike could have brought down the government. The Prime Minister said:

> ... you will defeat us. But if you do so have you weighed the consequences? The strike will be in defiance of the government of the country and by its very success will precipitate a constitutional crisis of the first importance. For, if a force arises in the state which is stronger than the state itself, then it must be ready to take on the functions of the state. Gentlemen – have you considered, and if you have, are you ready?

The strikers, as we know, were not ready. Mr Wesker comments:

> The crust has shifted a bit, a number of people have made fortunes out of the protest and somewhere a host of Lloyd Georges are grinning contentedly at the situation ... All

---

13. *The Secret Reins*, (Centre 42) *Encounter* No. 102, March, 1962. All quotations from Mr Wesker and Lloyd George are from the same source.

protest is allowed and smiled upon because it is known that the force – economically and culturally – lies in the same dark and secure quarters, and this secret knowledge is the real despair of both the artist and intellectual. We are paralysed by this knowledge, we protest every so often but really the whole cultural scene – particularly on the left – 'is one of awe and ineffectuality.' I am certain that this was the secret knowledge that largely accounted for the decline of the cultural activities in the Thirties – no one really knows what to do with the philistines. They were omnipotent, friendly, and seductive. The germ was carried and passed on by the most unsuspected; and this same germ will cause, is beginning to cause, the decline of our new cultural upsurge unless . . . unless a new system is conceived whereby we who are concerned can take away, one by one, the secret reins.

Although I found Mr Wesker's essay in the end disappointing, it did confirm for me that in England as elsewhere there are groups of people who are actively concerned with the problem. As we have seen, the political-economic structure of western society is such that the gears of creative intelligence mesh with the gears of power in such a way that, not only is the former prohibited from over initiating anything, it can only come into play at the behest of forces (vested interests) that are often in principle antipathetic towards it. Mr Wesker's 'Centre 42' is a practical attempt to alter this relationship.

I should like to say at once that I have no fundamental quarrel with Mr Wesker. My main criticism of his project (and I admit my knowledge of it is very hazy indeed) is that it is limited and national[14] in character and that this is reflected in his analysis of the historical background. He takes the 1956 production of Osborne's *Look Back in Anger*, for example, to be the first landmark in 'our new cultural upsurge'. A serious lack of historical perspective, the insularity of his view . . . these features are, I am afraid, indicative of a kind of church-bazaar philosophy which seems to underlie the whole project. Like handicrafts, art

---

14. I believe international policies have been attempted since this article was written. However, my criticism is still relevant.

should not be expected to pay. Mr Wesker calls for a tradition 'that will not have to rely on financial success in order to continue'. And so he was led to seek the patronage of trade unions and has begun to organize a series of cultural festivals under their auspices. While I have nothing against such festivals, the urgency of Mr Wesker's original diagnosis led me to expect recommendations for action at a far more fundamental level. Certainly, such a programme will not carry us very far towards seizing what he so happily refers to as 'the secret reins'. I do not think I am being overcautious in asserting that something far less pedestrian than an appeal to the public-spiritedness of this or that group will be the imperative of the vast change we have in mind.

Nevertheless, at one point in what remains an interesting essay, Mr Wesker quotes Mr Raymond Williams. Who Mr Williams is and from what work the quotation is taken I am unfortunately ignorant. I only wonder how Mr Wesker can quote the following and then go out and look for patronage.

> The question is not who will patronise the arts, but what forms are possible in which artists will have control of their own means of expression, in such ways that they will have relation to a community rather than to a market or a patron.

Of course it would be dangerous to pretend to understand Mr Williams on the basis of such a brief statement. I shall say simply that for myself and for my associates in Europe and America the key phrase in the above sentence is: *'artists will have control of their own means of expression'*. When they achieve that control, their 'relation to a community' will become a meaningful problem, that is, a problem amenable to formulation and solution at a creative and intelligent level. Thus we must concern ourselves forthwith with the question of how to seize and within the social fabric exercise that control. Our first move must be *to eliminate the brokers*.

At the beginning of these reflections I said that our methods will vary with the empirical facts pertaining here and now, there and then. I was referring to the tentative, essentially tactical nature of our every act in relation to the given situation, and also to the international constitution of what we might call the now underground. Obviously, all our operations must be adapted to the society in which they take place. Methods used effectively in London might be suicidal or simply impracticable in Moscow or Peking. Always, the tactics are for here and now; never are they in the narrow sense political. Again, these reflections themselves must be regarded as an act of the new underground, a prescriptive document which, in so far as it refers for the most part to what is yet to happen, awaits baptism by fire.

How to begin? At a chosen moment in a vacant country house (mill, abbey, church or castle) not too far from the City of London, we shall foment a kind of cultural 'jam session': out of this will evolve the prototype of our *spontaneous university*.

The original building will stand deep within its own grounds, preferably on a river bank. It should be large enough for a pilot-group (astronauts of inner space) to situate itself, orgasm and genius, and their tools and dream-machines and amazing apparatus and appurtenances; with outhouses for 'workshops' large as could accommodate light industry; the entire site to allow for spontaneous architecture and eventual *town planning*. I underline the last because we cannot place too much emphasis on the fact that *'l'art integral ne pouvait se réaliser qu'au niveau de l'urbanisme'*.[15] In the 1920s, Diaghilev, Picasso, Stravinski and Nijinsky acted in concert to produce a ballet; surely it does not strain our credulity to imagine a far larger group of our contemporaries acting in concert to create a town. We envisage the whole as a vital laboratory for the creation (and evaluation) of conscious *situations*; it goes without saying that it is not only the environment which is in question, plastic, subject to change, but men also.

It must be said at once that this quick sketch of our action-university is not the product of vague speculation. Not only are

---

15. *Documents Situationistes*, Guy-Ernest Debord. At present, town planning is determined by and tends to reinforce conventional functions, conventional attitudes. You sleep here, eat there, work there, die there. A revolutionary architecture will take no account of functions to be transcended (cf. Essay No. 2).

there numerous historical parallels, past situations, fortuitous or controlled, some of whose features are manifestly adaptable to our own project. During the past decade in many countries we have already conducted sufficient experiments of a preparatory nature: we are ready to act.

It used to be said that the British Empire was won on the playing fields of Eton. During the eighteenth and nineteenth centuries the British ruling class was formed exclusively in such institutions; the deportment they conferred on a man was vitally relevant to the growth of England at that time. Unfortunately, the situation at Eton and similar establishments did not continue to inspire its own improvement. Inertia set in. Forms that were once successful hardened until they were devoid of contemporary relevance. In the age of relativity we envisage the spontaneous university as filling the vital formative function of our times.

The Jewish settlements in Israel turned a desert into a garden and astounded all the world. In a flowering garden already wholly sustained by automation, a fraction of such purposiveness applied to the cultivation of men would bring what results?

Then, there was the experimental college at Black Mountain, North Carolina. This is of immediate interest to us for two reasons. In the first place, the whole concept is almost identical to our own in its educational aspect; in the second, some individual members of the staff of Black Mountain, certain key members of wide experience, are actually associated with us in the present venture. Their collaboration is invaluable.

Black Mountain College was widely known throughout the United States. In spite of the fact that no degrees were awarded, graduates and non-graduates from all over America thought it worthwhile to take up residence. As it turns out, an amazing number of the best artists and writers of America seem to have been there at one time or another, to teach and learn, and their cumulative influence on American art in the last fifteen years, has been immense. One has only to mention Franz Kline in reference to painting and Robert Creeley in reference to poetry to give an idea of Black Mountain's significance. They are key figures in the American vanguard, their influence everywhere.

Black Mountain could be described as an 'action university' in the sense in which the term is applied to the paintings of Kline *et alii*. There was no learning from ulterior motives. Students and teachers participated informally in the creative arts; every teacher was himself a practitioner – poetry, music, painting, sculpture, dance, pure mathematics, pure physics, etc., – of a very high order. In short, it was a situation constructed to inspire the free play of creativity in the individual and the group.

Unfortunately, it no longer exists. It closed in the early fifties for economic reasons. It was a corporation (actually owned by the staff) which depended entirely on fees and charitable donations. In the highly competitive background of the United States of America such a gratuitous and flagrantly non-utilitarian institution was only kept alive for so long as it was by the sustained effort of the staff. In the end it proved too ill-adapted to its habitat to survive.

In considering ways and means to establish our pilot project we have never lost sight of the fact that in a capitalist society any successful organization must be able to sustain itself in capitalist terms. The venture must pay. Thus we have conceived the idea of setting up a general agency to handle, as far as possible, all the work of the individuals associated with the university. Art, the products of all the expressive media of civilisation, its applications in industrial and commercial design, all this is fantastically profitable (consider the Musical Corporation of America). But, as in the world of science, it is not the creators themselves who reap most of the benefit. An agency founded by the creators themselves and operated by highly-paid professionals would be in an impregnable position. Such an agency, guided by the critical acumen of the artists themselves, could profitably harvest new cultural talent long before the purely professional agencies were aware it existed. Our own experience in the recognition of contemporary talent during the past fifteen years has provided us with evidence that is decisive. The first years would be the hardest. In time, granting that the agency functioned efficiently from the point of view of the individual artists represented by it, it would have first option on all new talent.

This would happen not only because it would be likely to recognize that talent before its competitors, but because of the fact and fame of the university. It would be as though some ordinary agency were to spend 100 per cent of its profits on advertising itself. Other things being equal, why should a young writer, for example, not prefer to be handled by an agency controlled by his (better-known) peers, an agency which will apply whatever profit it makes out of him as an associate towards the extension of his influence and audience, an agency, finally, which at once offers him membership in the experimental university (which governs it) and all that that implies? And, before elaborating further on the economics of our project, it is perhaps time to describe briefly just what that membership does imply.

We envisage an international organisation with branch universities near the capital cities of every country in the world. It will be autonomous, unpolitical, economically independent. Membership of one branch (as teacher or student) will entitle one to membership of all branches, and travel to and residence in foreign branches will be energetically encouraged. It will be the object of each branch university to participate in and 'supercharge' the cultural life of the respective capital city at the same time as it promotes cultural exchange internationally and functions in itself as a non-specialised experimental school and creative workshop. Resident professors will be themselves creators. The staff at each university will be purposively international; as far as practicable, the students also. Each branch of the spontaneous university will be the nucleus of an experimental town to which all kinds of people will be attracted for shorter or longer periods and from which, if we are successful, they will derive a renewed and infectious sense of life. We envisage an organisation whose structure and mechanisms are infinitely elastic; we see it as the gradual crystallisation of a regenerative cultural force, a perpetual brainwave, creative intelligence everywhere recognizing and affirming its own involvement.

It is impossible in the present context to describe in precise detail the day-to-day functioning of the university. In the first place, it is not possible for one individual writing a brief introductory essay. The pilot project does not exist in the physical sense, and from the very beginning, like the Israeli kibbutzes, it must be a communal affair, tactics decided *in situ*, depending upon just what is available when. My associates and I during the past decade have been amazed at possibilities arising out of the spontaneous interplay of ideas within a group in constructed situations. It is on the basis of such experiences that we have imagined an international experiment. Secondly, and consequently, any detailed preconceptions of my own would be so much excess baggage in the spontaneous generation of the group situation.

Nevertheless, it is possible to make a tentative outline of the economic structure.

We envisage a limited liability company (International Cultural Enterprises Ltd) whose profits are invested in expansion and research. Its income will derive from:

1 – Commissions earned by the Agency on sales of all original work of the associates.
2 – Money earned from 'patents' or by subsidiaries exploiting applications (industrial and commercial) evolving out of 'pure studies'. Anyone who has spent time in an art workshop will know what I mean. The field is unlimited, ranging from publishing to interior decorating.
3 – Retail income. The university will house a 'living museum', perhaps a fine restaurant. A showroom will be rented in the city for retail and as an advertisement.
4 – Such income as derives from 'shows', cinematic, theatrical, or *situationist*.
5 – Fees.
6 – Subsidies, gifts, etc., which in no way threaten the autonomy of the project.

The cultural possibilities of this movement are immense and the time is ripe for it. The world is awfully near the brink of disaster. Scientists, artists, teachers, creative men of goodwill everywhere are in suspense. Waiting. Remembering that it is our kind even now who operate, if they don't control, the grids of expression, we should have no difficulty in recognising the spontaneous university as the possible detonator of the invisible insurrection.

Sigma: A Tactical Blueprint

It is our contention that, for many years now, a change, which might usefully be regarded as evolutionary, has been taking place in the minds of men; they have been becoming aware of the implications of self-consciousness. And, here and there throughout the world, individuals and tentative groups of individuals are more or less purposively concerned with evolving techniques to inspire and sustain self-consciousness in all men.

However imperfect, fragmentary, and inarticulate this new force may presently appear, it is now in the process of becoming conscious of itself in the sense that its individual imponents are beginning to recognize their involvement and consciously to concern themselves with the technical problems of mutual recognition and, ultimately, of concerted action.

History is of societies geared to and through their every institution affirmative of the past, which tends, whatever its complexion, to perpetuate itself. Thus there is a natural inertia in history. Conventions, and the institutions which lend them authority, crystallize. Change is resisted, particularly changes in ways of thinking. The change which concerns us here was first explicit in modern science; the same change has been announced for close on a century in modern art. A whole new way of thinking became possible with the 20th Century. Just as the substantial, objective world was destroyed by modern science, so all modern art has turned on the conventional object and destroyed it. Modern art is expressive of the evolutionary change we are speaking about; modern science furnishes us with the methods and techniques in terms of which we can postulate and resolve the practical problems of adapting ourselves to history in a new, conscious, and creative way.

In looking for a word to designate a possible international association of men who are concerned individually and in concert to articulate an effective strategy and tactics for this cultural revolution (cf. *The Invisible Insurrection*, Trocchi), it was thought necessary to find one which provoked no obvious responses. We chose the word 'sigma'. Commonly used in mathematical practice to designate all, the sum, the whole, it seemed to fit very well with our notion that all men must eventually be included.

In general, we prefer to use the word 'sigma' with a small letter, as an adjective rather than as a noun, for there already exist a considerable number of individuals and groups whose ends, consciously or not, are near as damnit identical with our own, groups which are already called X and Y and Z and whose members may be somewhat reluctant to subsume their public identities under any other name. If these groups could be persuaded of the significance of linking themselves 'adjectivally' to sigma, it would for the present be enough. Moreover, in the foreseeable future, we may very well judge it prudent to maintain multiple legal identities; doing so, we may avoid provoking the more obvious kinds of resistance.

Actually dispersed as we are, and will be until several self-conscious focal-points (sigma-centres) are established, effective communications are vital. All individuals and groups the world over must be contacted and henceforth invited to participate. People must be located and activated: we are confronted with the technical problem of elaborating ways of gearing the power of all us individuals to an effective flywheel. This must be solved without requiring anyone to sink his identity in anything noxiously metaphysical.

In *The Invisible Insurrection* we touched on the kind of situation we wish to bring about. We conceived it to be a kind of spontaneous university. But the term 'university' has some unfortunate connotations and is, besides, too limited to include the entire complex of vital and infectious human processes we have in mind to detonate first here in England and subsequently throughout the world. The original spontaneous university (or sigma-centre) will be a fountainhead only. We are concerned with cities and civilizations, not with 'classrooms' in the conventional sense; nevertheless, we are at the beginning of it all and must commence with certain practical considerations. Our experimental situation, our international conference, must be located so that our 'cosmonauts' can either congregate or be in contact.

It is not simply a question of founding yet another publishing house, nor another art gallery, nor another theatre group, and of sending it on its high-minded way amongst the mammon-engines of its destruction. Such a firm (I am thinking in terms of the West for the moment), if it were successful in sustaining itself within the traditional cultural complex, would 'do much good', no doubt. But it is not the publishing industry alone that is in our view out of joint (and has no survival potential); to think almost exclusively in terms of publishing is to think in terms of yesterday's abstractions. A softer bit and a more resilient harness won't keep the old nag out of the knackery. Of course sigma will publish. When we have something to publish. And we shall do it effectively, forgetting no technique evolved in yesterday's publishing. (Or we may find it convenient to have this or that published by a traditional publisher.) But it is art too in which we are interested. With the leisure of tomorrow in mind, it is all the grids of expression we are concerned to seize. That is what we mean when we say that 'literature is dead'; not that some people won't write (indeed, perhaps all people will), or even write a novel (although we feel this category has about outlived its usefulness), but the writing of anything in terms of a capitalist economy, as an economic act, with reference to economic limits, is not in our view interesting. It is business. It is a jungle talent. We also wish to paint and we also wish to sing. We have to think of a society in which leisure is a fact and in which a man's very survival will depend upon his ability to cope with it. The conventional spectator-creator dichotomy must be broken down. The traditional 'audience' must participate.

We might even say we don't know what we wish to do; we wish, rather, continuously to consult with other intelligences on an international and experimental basis. Amongst other things, we believe in the vital relevance of pamphlets and pamphleteering, but it is not that we shall bring out twelve (the round dozen!) pamphlets on the 14th of September to 'launch' our imprint and proceed to send our private little ball spinning along the well-worn grooves of the cultural pinball-machine: that would be to invite the destruction of the intuition which drives us to articulate. Nor can we limit ourselves, as far as printed matter is concerned, to the traditional media. One interesting 'publishing' project, for example, would be to rent an advertisement panel in (say) four of the London Underground stations for a trial period of one year, and to print our weekly (or monthly) magazine poster-size. Obviously, the weekly poster could be placed in other spots as well. A broadsheet, personal size, could be sent to sponsors and subscribers who might value a facsimile collection of the posters. And why stop at London? (Undergrounds of the World, Unite!) The editorial job in such a project would be complex but not impractical. Thirty or forty writers sympathetic towards sigma could be solicited in advance. Other unconventional projects, which we shall discuss in more detail later, are advertising space in little magazines, in the personal columns of national newspapers, all manner of labels, matchboxes, etc., toilet paper (for the *New Yorker* reader who has everything), cigarette cards, the backs of playing cards, etc. Of course, we shall publish books as well; but the greater part of what we shall eventually decide to do will grow out of the conflux of creative ideas and goodwill that is sigma. To begin with, we must make a continuous, international, experimental conference possible; a permanent meeting of minds to articulate and promote the vast cultural change which UNESCO is prevented by its origins from effecting.

We must say to our sponsors: While we can envisage sigma's flourishing economically in the West, it is not primarily a business organization. We require a protected situation, a place to confer and corporately create. A great deal has already been done. But our strength lies not so much in what has so far been done purposively in our name as in *the availability of other intelligences to our transcategorical inspiration*. All over the world today are little conflagrations of intelligence, little pockets of 'situation-making'. Some of the first theorists called themselves '*Situationistes*'. Other individuals and groups who appear to us to have similar attitudes are presently being gathered into a comprehensive index which will serve as the basis for our communications. We have to evolve the mechanisms and techniques for a kind of supercategorical cultural organization. Some of its features we believe to be as follows:

(1) *Sigma as international index*:
The first essential for those whose purpose it is to link mind with mind in a supernational (transcategorical) process, in some kind of efficient expanding index, an international 'who's who'. It is a question of taking stock, of surveying the variety of talent and goodwill at our disposal. *Who* is with us? Who *knows* he is with us? Our general invitation might read something like this:

> We should like to invite you to take part in an international conference about the future of things. The brief introductory statement enclosed (*The Invisible Insurrection*) should give you an idea of what we are about.
>
> We have chosen the word sigma because as a symbol it is free of bothersome semantic accretions.
>
> Actually dispersed as we are, and will be until several self-conscious focal-points are established (in each of which an experimental situation is self-consciously in the process of articulating itself), effective communications are vital.
>
> Now and in the future our centre is everywhere, our circumference nowhere. No one is in control. No one is excluded. A man will know when he is participating without our offering him a badge.
>
> We have decided that as far as it is economically possible you should receive all our future informations. Sigma's publications are in general given away free to those who participate in its activities.
>
> The conference begins now and goes on indefinitely. We are particularly anxious to have your participation soon, as soon as possible.   sigma associates
>
> We are writers, painters, sculptors, musicians, dancers, physicists, bio-chemists, philosophers, neurologists, engineers, and whatnots, of every race and nationality. The catalogue of such a reservoir of talent, intelligence, and power, is of itself a spur to our imagination.

(2) *Sigma as spontaneous university*:
We can write off existing universities. These lately illustrious institutions are almost hopelessly geared and sprocketted to the cultural-economic axles of the status quo; they have become a function of the context they came into being to inspire. Of the American universities, Paul Goodman writes: 'Therefore we see the paradox that, with so many centres of possible intellectual criticism and intellectual initiative, there is so much inane conformity, and the universities are little models of the Organized System itself.' Secession, the forming of new models, this is the traditional answer, and in our view the only one. So Oxford broke away from the Sorbonne and Cambridge from Oxford, and 'the intellectual ferment was most vigorous, the teaching most brilliant, the monopoly of the highest education most complete, almost before a university existed at all'. (Hastings Rashdall: *The Universities of Europe in the Middle Ages*.) The bureaucracies of the universities mesh with the bureaucracy of the state, mirror it in little; and the specific disease of bureaucracy is that it tends to spawn more of itself and function as a parasitic organism, inventing 'needs' to justify its existence, ultimately suffocating the host it was intended to nurture. (Cf. the satire of William Burroughs.) The universities have become factories for the production of degreed technicians; the various governmental reports on them (particularly the Robbins Report), skating over the thick crust of centuries, call simply for more and more of the same.

The empty chapels of the Cambridge colleges are a significant symbol of the decline of the parent institution. Built originally to house the soul of the community of scholars, they are presently derelict. Quite recently, there was a newspaper report of a prize being offered to the student who wrote the best essay on what should be done with them. It was awarded to a student who suggested they could be converted to laboratories for science, dining halls and and residential quarters for the students, libraries, etc. In short, what was once the vital spiritual centre was to be turned over to material purposes; space is short, and imagination is shorter. That something immaterial, something intangible, had been lost, was overlooked. There would have been more hope for Cambridge, certainly more evidence of spirituality, if it had been decided to turn them into brothels.

Meanwhile, those who (rightly or wrongly) are deeply distrustful of the statistical method, clamouring for the abolition of the 11-plus examinations, tend to overlook the disastrous influence the examination-dominated curriculum has upon the attitudes and habits of the student population at our universities. The competitive system encourages the clever tactician, the glib, the plausible. It is certainly painful and perhaps even dangerous for a student to become deeply interested in his subject, for he is constantly having to get ready to demonstrate his virtuosity; the students at our universities are so busy practising appearances that one seldom meets one who is concerned with the realities. The entire system is a dangerous anachronism. Secession by vital minds everywhere is the only answer.

The more imaginative university teachers all over the world are well aware of these things. But they can do nothing until they can see a possible alternative. Sigma as spontaneous university is such an alternative. It can only grow out of the combined effort of individuals and groups of individuals working *unofficially* at a supernational level. A large country house, not too far from London (and Edinburgh, and New York, and Paris, etc.), is being sought for the pilot project.

Those who saw the photographs of Lyn Chadwick's personal 'museum' in the colour supplement of *The Sunday Times* some months ago, those who know something of the Louisiana Foundation in Denmark, of the 'semantic city' at Canissy in France, about the cultural activities in Big Sur, California, about Black Mountain College in North Carolina, about various spontaneous cultural conglomerations in California and New York in the late fifties, will have some idea of the vital significance of ambience. While a great deal of lipservice is paid to the significance of a man's environment (especially during the early formative years), our societies push ahead willy-nilly boxing people into honeycomb apartment blocks to meet the immediate requirements of industry. For the moment, there is little we can do about this, but we can take care that the structural features of our sigma-centres are geared to and inspiring of the future as we imagine it can be rather than the past and the present out of which men must evolve. Our experimental sigma-centre must be in all its dimensions a model for the functions of the future rather than of the past. Our architects, arriving at the site with the first group of associates, will design the architecture of the spontaneous university for and around the participants.

The site should not be farther from London than Oxford or Cambridge, for we must be located within striking distance of the metropolis, since many of our undertakings will be in relation to cultural phenomena already established there, and so that those coming from abroad can travel back and forth from the capital without difficulty. Moreover, we have always envisaged our experimental situation as a kind of shadow reality of the future existing side by side with the present 'establishment', and the process as one of gradual 'in(ex)filtration'. If we were to locate ourselves too far away from the centres of power, we should run the risk of being regarded by some of those we are concerned to attract as a group of utopian escapists, spiritual exiles, hellbent for Shangri-La on the bicycle of our frustration. Then, 'The original building will stand deep within its own grounds, preferably on a riverbank. It should be large enough for a pilot-group (astronauts of inner space) to situate itself, orgasm and genius, and their tools and dream-machines and amazing apparatus and appurtenances; with outhouses for workshops large as could accommodate light industry, the entire site to allow for spontaneous architecture and eventual *town-planning*.' Etc. (Cf. *The Invisible Insurrection*.) Here our 'experimental laboratory' will locate itself, our community-as-art, and begin exploring the possible functions of a society in which leisure is a dominant fact, and universal community, in which the conventional assumptions about reality and the constraints which they imply are no longer operative, in which art and life are no longer divided. The 'university', which we suspect will have much in common with Joan Littlewood's 'leisuredrome' (if she will forgive me coining a word), will be operated by a 'college' of teacher-practitioners with no separate administration.

The cultural atrophy endemic in conventional universities must be countered with an entirely new impulse. No pedagogical rearrangements, no further proliferation of staff or equipment or buildings, nor even the mere subtraction of administration or planning will help. What is essential is a new conscious sense of community-as-art-of-living; the experimental situation (laboratory) with its 'personnel' is itself to be regarded as an artefact, a continuous making, a creative process, a community enacting itself in its individual members. Within our hypothetical context many traditional historical problems will be recognized at once as artifical and contingent; simultaneously we shall realise our ability to outflank them by a new approach; and certain more vital problems which today receive scant attention or none at all, together with others which in a conventional context cannot even be articulated, will be recognized as more appropriate to any possible future of mankind on this planet . . .

We must choose our original associates widely from amongst the most brilliant creative talents in the arts and the sciences. They will be men and women who understand that one of the most important achievements of the twentieth century is the widespread recognition of the essentially relative nature of all languages, who realise that most of our basic educational techniques have been inherited from a past in which almost all men were ignorant of the limitations inherent in any language. They will be men and women who are alive to the fact that a child's first six years of schooling are still dedicated to providing him with the emotional furniture imposed on his father before him, and that from the beginning he is trained to respond in terms of a neuro-linguistic system utterly inadequate to the real problems with which he will have to contend in the modern world.

Our university must become a community of mind whose vital function is to discover and articulate the functions of tomorrow, an association of free men creating a fertile ambience for new knowledge and understanding (men who don't jump to the conclusion Kropotkin carried a bomb because he was an anarchist), who will create an independent moral climate in which the best of what is thought and imagined can flourish. The community which is the university must become a living model for society at large.

(3) *Sigma as international cultural engineering cooperative*:
(a) *The international pipeline*:
When sigma-centres exist near the capitals of many countries, associate artists and scientists travelling abroad will be able to avail themselves of all the facilities of the local centre. They may choose simply to reside there or they may wish to participate. If the visitor is a celebrity, it would probably be to his advantage to do any 'interview' work (audio or video) in the sigma-centre where 'angle' and editing can be his own. Sigma will then handle negotiations with local radio and television. The imaginative cultivation of this international pipeline would be a real contribution to international understanding.
(b) *Cultural promotion*:
This field is too vast to be treated fully here. It includes all the interesting cultural projects, conferences, international newspaper, publishing ventures, film and television projects, etc., which have been and will be suggested by associates during conferences. Many of these ideas, realised efficiently, would make a great deal of money. All this work would contribute to the sigma image.
(c) *General cultural agents*:
Some of the associates, especially the younger ones who are not previously committed elsewhere, will be glad to be handled by sigma. Obviously, we shall be in a position to recognize new talent long before the more conventional agencies, and, as our primary aim will not be to make money, we shall be able to cultivate a young talent, guarding the young person's integrity.
(d) *General cultural consultants*:
The enormous pool of talent at our disposal places us in an incomparable position vis-à-vis providing expert counsel on cultural matters. We can advise on everything cultural, from producing a play to building a picture collection. A propos the latter, one of our proposed services is to offer an insurance policy to a buyer against depreciation in value of any work of

art recommended by sigma. It may frequently be advisable, economically or otherwise, for sigma to encourage some established company to undertake this or that cultural project: that is to say, sigma will not necessarily wait passively to be consulted. A recent project in which sigma successfully took the initiative was the anthology on drugs and the creative process contemplated by three of our collaborators. With all the sensationalism with which this subject is invested in the world press, and considering the horrible possibility of more repressive legislation inspired by ignorance and fear, we felt the need for a definitive and responsible statement along the lines envisaged by us to be urgent. Sigma has successfully arranged for the appearance of this book under an imprint highly regarded by the 'establishment'. This is just one example of how sigma can *engineer* in the cultural field without actually involving itself, of how existing mechanisms can be adapted to our own purposes. (Obviously, further ideas ripe for commercial exploitation cannot be made public in this context.)

London 1964, the projected 'box-office'.

A shop with basement and upper part is to be found in London in the immediate future. Mr Trocchi intends to have his private quarters in the upper part for the time being. The shop and lower part will be converted into a kind of living-gallery-workshop-auditorium-office, where conferences and interviews can be held and where some of our techniques, found-objects, and publications can be exhibited. It will be our window in the metropolis, a meeting-place where our expanding index is housed, and a kind of general box-office for project sigma. Later on, when the pilot centre is established outside the city, the box-office will be doubly important.

Conclusion:

Perhaps the most striking example of the wrongheaded attitude towards art in official places is provided by the recent scuffle to keep the well-known Leonardo cartoon from leaving the United Kingdom. The official attitude has more in common with stamp-collecting than with aesthetics. The famous cartoon could have been sold abroad for around £1,000,000. For a small fraction of that sum, *perfect replicas* of it could have been made and distributed to every art-gallery in the country. It is small wonder that the man in the street has such a confused attitude towards art. This confusion of value with money has infected everything. The conventional categories distinguishing the arts from each other, tending as they do to perpetuate the profitable institutions which have grown up around them, can for the moment only get in the way of creativity and our understanding of it.

The basic shift in attitude described in the foregoing pages must happen. IT IS HAPPENING. Our problem is to make men conscious of the fact, and to inspire them to participate in it. Man must seize control of his own future: only by doing so can he ever hope to inherit the earth.

Letters to Hugh MacDiarmid

3 January 1964

Dear Sir,

Mr MacDiarmid is quite correct when he denies leading the song. Sidney Goodsir Smith, taking an unofficial stroll across the stage of the McEwan Hall after the pubs had closed for the afternoon (perhaps he had heard that whisky was to be found on the speakers' table?), led the singing. Unfortunately, the song had no more satirical point than a belch, and was as irrelevant as most of what was said on the platform that afternoon . . . it was simply a case of the blind drunk leading the blind.

But a more serious inaccuracy in Mr Levin's otherwise excellent article, and one which Mr MacDiarmid's letter pointedly fails to notice, was Mr Levin's counting Mr MacDiarmid among the rebels. For, whatever Mr MacDiarmid's views are now (and I heartily hope they have changed), in August 1962 he was indignantly denouncing such writers as Burroughs and myself as 'vermin' who should never have been invited to the conference, and in an article in the *Scottish Daily Express* on the Saturday on which the writers departed from Edinburgh he stated that the proper place for us was either an insane asylum or prison. Many of us, and no one more than myself were astonished at the vehemence with which a man we had always supposed was a rebel denounced us as dangerous perverts. But these are the facts. At the 1962 Conference the wielder of the long moral rifle of John Knox was none other than Mr MacDiarmid.

If now, in the light of what happened in 1963, Mr MacDiarmid is presenting himself as a defender of the freedom of the conference, we are entitled to ask: freedom for whom? Are the writings of Trocchi, Burroughs and the like – to use Mr MacDiarmid's own revealing phrase – still to be prescribed?

(*New Statesman*, 1964)

Alexander Trocchi

18 January 1964

Dear Sir,

It was quite evident from Mr MacDiarmid's first speech at the 1962 conference that he had decided not to tolerate me (and my 'ilk') before I had ever reached Edinburgh. In his absurdly haughty way he dismissed as immoral rubbish all post-war fiction concerned with the problem of 'identity' and international in outlook. Then, as now, his terms of abuse were those of a rabid nationalistic moralist. Confession implies a sense of guilt. When Mr MacDiarmid threw his 'drug-fiend-and-deny-it-if-you-can-type-literary-criticism' at me, I could hardly be expected to deny I used drugs. But my various statements about valid methods of extending the range of human consciousness could be construed as a 'confession' only by intellectual tadpoles already hopelessly immersed in the bitter waters of Mr MacDiarmid's moral universe. While some ladies of Edinburgh may derive comfort from the knowledge that Mr MacDiarmid's claymore will defend them against rape at future conferences, those of us who come after Freud and Wittgenstein, alarmed by statements which take the form: 'I am all for freedom . . . BUT . . .', will not be deceived by any of Mr MacDiarmid's assurances and denials, flat, round or square . . .

(*New Statesman*, 1964)

17 May 1964

Dear Mr MacDiarmid,

While there have been and will be aspects of life and art upon which we cannot be in accord, it seems to me there must be a few vital issues upon which we can hardly fail to be in agreement, and I, for my part, am most sorry that the particular circumstances in which we first met one another were such as to bring the former into prominence and distract our attention from the latter. Amongst this latter is our common revolt against the smug philistinism of many of our countrymen. That the good folk of the Edinburgh establishment should take pride in smothering the literary side of the festival this year is for both of us, I am sure, bloody shocking evidence of their barbarism.

I believe too that we are agreed that they shouldn't be allowed to get away with it, that it is a scandal and could be a dangerous precedent. I am writing to inform you that I shall be doing all in my own power to help Haynes make a success of an 'unofficial conference' and to express my personal hope that you will be with us, in your rightful place at the head of our shock troops, in Edinburgh this summer. I am certain we can do much more than was ever done 'officially', and at much less expense, if we can be together in this, for poetry and sanity, now. Next time I am in Scotland I hope I shall have the opportunity of meeting you privately. Really, I am not in the least anxious to continue a public sniping match with a man for whom I have always had the profoundest respect.

(Copy of the letter obtained from the papers of the Trocchi Estate.)

Letter to William S. Burroughs

12 October 1963

Dear Bill,

I meant to be in touch with you before we left. Instead, I arrived in Tangiers struggling in the awful ooze of someone else's determination. Tangiers flashed no more real across my pathetic horizon than a Raphael Tuck postcard on a windy promenade, and I was less free during those seventy-two hours than any bus tourist. So you and us and everything was pretty irrelevant from the beginning and after that unfortunate evening I had only one thought in mind, to get that family bit of mine back to London where I hoped to learn just what it all had to do with me anyway. And, as things have turned out (in spite of young Michael's[16] driving us head-on into another car 122 km from Dieppe) . . . Lyn is setting herself up apart to find something or other hitherto obscured, it seems, by my shadow. And how relieved I am! . . . to be able to give my attention to something else . . . Should we be together or not? It sounded like a valid question. But not for two whole bloody years. After seven hundred and thirty days and seven hundred and thirty nights it was time to put it in a bottle and consign it to the Gulf Stream for a quick passage through the North Arsehole . . . It wasn't Lyn I wanted to get rid of. It was her obsession.

I enclose a copy of the essay to acquaint you with the methods we have already evolved. We have arrived at the name sigma because it seemed semantically 'clean', being the symbol conventionally used in mathematics for the sum or the whole. Unlike most words, it has no other traditional connotations to suggest we're quick or slow, left or right, hare-lipped or cloven-hooved. The company was formed in a hurry with the minimum of three directors, Mike Fenton (whom it's too bad you didn't

16. Michael Hollingshead.

meet), Charlie Hatcher, and myself, a few days before I left England at the beginning of July, and that was pretty much all that happened until my quick trip back to England at the time of the Festival.

The trouble is, Bill, there is no interesting alternative to Calder in London. Or there won't be until sigma really gets going and we bring out most of the stuff under our own imprint. Well, that could happen very soon, particularly if I can count on the aforesaid apple. The first thing I'd like to have from you is your permission to go ahead and arrange for you to be registered as a director in the company. If you give me your OK in principle now (you'll want to read the articles, etc., before you sign anything) I can probably set things in motion, or, if you like, I'll make arrangements for this to be done whenever you next visit London. But I do feel I want your other-things-being-equal assurance of collaboration now. And I think, even though he's so far away at the moment, that we should invite Bob Creeley to accept a directorship too. I think you'll appreciate the significance of this preliminary international liaison, and how it will strengthen my hand for the spadework to be done here in England. The bricks and mortar of our enormous factory are contingent upon the eventual assent of our nuclear cosmonauts to operate it.

Last time I was in London I bumped into a cat from the West Indies[17] who offered a house in London. I am in it now. It's not a big house, but he's angling for another nearby and meanwhile you can count on a room in London when you come to inspect our operations. Meanwhile, if I ever get this bloody letter finished, I shall continue circularising our contacts everywhere. If there is anyone who should receive our literature who might be unknown to me, please send his name and address.

Now, as you know, one of the sources of income for the project is to be the commissions earned by the company in acting as agent to the participants. We can go ahead with that

---

17. This was Michael De Freitas, also known as Michael Abdul Malik and, notoriously, as Michael X.

now because, fortunately, we have Mike Fenton (whose business that is precisely) to get this aspect of the affair organized. But he's got to have something to handle. As soon as it gets known that sigma is handling a few of us successfully, others will come forward (and you and I can do a bit of propulsion from behind. So what I suggest is that you and I present a detailed account of the state of our affairs and authorize the company to go ahead and see what it can do for us for a trial period. At the moment we've both got Simon King amongst God knows how many other incompetents, and I think you'll agree he is a fucking joke. We've got nothing to lose, and with the heads around us who know yr work and mine, the markets, the key people etc. . . . . Please let me have yr thoughts and yr help, Bill, and I'm sure we'll have some fun yet in London.

(This letter has been edited.)

The Junkie: Menace or Scapegoat?

The basic varieties of drugs have been known to mankind for tens upon tens of centuries, but they have shot into focus during the last quarter of a century as a cultural menace, of the order of the Black Death of a plague of locusts. Never before was there ostensibly such large-scale panic.

I say *ostensibly* because undoubtedly this climate of hysteria is foisted upon the public by an irresponsible, evangelical and news-mongering press inspired by some of our more preposterous public opinion makers.

Almost daily we are confronted by sensational pseudo-problems luridly and melodramatically treated which, of course, distract one and all from the really vital questions facing us at this time. How many children have been driven more or less directly to destruction by an outraged older generation and its outrageous laws?

I have no doubt it will eventually come to be seen that the typical heroin addict, or junkie . . . the contemporary geek with his desperate craving and his ingratiating whine . . . is, in so far as he exists (and I fear he does), a straightforward product of a fear-ridden and puritanical society's need, its unconscious desire, *that he should exist*, and that he (the junkie) assumes his peculiar and unsavoury characteristics in reacting, as any human being would tend to react, to the various misguided sanctions which are imposed upon him.

Like the old American negro, born in the South, old Uncle Tom, he soon learns his role, to say 'Yes Boss!', pronto. Within the perilous and tragically limited perimeter imposed upon him by the sick imaginations of his fellow men, the junkie soon learns to get by with his ridiculous mask on, and, as men tend to become what they do, he sometimes forgets he was ever anyone else.

The Great Junkie Confidence Trick we have inherited almost without qualification from the United States. It goes like this:

A man uses heroin.

Ha! says Society. You are an ill and evil and desperate fellow! We shall keep you short of junk (heroin) and make you less desperate . . .!

The junkie, who has to contend with what is admittedly a dangerous drug, is forced now to contend with an unnatural scarcity of the drug to which he has already, let's say, become addicted. This artificial shortage, and the most degrading and difficult conditions of supply (he is often forced to beg, to cheat, to steal) magnify the original danger tenfold.

Desperate without the drug, or kept in permanent short supply by men moved more by morals than by medicine, the junkie uses his drug in a desperate way. His deepening desperation causes him to think almost exclusively of heroin. Either he has the drug temporarily and sees himself running out of it and using it more and more hysterically, or he is even more panic-stricken because he is without it.

Obviously, he must become a professional. Drug addiction tends to become his whole life. At one of our clinics he is at constant battle with his doctor to maintain his present level of supply. Sooner or later, he finds it is the stubborn policy of the clinic to get him to lower his consumption. He is a kipper. They insist upon 'curing' him.

This relentless struggle drains him of the vital energies he so badly needs to deal with the only *real* problem: HIS PERSONAL AND INDIVIDUAL CONTROL OVER HIS USE OF THE DRUG. We must repeatedly insist that the policeman's or the doctor's control over another man's use of the drug is, at best, interference, at worst, criminal coercion.

The victim of restraint, compulsion, bigotry, and all manner of excruciating pressures, the Junkie finally deteriorates morally. Society, with its entirely negative approach, actually creates the pseudo-problem in terms of which the junkie is often fatally embroiled.

Perhaps the fundamental fault in the British system of dealing with the question is the fact that if one wishes to use heroin at all, one is forced to show that one is addicted. In doing so one steps on to the terrible treadmill of which we have already spoken. Occasional users must either become addicted or run the various risks of obtaining what is often an adulterated product from a criminal source.

The present policy in this country derives more or less from the recommendations set out in the Brain Report (1965), a document in which one will look in vain for any really fundamental debate. Old prejudices . . . including that absurd and rigidly held one that only those who have no personal experience of narcotics are qualified to speak of them . . . were simply not questioned. The underlying attitude vis-à-vis heroin was, of course, entirely negative. That there might be something, just some wee virtue in the stuff (beyond the narrowly medical), it did not occur to anyone to ask. Perhaps that is not to be wondered at, considering the 'climate'. Though, unless one could derive something on the credit side it is difficult to see how anyone came to subject himself to either the criminal circumstances or all the indignities involved in becoming addicted. But, it is not really my purpose to argue for heroin at this time. I note the fact of the purely negative approach of Brain and his colleagues simply as one more symptom of the superficiality of the investigation.

There was a nasty (if unconscious) hypocrisy running through the report in so far as it dealt with the matter of heroin addiction. Consider this:

'Since compulsory treatment seems to meet with little success, there is little that can be done for these people beyond restricting the possibility of illicit supplies.' Done FOR what people? Users? As it had turned out, either you become a good dog who wants to become a kipper or your only source is illicit. And in the report there was talk of powers of compulsory detention and treatment. So despite the fact that 'compulsory treatment seems to meet with little success', the committee did in fact and effect call for just that. And what is worse, that particular recommendation was implemented when the clinics got going. The fact is that society, as represented by the Brain Committee, government, and press, was not thinking of 'these people' at all; *they* were treated throughout the report simply as a menace to themselves and other people, and the unimaginative conclusions were without exception expressed in terms of prescription.

There was a vagueness in the recommendations about what was to be 'done for' whom. But it was taken for granted that those who used heroin (use in the mind of the committee could only be misuse) should be regarded as junkies and 'notified to the authorities' . . . the grammar was no better than the intention which was to stick a most dangerous label on a person for police and medical purposes so that he could be legally subjected to the kipper-cure. When the change in the law came, those who were dependent upon the drug were forthwith dependent either upon criminal sources or upon the clinic they elected to attend. No longer was a user a private individual obtaining supplies in (some) confidence from the doctor of his choice. He was now publicly an 'addict' reporting to an assigned clinic at a fixed hour of an appointed day, there to be interviewed by a strange doctor, often young and entirely inexperienced, who tended 'to go by the book'.

The imposition of the fixed addict-image on an individual placed him in a situation in which, by virtue of the new laws governing addiction and the conventional attitudes of which these laws were an expression, he was all but condemned to respond in a stock way. This process is well known to modern psychiatry. The fact, for example that schizoid tendencies can be intensified by hospitalization has led to the idea of the 'anti-hospital'.

The clinic doctor, acting on the general principle that the lower a man's consumption of heroin the better, struggled from the very first (and psychologically crucial) consultation to get his patient to accept a prescription for the smallest possible amount of the drug. This tendency was accentuated by the public emphasis in the Brain Report and elsewhere, on 'the dangers of overprescription'. Thus from the beginning the new doctor provoked all manner of non-cooperative responses: the user was forced to resort to cunning, to lie, to cheat, to beg, to fawn, desperately trying to ensure himself of adequate supplies. Doctor and patient were henceforth involved in a battle of wits, in the very common and destructive pseudo-problem of which we have already spoken, in which all the energies which should have been brought to bear on the real problem were being wastefully dissipated.

It is not a question of blaming the doctors for the degrading predicament of the junkies, though as a profession I think they had a responsibility to counter the wave of public hysteria in reference to the heroin question with such facts as the far far more serious question of addiction to barbiturates. In this context I don't intend to deny the relative and various uses of such drugs as Apomorphine and Lomotil.

(A few years ago the *Evening News* reported 2,000,000 barbiturate addicts in England. Every schoolboy should know that compared to a barbiturate addict, a heroin addict smells like a rose.)

The only clear relationship between the use of heroin and the practice of medicine is the fact that only members of the medical profession (and, today, only under certain controlled circumstances) are legally able to sign a prescription for the drug. From this fact it surely does not follow that the doctor is the man best qualified to 'treat' the heroin user, addict or not. And why, indeed, do we assume that he needs 'treatment' at all in the medical sense? Doctors know very well it is a virtual impossibility to cure 'addiction to heroin' by any known medical means.

The fact is that it is simply not that kind of problem. If treatment is called for at all it is in a cultural or spiritual sense. And do we not all need that kind of treatment, all the drunks and punks amongst us?

My own close familiarity with the question of addictions over two decades in the United States and in this country has convinced me that there is a possibility of organizing a helpful kind of 'retreat' where addicts could learn either to come to terms with their addiction and to use their drug (if use it they must) in a controlled and unhysterical way, or even to move beyond addiction, using chemical means amongst others. But this will not be accomplished either by absolute prohibitions or by forcing the user into a state of mind in which nothing is significant except the either/or of heroin. In such a retreat . . . it may or may not be an actual geographical location . . . the junkie would be encouraged from the beginning to involve himself in other things and to get his 'problem' into some kind of rational perspective, indeed, to minimize it rather than the opposite. Simultaneously, the person would be encouraged to express himself in art and in a vital and active sexuality. Were I involved in such a project, I should certainly wish to have doctors amongst my colleagues, but more than anyone else I should wish to involve lovers and the sexually liberated.

Perhaps the most scandalous aspect of the whole question is the way in which the normal constitutional rights of a person tend more and more to be violated in the treatment he is accorded. In England, our junkies are Englishmen. They have the same legal rights as other Englishmen? Where are a man's legal rights once he is handed over to the doctors?

In *Cain's Book* (1959), I tried to make a stand in New York. 'I say it is impertinent, insolent, and presumptuous of any person or group of persons to impose their unexamined moral prohibitions upon me, that it is dangerous both to me and, although they are unaware of it, to the imposers, that in every instance in which such a prohibition becomes crystallized in law, an alarming precedent is created . . . Vigilance. Dispute legal precedent' (p. 41, Jupiter Books, Calder and Boyars).

Actually, what is trumpeted abroad as 'the heroin problem' is a peculiarly American affliction. It moves abroad with aid, armaments, and the American Way of life.

> Forty thousand soldiers
> Forty thousand spikes
> Stun me a little, Daddie
> Before I gut the kikes!

In England, I pray you will believe me, *we do not need it*.

Is it too much to hope that on this island old in democracy . . . is it too much to hope that to a younger and less prejudiced generation of Englishmen it might seem that the kind of invasion of inner space (of privacy, Daddie) that is perpetrated on all junkies is unjustifiable?

Those who lived at the time of Auschwitz seem nowadays quite at home with the smoke.

Notes from a Diary of a Cure, 1965

9th October 1965 or 1st Day: Beachhead established – 'Diary of a cure?' (Cocteau) – No, I refuse to regard it in this way – to do so is to accept the conventional hysteria surrounding the subject as meaningful response.

About 6 weeks ago, with the pressure of events, the intensity of my interest and involvement therein, I found I was using what, under *unexperimental conditions* . . . I felt was an excessive amount of heroin and cocaine . . . I began to feel that my consumption of these drugs was irresponsible, dangerous and perhaps potentially fatal . . . I knew I was *out of control* . . . I had always felt that heroin (among other drugs) wasn't intrinsically unmanageable. I wanted not to stop using the opiates 'for ever and ever' but to use them wisely and well. That would no doubt mean: occasionally . . . an absolute prohibition was every bit as dangerous and limiting as addiction . . . So I decided to leave town and set myself up at the seaside with drugs for about 24 hours after arrival (at normal rate of consumption – heroin 10–20 gr/diem and cocaine 2–7 gr/diem, carrying all my notes for *The Long Book* etc. and plenty of hallucinogens and various substitutes, no, various drugs which used in conjunction with one another, would serve to reestablish the 'normal' chemical balance of my metabolism without, on withdrawal of heroin, provoking withdrawal symptoms. That's to say: Methadone (physeptone), apomorphine, fentazin, daptazole, etc., to break the back of my habit and attain a state such that I could TAKE IT OR LEAVE IT (i.e. H only, C not addictive).

9pm – This evening, rather later than I had anticipated this beachhead was established in Herne Bay, Kent . . . counting the pills now, where I sit overlooking the sea – overhearing, I could say, for it is dark outside and the curtains are already drawn, I find I have 28 × 1/65th tabs which is rather less than 5 gr or a very 'thin' 12 hours . . . and instead of cocaine . . . I have none any longer . . . one very small dose of liquid dizisdrine. So, tomorrow, with the dawn, other things being equal, I should begin the experiment with LSD, 150 micrograms. *Et on verra* . . . Indeed, too soon.

11pm – 24!

10th Oct. – 21! How can I use 21 pills to bring myself down from the consumption of 100 approx/diem?

☩

The symbol, is, I find, contained in the blue silk mandarin's cloak I donned tonight. I feel it should give an air of formality to these desperate proceedings.

12pm – 11 pills left. We shall take a cup of Horlicks and then, to begin with 150 micrograms of LSD – perhaps then I shall get things in a clearer perspective – I can't say I am not worried, vaguely, about the ending of my stock of heroin . . . but, on the other hand, I cannot say I am VERY worried. I am not. I am old enough and I hope, wise enough, not to make any wild predictions . . .

4.30pm – There is one grain of heroin left – has been these last 4 hours. I feel if I can keep that grain there, in the bottle, under the Buddha

      all will yet be well
for   while the grain remained
      there is no heart
      laid waste
      with black despair

Thus I have donned the blue robe of the Mandarin and I await deliverance propped high in my bed overlooking the grey sea.

(Exploring in town, I had seen a copy of *Cain's Book* for sale, 20/- and heard two people talking about its author 'who will soon be dead – he's a drug-addict you know . . .' when a small girl asked me for my autograph, I wrote 'I who am about to die salute you . . .')

6.10pm – last fix taken, i.e. it no longer beckons from over there eh. I feel wonderful . . .

How I Came to Want to Get Off

Sometimes i scare myself. It is as though i am frantically trying to board a train which always goes just one mile an hour faster than i can run, stiffer in the knees now i am thirty-eight and not twenty-eight. i cannot live in the present because i am always anxious about the future because i tell myself i am. i am always going to do something – tomorrow. There are certain technical difficulties, of course. i want to be able to use this world as my personal play garden. All the time. Meanwhile, i am still nailed to the economic rack. That is the big game into which i was born underprivileged.

My father became gradually more ridiculous as he grew older: he was always demonstrating he was pleased to kiss the arse of his betters. And while my mother was not the least like him, she didn't seem to question some of his categories. If i am insane now, and some people speak and act as though they believe i am, it is hardly surprising. The system of values that was imposed upon me from the beginning after i was thrust screaming from a warm womb, that influenced me in my growing, was insane through the insane flux and reflux of the contradictory behaviour of my elders and the malodorous altar of nonsense, weakness, stupidity, and hypocrisy they ultimately worshipped at.

My father got a physical pleasure out of delivering a crate of lemonade to my philosophy professor – it was an achievement. He could now speak of that philosophy professor with familiarity before friends and rivals. i was taught early that men were divided into friends and enemies, into rich and poor, that the rich could do more or less what they liked in fairyland now, and the poor wiped their arses for them, but that in return for this service, the poor could do something more difficult than pass through the eye of a needle – later, after they were dead.

After you're dead, mummy? Because we were poor. Very poor. Poor, but proud, my mother would have said without a blush. Proud because poor? No, because we're good. Good?

Meanwhile, warm and sweet-scented ladies stepped out of long, black cars in the street and on the screen in my little-boy's dreams. Good? Wicked? Hush, not for you. it was possible, of course, for a poor boy to find a tinder box and marry a princess, wasn't it? Of course that's just a fairy tale, son. Like the rats granny talked about? Yes, just like them. But i saw a rat, mummy.

How can i grow up and marry a princess, mummy? If only my dear mother had said: i am a princess, darling, so it shouldn't be either difficult or necessary. She might have saved me a great deal of time. But my mother could never have said that, despite her justifiable pretensions to gentility. She was too humble. Not very 'umble – 'her's was humility, quiet, unobtrusive, polite' – utterly Christian. i often thought as a child she was the only Christian i ever met. i am horrified today to discover that i have no really coherent notion of what she was like. My relation to her seems to have been entirely intuitive, emotional and inarticulate. But i can remember that in spite of her usual dowdiness, which at the beginning sometimes embarrassed me in front of my richer friends, she seemed to command the respect of whoever was near her. Other children fled to my mother for a kind of reassurance they were unable to get from their own. Other parents, when they spoke of my mother, seemed to speak more gently, almost in awe. Meanwhile, my father roamed the corridors of the house like some mad, wounded beast.

It seems to me that a man must arrive at a point where he is entirely alone and the external world is merely an incoherent and contradictory mass of detail, and that he must begin at the beginning and build all over again his whole world structure. There is only that vast sea of evidence, of potential evidence, rather, for he is not possessed of any self-evident criterion of relevance. From time to time madmen in high places threatened us all with nuclear destruction.

Uncle Hamlet, Quite Gone Into Middle Age . . .

Christmas Eve, 1978

To sit down again after all these years, to take up where I left off, approximately at the end of *Cain's Book*, at which point it was obvious I had committed some kind of spiritual *hari-kari* . . . Oh, it's true I've written a few poems since then, and a few essays, but during the sixties I wanted to move things, not to write them. And do you know, I think I did move them? Even if for the moment I seem to have moved them right out of touch with me . . . what was to be said has been said . . . there was no more to say. Thus, when a few months later my publisher once again located me and with chequebook in hand asked me what it was I was now working on, it occurred to me to say that the book I . . . hmph . . . hmph . . . was now working on was a long one. When he asked me what the book was called, I said at once it was called *The Long Book*. That, give or take a year, my love, was fifteen years ago. By this time it must, one might think, be a very long book indeed. Well, it was a long living. I think I can say that.

The Long Book. All those notes. All those words. Ideas, unfinished thoughts, not so many reams of the stuff . . . into which, if I reach for a page, I am . . . sometimes . . . relentlessly drawn. After all, they *are* my own notes, and from time to time I can remember the circumstances in which they came into being. Ah yes, that was the time . . . and suddenly the bright impulse which took me back there is thwarted, extinct. Yesterday's bearings. But they are none the less true, I suppose, although sometimes the very sight of them makes me want to throw up . . . and no wonder, all those titles! All those plausible beginnings! What I am looking for, I told myself over the years, is a plausible end. Like the overdose with which I have been accredited how many times since I fled from New York? My God, I thought you were dead! Yes, indeed, the plausible happening, the plausible end . . . or even the implausible one, so long as I could write *fin* at some point or other, and the gesture be in some profound sense fitting.

But of course it was not to be. Plausible or implausible I had no end in sight, nor would have before dying, and then someone else would have to write it. Meanwhile, I was and am as usual kneedeep in the disordered thoughts of more than a decade. Uncle Hamlet, quite gone into middle age, and still undecided.[18]

18. This was written as a Christmas Eve note to Sally Child, his lover and companion.

Acknowledgements and Sources

The extracts from an unpublished autobiographical novel are from the Trocchi collection in the John M. Olin Library at Washington University, St Louis, Missouri. The following, also previously unpublished material, are reproduced from the same source: 'The Earthbound', 'Fragments from the Diary of a Man Found Gassed in a Glasgow Slum', 'Tapeworm', 'Eileen Lanelly' (from an unpublished novel, titled in draft *James Fidler*), 'Notes from a Diary of a Cure, 1965' and 'How I Came to Want to Get Off'.

'Peter Pierce', 'A Meeting', 'The Holy Man' and 'A Being of Distances' were published in *New Writers 3* (1965) and are reproduced here with kind permission of John Calder Publishers, London.

The extracts from *Young Adam* and *Cain's Book* are reproduced here with kind permission from John Calder Publishers, London.

'The Rum and the Pelican' was originally published in *Merlin*, Paris, Summer/Autumn 1954.

The 'Foreword to Vol. 5 of Frank Harris' *Memoirs*' was published in the Brandon House edition of the book, California, 1966 (under the pseudonym of Frances Lengel).

'A Note on George Orwell' appeared in *Evergreen Review*, New York, 1958.

'The Junkie: Menace or Scapegoat?' appeared in *Ink* magazine, London, 26 June 1970.

'Invisible Insurrection of a Million Minds' was first published in *New Saltire Review* magazine, 1962 as was 'Sigma: A Tactical Blueprint'.

'Wolfie' and 'Uncle Hamlet, Quite Gone into Middle Age . . .' are previously unpublished.

The letter to Jack and Marjorie Robertson was written in October 1950 for the *Scots Review*, Edinburgh.

The letter to Samuel Beckett is reproduced with kind permission of the Mills Memorial Library, McMaster University, Hamilton, Ontario.

The letters to Terry Southern and William S. Burroughs are reproduced from copies in the papers of the Estate.

The letters to Hugh MacDiarmid are reprinted here with permission from the *Times Literary Supplement* and the *New Statesman*.

Any queries regarding the Trocchi Estate should be addressed to Ms Sally Child, 13 Hornsey Lane Gardens, London, N6 5RX.

A Trocchi Bibliography

NOVELS

Helen and Desire, Olympia Press, Paris, 1953, under pseudonym of 'Frances Lengel'. Reprinted variously, and in French, Italian, Spanish, German, Dutch, Japanese, once as *Desire and Helen*, and by Castle Books, New York, 1959, as *Angela* under pseudonym of 'Jean Blanche'. Printed under Trocchi's own name by Brandon House, California, 1967, Olympia Press, London, 1971 and Tandem Books, London, 1972. Also a Collectors' Limited Edition by Olympia, date unknown.

The Carnal Days of Helen Seferis, Olympia Press, Paris, 1954, under pseud. of 'Frances Lengel'. Reprinted variously, and in Dutch, German and Italian, also in unauthorised edition as *The Return of Angela* by Castle Books, New York, 1959, under pseud. of 'Jean Blanche'. Reprinted under Trocchi's own name by Brandon House, California, 1967.

Young Adam, Olympia Press, Paris, 1954, under pseud. of 'Frances Lengel'. Reprinted with four stories as *The Outsider*, Castle Books, New York, 1960. First UK edition by Heinemann, London, 1961. Reprinted by Pan Books, London, 1963, New English Library, London, 1966, John Calder, London and New York, 1983. Also appeared in numerous unauthorised editions, and once retitled as *Seeds of Desire* from Castle Books, New York, 1959.

School for Sin, Olympia Press, Paris, 1954, under pseud. of 'Frances Lengel'. German, Dutch, Italian, French editions. Reprinted under Trocchi's own name as *School for Wives* by Brandon House, California, 1967.

Frank Harris – My Life and Loves; Volume 5; An Irreverent Treatment, Olympia Press, Paris, 1954. Reprinted variously, and in Dutch, German, Italian, French editions. Reprinted as *What Frank Harris Did Not Say* by Olympia Press, (Travellers Companion Series) New York, 1966 under Trocchi's own name, by New English Library, London, 1966, and by Brandon House, California, 1967. Also a Collectors' Limited Edition by Olympia, date unknown.

Thongs, Olympia Press, Paris, 1955, under pseud. of 'Carmencita de las Lunas'. Editions in German, Danish, French, Italian. Reprinted by Brandon House, California, 1967 under Trocchi's own name, and by Olympia Press, London, 1971.

White Thighs, Olympia Press, Paris, 1955, under pseud. of 'Frances Lengel', and by Keimeisha, Tokyo, 1955. Reprinted under Trocchi's own name by Brandon House, California, 1967.

Sappho of Lesbos, Castle Books, New York, 1960. First UK edition by Tandem Books, London, 1971. Reprinted by Star Books, London, 1986.

Angela (see *Helen and Desire*); Castle Books, New York, 1959 under pseud. of 'Jean Blanche'. This was a different version of the other *Angela*, completely rewritten by Trocchi himself.

Cain's Book, Grove Press, New York, 1961 (two editions). First UK edition by John Calder, London, 1963. Editions in Germany, France, Netherlands, Argentina, Spain, Italy, Denmark, often from several different publishers. Reprinted by Quartet Books, London, 1973. Third US edition by Grove Press, 1979.

TRANSLATIONS

Eleven Thousand Virgins; Memoirs of a debauched Hospodar by Guillaume Apollinaire, (from French) Olympia Press, Paris, 1953 under pseud. of 'Oscar Mole'. May have been reprinted under title of *The 11th Hour of Whips*. (No copy seen.)

I, Jan Cremer (with R.E. Wyngaard, from Dutch), Calder & Boyars, London, 1965. Reprinted by Panther Books, London, 1968, 1969, 1970 (twice).

The Girl on the Motorcycle by Andre Pieyre de Mandiargues, (from French), John Calder, London, 1966. Reprinted by Four Square, London, October 1967, and New English Library, London, November 1967, 1968 (three times).

The Bloody Countess by Valentine Penrose, (from French), Calder & Boyars, London, 1970, reprinted shortly afterwards, to tie-in with the film as *Countess Dracula*.

The Centenarian by Rene de Obaldia, (from French), Calder & Boyars, London, 1970.

La Gana by Jean Douassot, (from French), Calder & Boyars, London, 1974.

POETRY

Man at Leisure, Calder & Boyars, London, 1972, hardback and paperback editions.

EDITORIAL

Writers' Revolt (with Terry Southern and Richard Seaver), New American Library, New York, 1960.

Collected Merlin Magazine (1952–5) reprinted in hardcover volume by Kraus Reprint, Nendeln, Liechtenstein, 1970.

The Sigma Portfolio (duplicated) items 1–39, London, 1964–67.

My Own Business, London, 1970, poster-broadsheet.

SHORT STORIES

New Writers 3, Calder & Boyars, London, 1965 contains 'A Being of Distances', 'The Holy Man', 'Peter Pierce' and 'A Meeting', which had appeared in *The Outsider* (see *Young Adam*).

CONTRIBUTIONS TO PERIODICALS

Scots Review, Edinburgh, Nov. 1950–April 1951, monthly articles under the byeline; 'Paris Letter'.

Botteghe Oscura, Rome, 1951, long poem 'How At Thebes Tiresias The Prophet Told', 1952, 'A Being of Distances' short story.

Nimbus, London, 1952, poetry.

Tomorrow, London, 1953, short story reprinted.

Points, Paris, 1953, the short story 'Peter Pierce'.

Paris Review, New York, 1958, a section of *Cain's Book* titled 'The Citadel'.

Evergreen Review, New York, 1958, 'A Note on George Orwell'. 1963, reprinted both 'Invisible Insurrection of a Million Minds' and 'Sigma: A Tactical Blueprint' essays.

New Saltire Review, Edinburgh, 1962, 'Invisible Insurrection Of A Million Minds' essay.

International Situationiste Review, Paris, 1962 (and various other editions, and of the I.S. anthology) co-authorship of editorial. Reprint of 'Invisible Insurrection' essay.

Anarchy, London, 1962, reprinted 'Invisible Insurrection' essay.

Scotsman, Edinburgh, 1963, 'Don't Ask Your Grannie' essay.

Los Angeles Free Press, LA, 1963, reprinted 'Invisible Insurrection' essay.

New Society, London, May 1965, 'Lady Chatterley's Charade' (review); 'Drugs of Mind', 1970.

Ink, London, 26 June 1970, 'The Junkie: Menace or Scapegoat?'

International Times, London, June 1969, 'Watch That Gnome', essay.

The Olympia Reader, New York, 1966, extract from Frank Harris' *Memoirs* Vol. 5.

Sections of *Cain's Book* appeared in numerous American periodicals at various times, including 'Oyster', 'The Book Of Grass', 'The Addict' anthology, 'Out Of Our Minds' (Penguin), 'Man's Magazine', 'Drugs From A–Z'.

SCREEN CREDITS

Man with a Hat Director; Wadhawan, London, 1973. 40 mins, Producer, David Scheuer.

Marihuana, Marihuana Director; Wadhawan, London, 1973, 40 mins, Producer, David Scheuer.

Cain's Film Director; Wadhawan, London 1968.